WED BY NECESSITY

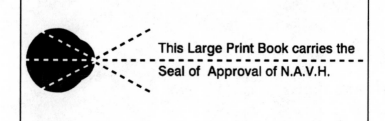

This Large Print Book carries the
Seal of Approval of N.A.V.H.

SMOKY MOUNTAIN MATCHES

WED BY NECESSITY

KAREN KIRST

THORNDIKE PRESS
A part of Gale, a Cengage Company

Farmington Hills, Mich • San Francisco • New York • Waterville, Maine
Meriden, Conn • Mason, Ohio • Chicago

LIBRARY OF CONGRESS CIP DATA ON FILE.
CATALOGUING IN PUBLICATION FOR THIS BOOK
IS AVAILABLE FROM THE LIBRARY OF CONGRESS

ISBN-13: 978-1-4328-4463-9 (hardcover)
ISBN-10: 1-4328-4463-6 (hardcover)

Published in 2018 by arrangement with Harlequin Books S.A.

Printed in the United States of America
1 2 3 4 5 6 7 22 21 20 19 18

Not that I speak in respect of want: for I have learned, in whatsoever state I am, therewith to be content.

— *Philippians* 4:11

To my readers. Your letters, emails and messages are a huge source of encouragement. You inspire me to strive to write emotional reads you won't want to put down. Thank you for supporting my dream job.

ACKNOWLEDGMENTS

A huge thank you to Stephanie White for her insight into horse wounds and care and for introducing me to her beautiful horses.

CHAPTER ONE

Gatlinburg, Tennessee
July 1887

As a holiday, Independence Day left a lot to be desired. Independence was a dream Caroline Turner wasn't likely to ever attain. Crumpling the note in her hand, she surveyed the crowd of people gathered to watch the fireworks display. Her blackmailer could be here tonight. He could be watching her every move.

The fireworks' blue-green light flickered over the sea of faces, followed by red, white and gold. She tried to shake the sinister feeling. Stuffing the wrinkled paper into the pocket hidden deep in the folds of her skirt, she schooled her features and made her way along the edge of the field to where the musicians were playing patriotic tunes. She wasn't about to give her tormentor the satisfaction of knowing he'd rattled her.

"Caroline, we're running low on lemonade."

"Then make more," she snapped at eighteen-year-old Wanda Smith. Surely the volunteers serving refreshments didn't need her input in every decision.

"We've misplaced the lemon crates."

At the distress in the younger girl's countenance, Caroline relented. "Fine. I'll look for them. You may return to your station."

It took her a quarter of an hour to locate the missing lemons. By then, the last of the fireworks had been shot off and attendees were ready for more food and drink. The celebration was far from over, yet she wished she could return home to her bedroom and solitude. The prospect of having to dole out more money to a stranger made her stomach churn.

She diverted to the drink table and helped serve the press of thirsty folks. The line eventually dwindled, and Caroline drifted over to watch couples dancing to lively music. The summer night air enveloped her, ripe with the scents of fried chicken, honeysuckle and cologne.

A trio of young women approached and engaged her in conversation. As usual, they wanted to know about her outfit, whether she'd had it made by a local seamstress or her mother had had it shipped from New York. Before they'd exhausted their talk of fashion, a stranger inserted himself into their group.

"Excuse me."

Caroline didn't recognize the hulking figure. Well over six feet tall, he was as broad and solid as an oak tree and looked as if he hadn't seen civilization in months. He was dressed in common clothing; his shirt and pants were clean but wrinkled. Dirt caked the heels of his sturdy brown boots. His thick reddish-brown hair was tied back with a strip of leather. If left unbound, it would likely skim the bottom of his collar. While he appeared to have a strong facial structure, his mustache and beard obscured the lower half of his face. His mouth was wide and generous. Sparkling blue eyes assessed her.

"Would you care to dance?" He spoke in a rolling brogue that identified him as a foreigner.

The other girls had fallen silent and were watching him in awed stupor.

"Are you speaking to me, Irishman?" Caroline raised her brows.

He flashed a lopsided grin. "I'm no Irishman. I hail from Aberdeen, Scotland. And yes, I'm wantin' to know if you'd like to dance."

The way he pronounced his *o*'s teased her ears. Interest stirred to life, and she considered accepting his invitation. Then reason prevailed. As a member of one of Gatlinburg's most prominent families, she couldn't allow her reputation to become tarnished. In the Turner family, missteps were frowned upon.

"I don't associate with drifters."

"I take it your answer is no then?"

Regret sharpened her tone. "I believe I made myself clear."

His gaze turned mocking as he sketched a bow. "Forgive me for intruding upon your time, fair lass."

"I'll dance with you," Vivian Lowe practically purred.

Caroline and the others gaped at her.

"Will ya now? I'm a fortunate man."

Then, to Caroline's chagrin, he shucked the large pack from his back and thrust it at her. "Watch this for me, will ya?"

She struggled beneath its unwieldy weight, glaring as he led Vivian in a routine with the form and grace of an accomplished dancer.

"Caroline Grace Turner, what are you doing standing here dillydallying?" Her mother marched to her side. "You're supposed to be overseeing the stations. Ida has run out of potato salad and the Jackson sisters spilled a gallon jar of tea on Mr. Williams." Louise's upper lip curled. "What is *that*?"

"Nothing, Mother." Letting the pack thunk to the dry grass, she shot one last disgruntled glance in the direction of the dancers and trailed behind her mother like the dutiful daughter she was supposed to be.

Duncan McKenna should've known better than to ask the cool blonde to dance, but full of relief that his long journey was at an end, he'd given in to a spurt of optimism. He should've guessed that the alluring mystery in her navy-hued eyes and the sweet curve of her mouth were too good to be true. He watched her dump his belongings, her haughty features registering distaste, and march off with the silver-haired matron.

Lanterns suspended from stakes throughout the fields emitted soft light. As she passed one, the diamonds draped around her neck and wrists glittered and the silken, pearl-like fabric of her billowing skirts shimmered. The elegant dress displayed her statuesque, pleasing figure to perfection. A shame her attitude didn't match her outward beauty.

"Was Caroline right? Are you just passing through?"

Duncan switched his attention to the coy brunette in his arms. "Your friend was mistaken. I'm plannin' on stickin' around for a bit."

Her face brightened. "That's wonderful news. I'm Vivian Lowe, by the way."

"Duncan McKenna."

The music came to an end, and she made no effort to hide her disappointment. "I'm free for the next dance." Her shining hazel eyes implored him to extend their time together.

"If I hadn't ridden fifteen miles today, I would be honored to be your partner again." He smiled to soften the blow.

Her gloved hand latching on to his forearm, she leaned closer than good manners dictated. "Let me purchase you a lemonade then. You must be parched after so long a journey."

"Maybe another time."

Vivian accepted his excuse with a barely concealed pout. "I look forward to seeing you again, Duncan McKenna."

Bidding her goodnight, Duncan went to reclaim his belongings. He'd met forward young ladies in almost every town he'd sojourned in and had avoided them like the plague. The woman he desired for a wife and helpmeet wouldn't be so desperate for male company that she latched onto random strangers.

A young lawman waited beside Duncan's pack, boots planted wide and arms crossed beneath a glinting silver star, no doubt bent on interrogating him. Caroline's assessment wasn't far-fetched. Small towns tended to be suspicious of strangers.

"Good evenin' to ya." He held out his hand. "Duncan McKenna's the name."

"Ben MacGregor." With hair more deeply red than his own, and green eyes that seemed inclined to mischief, the man could've hailed from the same bonny isle as Duncan. His accent bore an easy Southern cadence, however. "I don't recall seeing you around these parts before. Family in the area?"

Resettling his pack on his shoulders, he shook his head. "I'm here for work. Albert Turner hired me to care for his horses."

"You're the new stable manager? I heard he found someone to replace old George. Welcome to Gatlinburg." His smile turned rueful. "I see you've already met Albert's daughter."

Duncan surveyed the milling crowd.

17

"Who? Vivian?"

"Ah, no. Caroline Turner." Ben jerked his chin in the direction of the refreshment tables. The blonde was there in what appeared to be a supervisory role. The girls enduring her instructions clustered together, their expressions reminiscent of those in the presence of royalty.

The exhaustion he'd been keeping at bay poured through him. His body begged for a dark room and a soft mattress where he could stretch out and sleep without having to listen for wild animals on the prowl or two-legged creatures up to no good. The anticipation over his new employment waned. He would have to cross paths with the snooty socialite on a regular basis.

"Does Mr. Turner have any more daughters I should be aware of?"

Ben tucked his thumbs in his pockets. "No, and we should count ourselves fortunate on that score." At Duncan's continued scowl, he chuckled. "Caroline's not so bad once you get to know her."

Before leaving Boston and his family behind, he'd known scores of women exactly like her. He had no wish to associate with more.

"Come with me," Ben said. "I'll help you locate Albert."

They wove their way through the throng of youngsters and adults. As they neared the table Caroline was stationed behind, her almond-shaped eyes lit on his and with a disapproving frown, she turned away. Duncan could well imagine her reaction when she learned the news of his employment and hoped he was around to witness it.

Caroline descended the stairs much later than usual the next morning. Disturbing dreams had troubled her sleep. Lack of rest wasn't the only reason she'd lingered in bed. Today she would make yet another trip to the bank, enduring the clerk's censorious stare as she made up another false story about an expensive bauble she wished to purchase. Then she'd ride out to the north side of the property, where she'd leave the demanded amount. She wondered how long this would continue. Eventually she'd run out of money, and then what?

As she neared the dining room, the rich aroma of hot coffee mixed with chicory wrapped around her. Her father had gone to New Orleans last month and purchased multiple tins. Her anticipation vanished the moment she crossed the threshold. The hulking Scotsman from last night's festivities was seated at her table. A china plate piled high with Cook's usual breakfast offerings was in front of him.

"You."

He appeared marginally tamer this morning, with the charcoal-gray shirt molded to the impressive breadth of his shoulders looking clean and pressed. In the light streaming through the windows, his hair had the rich sheen of mahogany. Once again, he'd restrained it with a strip of leather. He looked like a man who spent much of his time apart from society, nothing like the distinguished Charleston businessmen who usually used her home for a mountain retreat.

Shockingly, it was his untamed quality that appealed to her. Caroline's world was constructed of rigid rules and expectations. Duncan McKenna seemed to live to please himself. A heady prospect. The fact that she'd never partake in such personal freedom stoked her bad mood.

Lifting his head, he did a lazy inspection of her with his cobalt blue gaze.

"Good mornin', Caroline." His voice was deep and thick. The way he pronounced her name, with a slight roll of the *r,* sounded like music.

She advanced to the table and gripped the top rung of the chair opposite him. "I want you to leave."

He took a long draw of coffee, then plucked a sausage link from his plate and bit off half. Grinning as he chewed, he said, "*'Tisna* your house, is it, but your father's. I'm here on his approval."

"My father doesn't make a habit of inviting drifters to share our table. What did you do? Follow me here last night? Did you sleep in the woods and wait for your opportunity?"

His grin faded. "I'm no' a drifter."

Her nails dug into the polished wood. Her mother would throttle her if she marred the furniture. Inhaling deeply, she lowered her arms to her sides. She would not allow him to provoke her. Dealing with irritating people and situations was commonplace.

"Who are you then?"

Determined footsteps echoed in the hall and her father entered, newspaper rolled and tucked beneath his arm. His salt-and-pepper hair was combed off his high forehead. Dressed in a severe black suit, a gold tack pinned into his red tie, he'd long ago perfected the image of a successful businessman.

Caroline used to be in awe of him, of his accomplishments and the respect he had commanded in their former home of

Charleston, the state of South Carolina and beyond. Now, whenever she was in the same room with him, she questioned if his character was as sterling as she'd thought. Was his success based on honest practices? Or was he, like other kings of industry she'd read about, pursuing wealth at the expense of integrity? The documents the blackmailer had provided as an impetus to meet his demands were upstairs in her room. Copies, of course, in case she was tempted to destroy the evidence. But were they copies of authentic documents or were they falsified?

Albert spared her a brief glance. "Ah, Caroline, I see you've met Duncan. He's taking George's place." Striding over to the silver urn, he dispensed coffee into his cup and stirred in a generous portion of cream. "How did you fare last night, Duncan? Does the cabin suit you?"

"Aye, sir. I slept like a bairn."

George? Cabin? "Y-you hired him?"

Mr. McKenna's gaze, bright with humor, shifted to her. He ducked his head, but not before she saw his slow grin. He was enjoying her shock.

"Yes, Caroline." Looking down his hawkish nose at her, Albert addressed her as one would a difficult child. "Mr. McKenna is

22

our stable manager now. He came highly recommended from the Stuarts."

"Your friends in North Carolina?"

He nodded. Leaning against the sideboard, he said, "I expect you to make him feel welcome. In fact, you can give him the grand tour of the property. I've got a meeting at the bank this morning."

"Bank? Why are you going there?" Anxiety rose up to choke her. "Is there a problem?"

His brows pulled together over his nose. "You're acting strangely this morning. Perhaps you need to eat your breakfast instead of peppering me with questions." He started for the door, pausing but for a moment to address Duncan. "We'll talk later."

Duncan dipped his head. "Aye, sir."

When they were alone again, he motioned with his fork and winked at her. "I recommend the flapjacks."

She stiffened. "I don't need your recommendations, Mr. McKenna. Cook has been with us since I was eleven." Stalking over to the sideboard, she filled her plate without paying attention to what she was doing, her thoughts focused on one thing — her life had just gotten more complicated.

When she took the seat across from him, he blinked in surprise. "A hearty appetite, I see. Wouldn't have guessed it. But then, I learned a long time ago not to judge people on their appearance."

The arrow hit home. Sipping her tea, she wished he'd leave.

"Does Cook have a name?"

The cup rattled as she replaced it in the saucer. "Of course she does."

"What is it?"

Caroline raked her memory and came up empty. The buxom, wiry-haired woman who prepared their meals had always been referred to as Cook. "If you're so interested, why don't you ask her?"

He smirked, his gaze condemning. Duncan McKenna thought she was a snob.

"You don't know it. To you, she and the other staff aren't people. They're simply fixtures here to make your life easy."

His condemnation shouldn't sting. He was a crude, ill-educated stranger who was clearly envious of those who'd achieved success.

"You don't know anything about me, Mr. McKenna. Who's the one judging now?"

Surging to her feet, she tossed her napkin over her plate and opted to escape. These days, trying to protect her father's reputation consumed all her energy. She didn't

24

have the capability to cope with an infuriating employee on top of everything else.

CHAPTER TWO

He'd driven her from her breakfast. Not exactly gentlemanly behavior. Nor was it wise to provoke the boss's daughter.

Duncan scraped his chair back and hurried into the high-ceilinged, papered hallway in the center of the house, catching up to her on the veranda that ran the length of the rear exterior. Pots of cheerful yellow blossoms lined the white railing and flanked the steps. White wicker chairs were arranged to take advantage of the pastoral view, verdant fields that gave way to forest framed by majestic, blue-toned mountains.

"Caroline, wait."

On the crest of the steps, she slowly pivoted. Her delicate features were arranged into a controlled mask, but he could see the rapid pulse leaping at her neck. She wasn't as nonchalant as she'd like him to think.

"I don't recall giving you leave to address me by my first name."

"You were right back there. I don't know you and have no business commenting on your character." He jerked a thumb over his shoulder. "You *didnae* touch your food. I'll leave you alone to enjoy your breakfast."

She regarded him with a less-than-friendly gaze. Despite her attitude, she presented a vision that, if a man wasn't careful, could blind him to her obvious faults. Her sapphire-blue dress, a perfect choice for her fair complexion, draped over her figure like a glove. Her white-blond tresses were arranged in a sophisticated style, parted down the side and swept into a tight chignon at the back of her head. There were no diamonds today, only a ribbon choker about her neck and a blue-and-white cameo nestled in the dip of her collarbone.

"I lost my appetite." Presenting her back to him, she pointed to the stables situated close to the house. "Let's get this over with."

A dignified figure rounded the house and made to intercept them. The epitome of studied elegance, the lady was an older, more pinched version of Caroline. Her eyes weren't nearly as stunning, the color a washed-out, watery blue, and her blond hair was threaded liberally with silver. He didn't need Caroline's introduction to make the connection. Louise dismissed him with a single glance.

"Caroline, what are you doing?"

"Father asked me to give Mr. McKenna a tour of the property."

"We have to plan our menus for next week."

"Can we do that after lunch?"

Her mouth puckered and lines fanned out above her upper lip. "I suppose I can rearrange my schedule." Squinting, she fussed with her daughter's sleeves, plumping the fabric. "This color is all wrong for you."

Pink rose in Caroline's cheeks. "No one is going to see me in it, Mother."

He caught the implication. No one that counted, himself included. As a hired employee, his opinion about such things didn't matter. They viewed him as unimportant because they assumed he was poor and uneducated. Bitterness surged. He'd happily left this sort of narrow-minded attitude behind in Boston.

"I told you to stick to pastels."

"We're boring Mr. McKenna." Caroline's smile was brittle. "We'll discuss this later." Head held high, she started for the nearest stable entrance.

"Excuse us, Mrs. Turner," Duncan said.

Her nose wrinkled in distaste and she disappeared into the house.

Duncan entered the long building. The air was sweet with the scent of hay. High windows had been opened to let the breeze circulate. Dust motes danced in the square of light spilling through the open entrance.

Speaking in brisk tones, Caroline showed him the tack and equipment rooms on his left. A sturdy ladder led to a hayloft that extended the length of the building. The cobblestones beneath their feet were worn to a shiny patina and swept clean. Box stalls flanked either side of the wide center aisle. Only about half of them were occupied. One by one, she introduced him to the ten horses they owned. When she got to the last one, affection lightened her voice.

"This pretty lady is Rain." Pulling a carrot from her pocket, she fed it to the mare and ran her hand lovingly along its neck.

Duncan found himself captivated by the pure joy Caroline radiated and the way it softened her. He wouldn't have pegged her for an animal lover. His conscience pricked him. The Turners weren't the only ones capable of making judgments.

Joining her, he greeted Rain, taking in the healthy state of her dapple-gray coat and black mane. "She's yours?"

"Yes. I was unhappy when we first moved here from Charleston. My father bought her in hopes of appeasing me."

"How old were you?"

"Fifteen."

Old enough to have strong ties to her former home. As much as he preferred his current life, there were things — and people — he still missed.

"Did it work?"

Her rose-hued lips rolled together, pressing down. "Rain is my one bright spot."

Before he could question the cryptic statement, she stepped back, businesslike once again. "As you can see, we have ample space to board our frequent visitors' animals. Next week we have several guests joining us. You'll have extra duties."

"I can handle it." He shrugged. "You have an impressive setup."

She lifted her chin. "Ours are the largest, most well-equipped stables in Gatlinburg."

Duncan refrained from telling her that the McKenna stables were triple this size.

An adolescent boy walked in the far entrance, thin arms straining with a pair of buckets. Duncan strode to help him.

"Thank you, sir, but I can manage." His brown hair was cut short, and there was a gap between his front teeth. "Good morning, Miss Caroline."

"Anthony, I'd like you to meet your new

boss, Duncan McKenna."

The lad snapped to attention, chest puffed out. "Glad to meet you, Mr. McKenna."

"Likewise." Duncan pointed to the buckets. "Sure you won't be needing assistance?"

"No, sir."

"I'll return shortly to see to Rain," she told Anthony. "You may turn the others out to the paddocks."

"Yes, ma'am."

Duncan stopped beside a room she'd failed to show him. He touched the handle. "What's in here?"

"Personal storage." She made a dismissive gesture and continued walking.

He thought it odd to keep such items in a stable, but he chose not to question her.

They exited into the sunshine. The humidity closed in around him. If Tennessee's climate was anything like North Carolina's, he was in for some sweltering summer days. He reached up and tightened the strip restraining his hair. He needed to cut it. His parents and brothers wouldn't recognize him. After working in the great outdoors these many months, his skin had taken on a cinnamon hue, and he'd acquired more freckles on his forearms. He'd let his hair grow to his shoulders, and his beard was thick. He stroked it now, thinking it was

31

probably time to shave it off.

Caroline caught the gesture and frowned.

He mentally shrugged. Or not.

She showed him the various sheds, smoke-houses and other buildings. To his surprise, she was knowledgeable about the farm's workings. At the barn, which was half the size of the stables, she introduced him to another employee.

The gentleman had stooped shoulders, flyaway black hair and skin like leather. His Native American heritage was obvious, and Duncan wondered if he were Cherokee. His brown-black gaze, when it lit on Caroline, brightened like the sun coming out from behind the clouds.

"Wendell takes care of the livestock," she told him matter-of-factly. "But his primary task is making sure the landscaping is up to Mother's exacting standards."

"Miss Caroline is the true gardener around here," Wendell said with obvious pride.

Bending to pat the orange cat sniffing at her skirts, she frowned. "Don't let my mother hear you say that."

Duncan watched the exchange with interest. He couldn't imagine pristine Caroline Turner getting her hands dirty.

"We have to continue on, Wendell."

After he shook hands with Wendell, Caroline led Duncan outside. To their right, chickens pecked at the ground inside their pen. She checked the watch pin attached to her bodice, and her features grew pensive.

"You'll have to explore the rest of the grounds on your own." Without another word, she headed in the direction of the house.

"You're abandoning me midtour then?"

She turned and shaded her eyes with her hand. "I have an important matter to tend to."

"A shopping excursion that can't wait?" Plunging his hands in his pockets, he strolled to her side. "Or a gossip session with your friends? Is it your habit to abandon your duties, Caroline?"

That pulse at the base of her throat leapt again. Her fascinating eyes, however, remained frost-edged. "I don't know how you conduct yourselves over in Scotland, but around here, the hired help is expected to treat their employers with utmost respect. My father has high expectations, Mr. Turner. Fail him and you'll be cut loose."

Duncan wasn't sure why he was intent on baiting this woman. The only reason he could think of was that she was a handy target for the anger he'd thought he'd released long before now. He wanted to tell her that money and prestige didn't make her better than him. He was tempted to tell her that her family's wealth was a drop in the bucket compared to the McKennas'. He did neither. He'd rather have her honest dislike than fake regard.

Duncan liked what he'd seen so far of this part of the country. While he didn't plan on settling here, he didn't intend to ruin what time he did have.

"I *didnae* step off the boat yesterday."

"You could've fooled me."

With that parting shot, she left him standing there, making him wonder what it was that made her so unhappy.

The isolation of this part of their property unsettled Caroline. The forest had closed in after she'd passed the stable manager's cabin — Mr. McKenna's home for the foreseeable future — and the terrain had become steeper. At the gurgling, rock-strewn stream, she slid to the ground and, keeping hold of the reins, inspected her surroundings. She couldn't see any signs of other human life. Lofty trees marched in uneven succession in all directions. The forest was mostly a study in contrasts of brown earth littered with decomposing leaves, darker brown trunks and vivid green foliage — from leafy bowers twitching in the breeze to ferns growing in profusion on the forest floor to lichen patches on trunks and moss ringing the trees.

A testament to God's artistic perfection, the Smoky Mountains were wild and beautiful but not without hidden dangers. Somewhere nearby, someone lurked, possibly watching her.

Her hands clammy, she removed the black pouch from her pocket. She picked up her skirts and, picking her way across the rocks, laid it on the remains of a tree stump. Like every time before, she questioned if what she was doing was right. Should she confront her father? They'd never had a close relationship. Questioning his integrity would wound his pride and drive him farther away. But how long could this continue? Her funds weren't unlimited.

The blackmailer had working knowledge of the Turner factories in Charleston. He knew that despite her father's semi-retirement, he still had control of operations. He also knew Caroline had access to her inheritance. In January, she'd received the first note threatening to expose her father's unsavory business practices. If valid, the claims in the documents had the potential to crumble the Turner empire. Over the years, her father had cultivated a reputation of providing the very best in skin care.

Their products — ranging from soaps and emollient creams to perfumes and bath oils — had become synonymous with opulence and self-indulgence. Only the wealthy could afford them. The exorbitant prices were justified by their exotic, hard-to-obtain ingredients. Caroline's blackmailer maintained that, while Albert had initially adhered to such practices, he'd recently taken to forgoing the expense of locating and transporting said ingredients and substituting them with common chemicals. Until Caroline could find a way to substantiate these claims, she would meet his demands.

She was halfway across the stream when a rustling sound to her right made her stumble. Her boot sank into the cold water. Sucking in a sharp breath, she completed a jerky revolution, searching the woods below and rocky outcrops above. Had he decided to expose his identity? Would he do her physical harm?

But the source of her fright turned out to be a bandit-faced raccoon scouting for a meal. Caroline rushed to the other bank and clumsily mounted Rain, ready to be gone from there. Half an hour later, once again in the safety of her home, she was too distracted to give her mother's disparaging comments about her muddy boots and bedraggled hem much thought. Caroline absentmindedly changed into a lavender outfit that would please Louise's sense of style.

On a whim, she eased the bulging satchel from beneath her bed and ran her fingers along the supple, caramel-hued leather, stirring the dust on its surface and causing her to sneeze. Inside, there were a couple of outfits, grooming accessories and a wad of money. While the satchel had never been used, it wasn't new. She'd purchased it three years ago as a sort of promise to herself that, if her life became intolerable, she'd leave this town for good and never look back.

So far, she hadn't worked up the courage to use it. Or maybe she hadn't reached her breaking point yet.

Movement in the hallway startled her. Shoving it back under the bedframe, she intercepted their housekeeper in the hallway. Shy and skittish as a mouse, the young woman was dependable and hardworking. Louise fretted at times that she didn't pay attention to details, however.

"I'm going to freshen up your room, Miss Caroline." She indicated the mound of clean bedding in her arms.

"All right, Sylvia."

See? She did know her employees. Duncan McKenna was wrong about her. He had to be, because the picture he painted of her was most unflattering.

On the landing, she cupped the cone-shaped knob on the handrail. "Thank you, Sylvia."

The housekeeper's slim face registered surprise. She tucked a tendril of dark hair beneath her mobcap. "Oh, miss, there's no need to thank me. It's my job."

Caroline spent the remainder of the day making out menus and reassigning guest rooms for their arrivals the following week. They may have left Charleston years ago, but their ties to that city remained intact. Business associates and friends visited throughout the year, so much so that her home sometimes felt like a hotel. The news that Isaiah Marsh and his son, Theo, had been added to the guest list wasn't exactly welcome. Isaiah was boisterous and tended to make crude jokes. Theo wasn't anything like him. The thirty-year-old heir to a fortune was suave, handsome and smart as a whip. A definite catch. It was the calculating aspect of his personality that gave Caroline pause. He was one of a carousel of suitable bachelors her mother had attempted to pair her with. In Louise's opinion, any single man between the ages of twenty and forty with the right pedigree and desired amount in their bank account was suitable husband material. Thankfully, Theo was as uninterested in wedding her as she was him.

Marriage didn't strike her as an institution she wanted any part of. As far back as she could remember, her parents' strained relationship had been marked with indifference on her father's part and nagging reprimands on her mother's. They didn't esteem each other. There'd been few displays of affection. She hadn't realized there was anything amiss until her adolescent years, when she'd noticed her friends' parents' behavior differed from her own. The situation had only worsened with the move to Tennessee, but her mother's complaints to Albert had fallen on deaf ears. So she'd determined to become the social queen of Gatlinburg, and Caroline was expected to play her part as reigning princess.

Her nerves were frayed by the time dinner rolled around. Her father had extended an invitation to the banker and his wife, Claude and Merilee Jenkins, as well as the reverend and his wife. As they gathered around the sumptuously laid table, the silver candle-holders polished to a high shine and candle-light reflected in the mirrors on the walls, Caroline prayed that Claude wouldn't mention her frequent visits to the bank.

She had gone to the kitchen to ensure the soup was ready to serve when Duncan Mc-Kenna slipped inside the rear hallway. She stopped short to avoid a collision with the Goliath. He put out a hand to steady her. The feel of his rough skin against hers evoked a strange fluttering sensation in her middle.

Caroline jerked out of his grip. "You picked a bad time to speak with my father. He's entertaining guests."

The scent of Ivory soap clung to him. The waning sunlight entering the hallway set his hair and beard aflame. The effect of it all, combined with those startlingly blue eyes, made him more striking than any other man she'd encountered, even with the beard.

He didn't make his apologies and exit as expected. He remained exactly where he was, his potent gaze sweeping her person before lifting once more to her face, giving her the impression he saw much more than was on the surface.

"I'm not sure I agree with your *mathair.*"

"Excuse me?"

"The color of your dress," he stated. "I liked the one you had on this morning better. The dark blue matched your eyes and brought a bloom to your cheeks."

Other men had paid her compliments. Theirs hadn't filled her with a giddy contentment and longing to hear more.

It's the accent, she told herself.

"You're being familiar again, Mr. McKenna. We are about to have dinner. You'll have to come back in the morning. *After* breakfast."

His nostrils flared. Hands on his hips, he bent closer, his sculpted mouth filling her vision. "Tell me something, Caroline. What is it about me that offends you so? Is it because I, a lowly working man, dared to ask you for a dance?"

Her father's voice dispelled the tart response forming on her lips.

"Ah, there you are, Duncan. There are some people I'd like you to meet."

Caroline shifted out of the Scotsman's way.

He smoothed his beard. "I don't wish to intrude, sir."

"Nonsense." Albert made a dismissive motion. "Caroline, put another setting at the table."

Squashing her objection, she dipped her

41

head. "Yes, Father."

Before Duncan made to move past her, he looked at her, lips trembling with amusement. Her skin flushed hot. And to think, mere moments ago, she'd been drawn in by what she'd assumed was sincere admiration. This stranger had a habit of laughing at her expense. As the men disappeared into the dining room, she wondered if complaining to her father would do any good. Duncan McKenna was proving to be troublesome in more ways than she'd first anticipated.

CHAPTER THREE

Duncan slid the succulent beef into his mouth and savored the mushroom gravy it was coated in. He hadn't enjoyed a spread like this since before he'd set out on his own. The dining room was a sumptuous, understated display of elegance in hues of silver and blue. Dark, heavy furniture contrasted with papered ivory walls. Suspended above the table, the chandelier sparkled with a hundred crystals. Candles that were interspersed among serving platters shimmered off the silver-rimmed china. If not for his upbringing, he'd have been intimidated by his host's obvious wealth and social connections.

Albert sat at the head of the table. Louise helmed the opposite end.

"How long have you been in the country?" Reverend Monroe, a serious man who wore compassion like a second skin, asked from the far end beside Louise.

"Ten years. My grandparents came five years before that and, once settled in Boston, encouraged my father to join them. I was sixteen when we left Scotland. I *havnae* been home since."

"Scotland or Boston?" Louise chose to belatedly acknowledge his presence with a sardonic question.

"Scotland is the jewel of my heart. I will always consider it my home." His gaze was drawn to the woman seated opposite. Caroline poured a thin stream of cream into her teacup. He had yet to catch her eye. That she resented his presence was obvious. "As for Boston, I *havnae* visited that city since I left, either."

While he yearned to roam the rolling green hills of his native land once more, his feelings about the bustling city where his soul had nearly succumbed to darkness were more complicated.

Claude Jenkins sat on Duncan's left. "What made you decide to travel?" he asked.

His wife leaned forward to address Duncan across Claude's barrel chest. "You're plenty old enough to settle down. Aren't you interested in finding a wife? Starting a family?"

"I was engaged once," he admitted. "It

didn't work out."

Over the lip of her china cup, Caroline's navy-hued gaze swerved to his. Her curiosity was plain. Was she wondering what type of woman would agree to marry him?

Mrs. Munroe made pitying noises. The reverend wore an expression of confidence. " 'Delight thyself also in the Lord, and He shall give thee the desires of thine heart.' Keep praying. God will lead you to the right woman in His time."

Before Duncan could respond, Caroline lowered her cup and spoke. "You didn't answer the other question. Why did you leave Boston? What would possess a person to leave their friends and family behind?"

He got the impression her aim wasn't to provoke him but to glean an honest answer. Surely the lady wasn't thinking of leaving her privileged life?

"America is a land of abundance," he said. "Varying landscapes. Fascinating people. I yearned to explore more of it."

He spoke the truth, just not its entirety. Edwin Naughton's face as he lay dying flashed in his memory, and the familiar shaft of guilt and regret gutted him. He may not have caused his valet's death, but it could've been prevented if Duncan had taken action. Sometimes, when he thought back on his former life, he didn't recognize the man he used to be.

Albert nodded sagely. "The desire for adventure is built into a man's character, as is the drive to conquer his world."

"My father encouraged me and my brothers to do just that."

"I only hope you've had enough to satisfy you for a while." Albert's smile was polite and entirely professional. "We'd like to keep you around as long as we're able."

Caroline suffered a coughing fit just then. Covering her mouth with her napkin, she mumbled an apology.

Claude asked about his travels, about the people and places he'd seen, and so Duncan regaled them with the more interesting and humorous bits. Neither Louise nor her daughter remarked on his speech. While the older woman regarded him as one would a pesky rodent inside the flour bin, Caroline followed the conversation with barely concealed interest. Well aware *he* wasn't her favorite topic, he surmised that stories of other places intrigued her. The Turners had the means to travel, but perhaps she'd chosen to stay close to home.

Louise rose to her feet and, diverting her guests' attention, announced that dessert and coffee would be served in the parlor.

46

Duncan intercepted her reluctant glance his way and decided to offer his thanks for the meal and return to his cabin. While Albert and the other couples had made him feel welcome, the Turner females would clearly like to be rid of him. His proud Scottish heritage welled inside him. In his younger years, he would've stayed to spite them. He'd changed in more ways than one. No use sticking around where he wasn't wanted.

Duncan hadn't meant to eavesdrop. He'd come inside to discuss the ordering of supplies when he'd heard Caroline utter his name. In the hallway outside Albert's study, he hesitated, debating whether to step into the open doorway and announce his presence or leave the way he'd come.

"Why him?" she lamented. "Why not hire someone local?"

"Because no one local has his qualifications." Exasperation colored his tone. "George had been struggling the last few years to accomplish his tasks. I kept him on as a courtesy. McKenna's just the man to restore things to their rightful order."

"Father, you haven't heard the way he speaks to me. Mr. McKenna has the manners of a . . . of a . . ." she said, floundering. "He's infuriating!"

Holding his hat in his hands, Duncan fought his rising temper, fingers crushing the crown. How dare she? If she cost him this job . . . Of course, there'd be others. But he'd just got here. He wanted to explore, meet the locals. Rest from his long journey over the mountains separating North Carolina and Tennessee.

"He seems like a perfectly reasonable man to me. Has he made untoward advances?"

Silence. Duncan's whole body tensed. If she lied, he'd be run out of town.

"No," she said at last.

His head fell back and he offered a silent prayer of thanksgiving.

"Give it some time." Albert's leather chair creaked. "This time next week, you'll be too busy entertaining our guests to exchange more than a dozen words with him. Your mother tells me Theo Marsh is looking forward to seeing you again."

"Mother is engaging in wishful thinking." She made a huff of displeasure. "What about after everyone leaves? How am I supposed to go about my daily life with him around, waiting to antagonize me?"

"I'm sure you're exaggerating. Duncan comes on the highest recommendation. We need him."

"But —"

"I suggest you apply your energy to what you do best — parting me from my money."

Duncan pivoted and walked lightly down the hall, bent on escape. Anger firing his blood, he pushed into the sunshine and smashed his hat on his head. He felt like kicking something. Or planting his fist into a wall. He settled for hefting grain sacks from the delivery wagon to the feed room. The physical labor helped expend the resentment burning through his veins. He was mucking out the stalls when she strode through the entrance.

"Why are you doing Anthony's job?"

The temper he'd wrestled with his entire life begged to be let loose. Calling on his self-control, he tunneled the pitchfork into the straw.

"Why does it bother you?" he bit out.

"Forget I asked."

He continued working while she saddled her mare. As she made to lead Rain outside, he couldn't maintain his silence any longer. Fingers still curled about the pitchfork, he moved into the aisle. She slowed, her demeanor wary.

"I heard you talking to your father about me."

Color brushed her cheekbones. "You were eavesdropping?"

"That *wasnae* my intent, I assure you. Nevertheless, I heard what you said, and I want you to know I plan on keeping this job. I'm no' keen on traversing those mountains again anytime soon."

Averting her face, she caressed Rain's neck. "I realize you have to earn a living," she conceded. "And since my father is resolved to keep you around, I suggest we agree to steer clear of each other."

Surprise stilled his tongue. She was offering a practical solution?

He became enthralled by the affection shining in her eyes as she gazed at her beloved horse. What would it be like if she were to turn that affection on him? Yearning arced through him like a bolt of lightning, rooting him to the ground. He didn't like Caroline, so why entertain such thoughts about her?

Had to be loneliness. He'd broken off his engagement to Maureen Craig a few weeks before he'd left Boston, which was well over a year ago now. He hadn't courted a woman since. Of late, he'd been thinking more often about finding a wife, settling into married life and starting a family.

He cleared his throat. "I, ah, believe that's reasonable."

Their gazes meshed, and he found himself

searching for answers. What made this woman tick? Was there more depth to her than he'd first thought?

"Then we have an agreement," she said. "You stay out of my way, and I stay out of yours."

His fingers curled into the wooden handle. "Aye."

Focused on her exit from the building, he didn't hear Wendell approach and nearly jumped out of his skin when the man spoke directly behind him.

"You misunderstand Miss Caroline."

Turning around, he said, "Good morning, Wendell. Can I help you with something?"

Wendell's brown-black gaze was knowing. "Miss Caroline is like a cactus fruit. Prickly on the outside but soft and sweet on the inside."

"There's nothing sweet about that woman."

"A wise man learns to look beyond the obvious. She hasn't had an easy life." His attention moved beyond Duncan's shoulder to the grand Victorian-style house visible through the entrance, the sun bathing its green exterior and white trim in golden light.

Duncan had sensed that all was not well between Caroline and her parents. Didn't mean she had the right to treat others, mainly him, as if they were the dirt beneath her high-priced boots. Being around Caroline was like looking into a window to his past. He used to think like her. Before he'd become a follower of Jesus, he'd bought the lie that earthly riches and achievements gave him value. He'd treated those he considered his equals with respect. Those who were poorer, who were of the working class or not members of the right family, he'd ignored altogether. He cringed with shame every time he thought about his boorish behavior.

"Give her a chance," Wendell advised, bringing him back to the present.

The man's words stuck with him the rest of the day. As the days rolled past, he couldn't get them out of his head. Was she hiding her true self behind that aloof exterior? Or was she exactly what she presented to the world?

Disgusted with his preoccupation, he went out of his way to avoid her. A week passed without them having to exchange more than a simple greeting. There were no more dinners in the Turner house. Whenever he needed to confer with Albert, he waited until he was certain she was out of the house. And any time she entered the stables, he found an excuse to tend to tasks else-where. It wasn't an ideal situation, but it maintained a tenuous peace between them.

That Friday, he ate his lunch as usual on the porch steps of his temporary home. Situated across the fields and tucked deep in the woods, the cabin couldn't be seen from the main area of the property. About a ten-minute walk from the main house, the cabin was self-sustainable with a vegetable garden, smokehouse, chicken coop and a decent-sized barn. The home itself consisted of one room, with a bare-bones kitchen — a cast-iron stove in decent condition, a lop-sided hutch and a handful of shelves to hold pots and other utensils — and a bed pushed against one wall. Two chairs were situated at the square table made of pine. The place might not be fancy, but it suited his needs.

Finished with his lunch, he started along the path toward the Turners' house, whis-tling a jaunty tune he'd learned as a child. When he emerged into the fields, instead of heading to the stables, he decided to explore the section of the property Caroline had failed to show him. According to Anthony, there was a pond large enough for fishing and swimming that Albert had given them permission to use.

Shin-high grass whispered against his pant

legs as he strolled past the grazing fields and paddocks, past the vegetable garden with its neat, even rows that were pungent with the smells of sun-warmed tomatoes, green peppers, cantaloupe and toiled earth. He entered the apple orchard next. A small one, compared to the farm he'd worked before this, but ample for their needs. The orchard gave way to mature oak and maple trees that were more distantly spaced than in the forest. Ahead in a meadow dotted with a riot of wildflowers, sunlight shimmered off the glass-like surface of the pond.

Enthralled by the serene view, he didn't at first notice he wasn't alone. But as he neared the water's edge, he spotted the green canoe floating atop the surface. Duncan blinked at the unusual sight of Caroline at rest.

She lay very still, a folded shawl cushioning her head and her hands folded over a leather-bound book, her chest rising and falling in an even rhythm. Water gently lapped the sides of the craft. Overhanging branches cast her upper body in shade, while the afternoon sun painted her in buttery light from the waist down.

In the delicate peach dress, with her countenance smooth, the long, curved lashes kissing her skin and her dusky pink mouth soft and slack, she looked as if she belonged in a painting.

A funny feeling took root in his chest. *This* girl, the one who wasn't looking at him with lips curled and eyes as wintry as the North Pole, was someone he might like to get to know. Too bad it was a mirage.

Intending to leave as quietly as he came, Duncan turned to leave. But then his nose twitched, and he sneezed suddenly and violently. With a startled cry, Caroline bolted upright and scrambled to her feet, barely catching her book before it fell. The canoe rocked.

"You!"

Sidling down the grassy slope, he put up a warning hand. "Careful, lass. You could —"

"How long were you watching me?" Color raced along her cheekbones, her expression aghast.

"No longer than five or ten minutes," he quipped, unable to resist teasing her. "Maybe fifteen. Did you know you snore?"

She sputtered. "I do *not* snore!"

She shifted and the canoe dipped.

"Caroline . . ."

Arms flailing, she went right over the edge backward into the blue-green water. Duncan fought the urge to laugh. Wading into the shallow water, he reached her in four long strides.

"My book!" Ignoring his outstretched hand, she dove for it, grasped it with trembling fingers. Mouth pursed in a flat line, she flipped through the now-sodden pages. "It's ruined."

"I'll replace it," he said. "Give me your hand."

She inspected the sodden fabric of her dress. "Mother is going to have an apoplectic fit."

"You have dozens of other dresses in your wardrobe, I'm sure."

"Our guests are arriving later this afternoon. I'll have to redo my hair!"

"It's not the end of the world." His fingers closed around her upper arm. It was impossible not to notice the warm suppleness of her skin. "Come on."

She shrugged him off. Chest heaving, she crossed her arms and delivered a withering stare. The effect was ruined by the darkened strands plastered to her nape and cheeks. Her hair arrangement drooped, and there was more than one leaf lodged in the mass.

Her fair beauty was undeniable. He tried to imagine what she'd look like with eyes soft with approval and her mouth curved in a sincere smile. He couldn't quite manage it.

"This is your fault," she spat. "If you hadn't been spying on me, this wouldn't have happened."

"I wasn't spying on you." Water lapped at his thighs and seeped into his boots. Even so, his temperature ratcheted up a notch. Would she run to Albert with this, too? "Since you neglected to show me this part of the property, I decided to have a look for myself. I *didnae* ken you were here."

"We had a deal." She poked his chest. "This isn't what I'd call abiding by your word."

"Do you not know when a man is teasing you? I haven't the time or the inclination to stand around and watch you sleep."

Her features pinched and, with a groan of frustration, she pushed past him. She slogged through the muck. Mud clung to the fine peach fabric. By the time he reached the bank, she was already marching through the meadow, boots squelching with each step, outrage obvious in her rigid posture.

A smile lifted the corners of his mouth. He knew it was wrong, but he kind of liked seeing Caroline with her hackles up.

CHAPTER FOUR

Caroline was still burning with embarrassment when she reached the house. Oh, he'd tried to mask his amusement, but it had been there in his eyes. He enjoyed seeing her squirm. In the hallway, she removed her boots and wet stockings, and wrung the excess water from her petticoats and overskirt. Beneath the anger, there existed a disturbing ache for something she couldn't quite name. As she hurried up the staircase to the second floor, she remembered the shocking solidness of his wide chest. It had been like poking her finger into a wall of iron. Iron sheathed in warm, firm flesh, she amended.

She entered her bedroom and braced herself for hysterics.

"Can I help you, Mother?"

Louise turned from where a half-dozen dresses were laid out on Caroline's bed. The wardrobe doors had been thrown open.

"We must choose your outfit for tonight . . ." Her jaw sagged in a most undignified manner. "Look at you! You're a mess! What happened?"

"There was a mishap at the pond."

Her hands pressed against her cheeks, Louise inventoried the damage. "You'll have to bathe again. I hope there'll be enough time for your hair to dry. You know how difficult it is to work with if it isn't."

"Yes, Mother."

"Tonight has to be perfect. Theo's interested, but according to his father, he's balking at matrimony. You must dazzle him in order to wring a commitment from him." Twisting back to the bed, she fingered a beaded ivory gown. "This one is lovely, but it will draw attention to your wide hips."

Looking down, Caroline skimmed her hips with her hands and grimaced. It was a common complaint of her mother's.

"If only you had inherited my physique." Louise tutted, "instead of Albert's mother's. Ah, well, there's nothing to be done about it. Let's hope the Turner name is enough to draw him in."

The familiar feeling of not measuring up, of not being good enough, coiled inside her chest, slowly suffocating any measure of contentment she was able to eke out of her daily life.

She hugged her middle. "I don't wish to marry Theo Marsh."

"You're not a fresh-faced eighteen-year-old." The skin around her watery blue eyes tightened. "You can't afford to be picky at this stage. Theo will be considered a good catch."

"You wouldn't mind that I'd be living in Charleston? What about my responsibilities here?"

"I'm perfectly capable of handling Gatlinburg's affairs." Rifling through the dresses, she lifted a floaty creation of seafoam green and studied her daughter with a critical eye. "This one might do."

Caroline drifted over to the large four-poster bed. "You wouldn't see me very often," she persisted. "A couple of times a year."

Louise cast her a sharp glance. "What's the matter with you? You're not getting sentimental all of a sudden, surely."

"No, of course not."

She'd stopped yearning for hugs and bedtime stories long ago.

"Good." She picked up the pale green dress. "Wear this one. I'll send Sylvia and Betty up with the tub." She sniffed. "You may borrow a sample of your father's latest soap — he's calling it Parisian Citrus — a blend of grapefruit, orange and tangerine with white musk from France. Hopefully that will be enough to rid you of the lake stench."

Caroline's gaze slid to her dressing table and the bottom drawer where she'd stashed the documents. Was the white musk truly from France?

"It's been years since I've toured our facilities," she rushed out. "I think a trip to Charleston would be perfect this time of year, don't you? We could go as soon as the Marshes and Lightwoods leave. I'd like to visit our old neighborhood, perhaps attend services at our church. I'm sure we could fit in a trip to the factories."

"You know your father resents anything he sees as interference in his business. If I delve beyond the most basic of inquiries, he gets testy. It's not a woman's world, he says. There is the issue of safety to consider, as well."

"He allowed me to visit as a child."

"You've forgotten the filthy conditions." Her nose wrinkled. "And the smell, at times, can overwhelm a body."

"I haven't been out of Gatlinburg for two years, Mother. I'd like a change of scenery."

Being in Charleston would give her the

opportunity to discover if the information in those documents had been fabricated. She could pretend interest in the family business and gain access to the offices, the machinery, storerooms where they kept the ingredients and even the laboratory where new compositions were tested.

"Then stop balking at the issue of marriage. If you want out, Theo is your ticket."

With that, she swept out of the room.

Caroline sank onto the mattress, testing the idea of taking her satchel and going alone. If she hoped to be free of the blackmailer's evil plan, she had to find out the truth. Her father saw her as an empty-headed heiress, good for hosting dinner parties and little else. He wasn't going to divulge his deepest secrets to her.

Snaring Theo was a short-term solution. Sure, she'd get to Charleston. She just wouldn't get out. She'd be locked into a loveless marriage like her parents', an intolerable proposition.

Once she was clean and her hair dry, she dutifully donned the seafoam green gown, choosing pearl-and-emerald earbobs and a matching necklace to accompany it. She sat for an hour while Betty brushed her hair and twisted the mass into a tidy twist. Then, pasting on her best smile, she descended the stairs and entered the parlor. All the guests turned to greet her. Theo, distinguished in his black suit, his short dark hair brushed off his handsome face, waited until everyone had drifted back to their original conversations to take his turn. Lifting her hand to his lips, he kissed her knuckles. His gray eyes gleamed with appreciation.

"You're even lovelier than the last time I set eyes on you," he drawled. "I'm glad my father insisted I come."

Unexpectedly, Duncan's mocking blue gaze entered her mind. She blinked it away. "You'd rather be somewhere else?"

He lowered her hand but didn't release it, his thumb stroking her knuckles. While pleasant, his touch didn't evoke butterflies in her tummy or prickles of excitement along her skin. Duncan didn't have to make contact for that to happen. All he had to do was come close. Irksome man!

"I had planned a hunting trip with my friends. But Father's been in correspondence with Albert, and he hinted how lonely you've been. I thought I'd see if I could remedy the situation."

The strange light in his eyes made Caroline uncomfortable. Intuition warned he didn't have serious intentions.

Pulling out of his grip, she lifted her chin.

"I'm afraid you gave up your hunting trip for nothing. Your father was misinformed. If I were lonely, I wouldn't need you to assuage it. I have plenty of pets already."

Glancing about to ensure they weren't overheard, he leaned close, a hardness entering his gaze. "Careful, Caroline. Your reputation as a cold, bitter shell of a woman means your options are few. A light flirtation with me would go a long way in convincing others that you're not a lost cause."

His words sliced into her, mainly because she sometimes did feel hollow inside. Maybe he was right. "My mother thinks I should aim for a marriage proposal from you."

His head jerked back in horror. "Marriage? To you?"

The couple standing beside the fireplace turned to stare. Humiliation surged. Louise's glass halted halfway to her mouth. Disapproval wrinkled her skin, and her gaze seemed to scream what Caroline had always suspected — *you're a mistake, a complete failure as a daughter.*

She turned away and hurried for the nearest exit, desperate for privacy.

Outside, the brisk, moisture-heavy wind tugged her hair and skirts. Jogging to the stables, she made for Rain's stall and began readying her for a ride. All she wanted was to be on her horse, climbing high into the mountains, with nothing around save for the birds and trees.

"What do you think you're doing?"

From the aisle behind her, the rolling accent lashed at her. She didn't have the strength to deal with Duncan right now. Not looking at him, she fought threatening tears. "Going for a ride, what does it look like?"

His boots scraped along the cobblestones as he came nearer. "Postpone it. The sky is about to unleash its fury."

"Can't." She settled the thick pad across Rain's back.

His hard hand clamped on to her arm and spun her around. In the barn's dim interior, his eyes blazed blue brilliance. "Going out right now is a foolhardy act."

Caroline averted her face so he couldn't see how upset she was. "Apparently I am a fool."

He was silent a long beat. "What?"

Injecting steel into her voice, she said, "Release me at once, Mr. McKenna. This is my horse, my choice. Besides, you don't know this area like I do. This is a passing rain shower, nothing more."

His hand fell away. With a muttered exclamation of displeasure, he stalked off. So she was stunned to see him on Jet minutes later, his Stetson tugged low over his eyes.

"Why —"

"Seeing as how you're determined to go despite my warning," he bit out, "I'm obliged to accompany you."

"I'll be fine."

"It's no' you I'm worried about. It's the horses."

Caroline pressed her lips into a tight line and, nudging her heels into Rain's flank, guided her toward the woods. She didn't want him around, but it didn't look as if she had a choice in the matter.

The satchel flashed in her mind. Freedom from her parents' displeasure, from her current lifestyle and her disappointment in herself, dangled like a rare, delicious fruit ripe for the picking. There was no reason to stick around any longer. Leaving Gatlinburg was the answer to her problems.

The deeper into the mountains they traveled, the more convinced Duncan became that their outing would end in disaster. Like a whistling locomotive, the wind barreled through the shallow valley, whipping the trees rooted into the steep inclines on either side into a frenzy. Both horses were on edge. If either of them had possessed nervous

66

dispositions, he or Caroline would've already been tossed from the saddle. The strip of sky visible above them was a churning, purple-gray mass of impending doom.

Anger simmered beneath his thin veneer of control. Caroline rode ahead of him, as silent and stiff as a marble statue. Maureen had acted similarly whenever she was miffed, which had been often. When he proposed again, it would be to a sweet, easy-to-please lass of poor means. Money complicated matters.

"What's put a bee in your bonnet?" he called. "Someone not act as you wished them to?"

The slope of her shoulders went rigid, but she didn't answer him.

"Whatever's upset you, 'tisna worth risking the horses. Let's turn back."

She angled her head so that he could see her profile. "I didn't ask you to accompany me. Leave if you want. I'm not ready."

A raindrop splattered on his sleeve. Shifting his Stetson up his forehead, he eyed the sky again. On a typical midsummer evening, they'd have several hours of daylight left. Not this night.

"It will be dark soon." He tried to reason with her. "We don't have lanterns."

Frowning, she lifted her head to the

heavens. Was she finally going to act sensibly?

"You don't wish any harm to come to the horses, do you?" he tacked on.

With a low command, Caroline brought Rain to a halt. He did the same with Jet, smoothing his palm along the animal's quivering muscles.

"I suppose we have no choice, do we?"

The resignation in her voice aroused questions. When she circled around, he glimpsed the depth of her melancholy. Something was troubling her. Something more than a mix-up with the hors d'oeuvres or a snag in her stockings.

Rain began to fall in discordant patterns. Tugging his brim lower, he said, "Stay close. We may have to find shelter if this gets out of hand."

Not waiting for her response, he maneuvered Jet around on the tight path. Thunder roiled through the valley. The storm wasn't on them yet. Seeking God's assistance, he prayed they'd reach the Turners' safe and sound. The clouds opened up, releasing sheets of moisture that drenched him in seconds. Riding behind him on the trail, Caroline was unprotected in her fancy evening gown.

Duncan didn't have time to worry about

her comfort. Squinting to see his way ahead, he searched for the rocky outcrop they'd passed fifteen minutes earlier. No point trying to continue in this onslaught. They'd wait out the storm until it was safe to ride again.

He glanced over his shoulder every few minutes. While her misery and worry were apparent, she remained in control of her horse, and he admitted she was an adept horsewoman. One point in her favor.

The thunder pealed again and, this time, the intensity of it shook the ground. Jet balked. Duncan tightened his grip on the reins. Lightning cracked like a whip, striking a tree close to the path. Caroline screamed.

Twisting in the saddle, Duncan found his chest seizing with horror as Rain reared, front hooves slashing the air, eyes rolling in their sockets and nostrils flaring. And suddenly Caroline was sliding off. Rain's rear leg caught the lip of the path, the soft earth crumbling beneath her hoof. The large gray went down, taking Caroline with her.

"Caroline!"

Vaulting to the ground, he paused long enough to secure Jet to a tree limb before scrambling down the slight slope. The interwoven treetops above kept some of the rain at bay. Soaked to the skin and splattered with mud, she struggled to sit.

He crouched beside her, searching for visible injuries. "Are you hurt?"

"I'm fine." Her wince communicated otherwise. "Please, see to my horse."

Duncan twisted and saw Rain farther below them. She was on her feet, at least.

"Are you sure nothing's broken?" He turned back. "What about your head? Did you strike it?"

Her hair hung like twisted wet cords and her eyes were large and anxious in her pale face. "I'm bruised, that's all."

Thunder rumbled through the valley again. Duncan hurried to check on her horse. A gash the size of his fist had opened up her side, likely from a broken-off tree limb. It was deep and raw and would be prone to infection. A fresh wave of anger washed over him. A fine, dependable animal was hurt because of Caroline's selfishness.

She navigated the slippery terrain to join him, her hands skimming the horse's good side. "Is she all right?"

"I'm afraid not," he gritted. "Take a look for yourself."

Her forehead crinkled in bewilderment. Coming around to where he stood, she saw the injury and gasped. "Oh, Rain." Her arms went around the horse's neck, and she buried her face in the gray coat.

Duncan hardened his heart. This was her fault. She'd disregarded his warning, and her horse had gotten injured because of it.

The storm's fury intensified. The sky lit up with successive lightning streaks. Tethered to the distant tree, Jet pranced to the side and tossed his head.

"Let's get these horses out of the elements."

A shudder racked her. Moisture clung to her exposed shoulders and arms. Taking hold of the reins and speaking in soothing tones, she led Rain up the ridge.

Cold leached into her from the rock against which she was wedged. Her head resting on her bent knees, face hidden in the dirty layers of her skirt, she was mired in shame. Beneath the rocky outcrop he'd discovered, Duncan stood apart from her, preferring the horses' company to hers. She didn't blame him.

The thunder and lightning had grown distant, but the rain's relentless pursuit remained constant. It pounded the earth, splattering mud in all directions. At least here, in this cramped space, they'd have the chance to dry out before heading home.

She couldn't stop shaking. The scene replayed in her mind yet again, the lightning striking within feet of them, the sensation of falling through the air and slamming into the ground, expecting to be crushed at any moment beneath her horse. She offered up a prayer of thanksgiving that Rain hadn't suffered a life-threatening injury. If she'd broken a leg or dislocated a shoulder, Caroline would've been returning home without her.

There was still a possibility of infection. She'd never forgive herself if that happened. And neither would Duncan. Caught up in her problems, she'd ignored his advice and put them all at risk.

The weight of her burdens threatened to suffocate her. Her father's indifference, her mother's disappointment, Theo's scorn and Duncan's contempt congealed into a single, sharp accusation. Caroline couldn't please any of them. The need to be far from Gatlinburg was a living, breathing thing.

Registering movement, she kept her head down until Duncan sank to the ground and nudged her.

"Here. Put this on."

Threading the damp strands out of her eyes, she focused on the bundle of material. Darkness had fallen. His features were wreathed in shadows, his eyes gleaming and the crimson-red undershirt snug against his upper body.

"It's no' completely dry," he said with a hint of impatience. "But at least you'll be covered."

She slipped her arms into the too-long sleeves of his shirt and overlapped the side panels over her midriff. A cedar scent clung to the fabric. "Thank you."

He shifted his legs and, resting his forearms on his bent knees, linked his hands. The man took up a lot of space. He was big and close, his upper arm butted against her shoulder, and Caroline was acutely aware of their seclusion. His body generated blessed heat that she yearned to share in. She glanced over, inexplicably fascinated by the patterns of faint veins on the backs of his hands, the thickness of his wrists and the fine spattering of freckles on his corded forearms. Regardless of the enmity that existed between them, Caroline accepted that the rugged Scotsman affected her on a level she hadn't before experienced. She would've liked to trace those freckles, test the texture of the fine auburn hairs and curl her hand into his, drawing strength from him when her own seemed to have failed her.

"As soon as the rain stops, I'll search for kindling that isn't completely waterlogged and try and start a fire. *'Twill* be a long night."

Disquiet muddled her thoughts. The fact that spending time alone with Duncan didn't bother her set off alarm bells. *Admit it. He fascinates you.*

"We can't stay here."

He swiveled his head her direction. "There's no moon, and we *dinnae* have lanterns. I'm no' about to risk further harm to the horses or ourselves to satisfy your whims."

Hurt lanced through her. "My parents will be searching for me."

"Let them. Unlike us, they'll be prepared to travel by night."

Caroline stared straight ahead, trying to picture her parents in a panic. She couldn't quite manage it. Would they even try and locate her? Or would their guests' comfort trump hers?

She twisted her hands into a tight ball. "Rain's going to be okay, right?"

"As long as we're diligent in her care, I'd say she has a good prognosis." His voice was brusque, his manner aloof.

Caroline's mind explored the nine years of friendship she'd shared with Rain. Her heart squeezed with regret.

"I'm sorry," she managed to say in a strangled voice. "I should've listened to you."

"Feeling sorry won't change anything. 'Tis a hard lesson you need to learn, Caroline Turner. The world doesn't spin on your orders. Cease thinking of yourself first, and mayhap another accident like this can be avoided."

CHAPTER FIVE

Something coarse swatted his face. Duncan registered hard, mineral-rich earth beneath his cheek and, blinking open gritty eyes, frowned at the nearness of a horse's hoof. Levering himself to a sitting position, he noted the purple and pink fingers stretching across the dawn sky. The spot where Caroline had been was empty. Jet and Rain stood there, poor excuses for chaperones. He hadn't meant to drift to sleep, had only closed his eyes for a moment, thinking to rest until the storm abated.

Shifting, his stiff neck protesting movement, he spotted her in the distance. When she'd left the cover of their outcrop, he hadn't a clue. She was seated on a dead tree with her back to him, her shoulders hunched forward, her head bowed. Her white-blond hair spilled halfway down her back, a beacon in the dim light.

Duncan stood and stretched the kinks

from his body, silently praying for the Lord to grant him patience. A bit of compassion wouldn't hurt, either. Not that long ago, he'd shared Caroline Turner's outlook, a fact that shamed him and was probably the reason she burrowed beneath his skin like an irritating splinter.

Inhaling a cleansing breath of rain-freshened forest, he approached, navigating the muddy ground with care.

"Good mornin'."

Caroline's head whipped up. Her eyes told the story of her misery. She was in a bedraggled state. Below where his heather-gray shirt swallowed her top half, her seafoam green skirts were wrinkled, soiled and torn in places. Her hair was uncombed and limp. And yet, she was lovelier in this moment than he'd ever seen her.

Unsettled by the thought, Duncan spoke more gruffly than he'd intended. "You should've woken me."

Her wretchedness intensified. "My eagerness to get home has waned since last evening." She picked at the dirt beneath her nails. "I'm not looking forward to explaining all this to my parents."

A frisson of unease slithered along his spine. As a newcomer, he didn't have a solid reputation built up to support his word.

Caroline was his employer's only child. And she'd already complained about him to Albert. Kneading the knots in his neck, he tried not to think about the possible ramifications of the night they'd passed in isolation. The two most obvious scenarios involved irate men with guns running him out of town or, worse, a preacher ready to perform a wedding ceremony. He'd take the men with guns any day.

"No use delaying the inevitable."

With a slow nod, she took her time getting up.

Duncan moved closer. "You said you weren't hurt."

Her features were drawn. "I'm bruised. Nothing's broken."

Worry lodged in his chest, taking him by surprise. "The ride back *willnae* be comfortable, I'm afraid."

"I know."

At least she wasn't a whiner. Maureen would've been assaulting his ears with complaints he could do nothing about.

The journey wasn't easy for either of them. They'd agreed to ride together in order make it more bearable for Rain. The rigid way Caroline held herself testified to her discomfort, as did her frequent, sudden inhales as Jet navigated the uneven terrain.

As for Duncan, his concentration was all but shattered. Riding with an alluring female in his arms wasn't exactly an everyday occurrence.

Her hair tickled his nose, causing him to sneeze. His chin and her skull had connected so many times he'd ceased murmuring apologies. The worst was whenever the terrain sloped unexpectedly, and her bare, smooth hands latched on to his, holding on for dear life. By the time his cabin came into view, Duncan was ready to spring from the saddle.

She stirred from her quiet contemplation. "Maybe we should part ways here."

"We'll endure the inquisition together."

"It will look better if I arrive alone."

"My mother raised me to be a gentleman, Miss Turner. Besides, your father will have questions for me."

He hoped Albert Turner would be satisfied with his answers.

Riding into the stable yard, Caroline forgot the curious sensations stirred by the Scotsman's nearness. The stirrings of hunger pangs faded. Her hope that their arrival would go unnoticed withered. Horses and men milled about, local farmers who should be tending chores but were no doubt here at the behest of her father. Almost as one, they turned to watch Jet's ambling approach and Rain following behind, their initial expressions of surprise changing to speculation.

Duncan's arm circled her waist, balancing her against his chest, and she felt his muscles go taut. His beard snagged her hair again, and a long exhale feathered across her ear. Too late, she remembered that she still wore his shirt, leaving him with nothing but his undershirt. Her skin pricked under the weight of their suspicions.

She recognized the commanding figure on the porch steps as the town's sheriff, Shane Timmons. He was conversing with her father and Isaiah Marsh, Theo's father. The trio noticed the hush encompassing the crowd at the same time. Her father's features pinched into prune-like proportions. A feminine exclamation drew Caroline's attention to the shadowed seating area. Her mother moved as if weights were attached to her legs.

As Duncan halted their progress and silently slid to the ground, Caroline braced herself for an ugly scene. He reached for her, his hooded gaze wary, his demeanor somber. He'd lost the leather strip he used to hold back his hair. The auburn waves skimmed his bearded jaw, as shiny as a new copper penny.

She registered the sureness of his hands around her waist and took an odd comfort from his nearness. Her boots met the ground, and her knees threatened to buckle. She gasped at the stabbing pain in her right side and the soreness up and down her body.

He didn't immediately release her. "You okay?"

Biting hard on her lower lip, she nodded.

When he put a wide gap between them, resignation firming his mouth, she felt ridiculously bereft.

Her father met them in the yard, his harsh visual assessment of their state of dress making her feel like an errant child. The sheriff joined them, while Louise remained on the landing, using the banister to support her weight. That she wasn't launching into an earsplitting tirade gave Caroline pause.

"You owe me an explanation, Mr. Mc-Kenna."

Caroline stepped in front of Duncan. "It's my fault, Father. I —"

"Hush, Caroline." Albert's gray eyes were cool. "If I'd required your input, I would've asked for it."

She flinched. Some of the men in the group shifted their stances, elbowing each other and whispering. Humiliation made her throat close up.

A gentle, work-roughened hand encircled her upper arm and eased her back a few steps. Duncan. She couldn't bring herself to meet his gaze.

"The lass and I are guilty of nothing more than poor judgment. We took the horses out for a ride last evening and got caught in the thunderstorm. Her mount suffered an injury. It was my decision to take shelter and wait for morning light to return home. You have my word of honor that your daughter's virtue remains unblemished."

Caroline wished disappearing was an option. Her gaze on the flower beds, she berated herself once more for not listening to Duncan. First her horse had been injured, and now they were being made a spectacle of. Gossip this juicy wouldn't die down for months. What else would become of one bad decision?

"That may be." The hint of disbelief in her father's voice shocked her. "However, you can agree how this looks. I won't have my daughter's reputation forever tainted because of your actions."

Was Duncan about to lose his job? In any other circumstance, she'd be relieved to be rid of him. But he clearly needed the income. Who knew? Maybe his family members were destitute, and he sent money home to support them.

She forced her lips to move. "It wasn't his decision to go. Duncan tried to persuade me to wait. He went along for the sole purpose of keeping the horses safe."

Albert's brows lifted. "I would hope he was interested in keeping my daughter safe, as well."

"Of course Miss Turner's well-being is a priority." Duncan's voice rang with sincerity. "That was one reason I *didnae* risk traveling through the night. She got bucked off her horse once. *Wasnae* wise to continue."

She recalled his very real concern that morning. Despite his annoyance, he'd been gentle as he'd helped her onto Jet's broad back.

Sheriff Shane Timmons spoke up. "Are you all right, Caroline?"

The compassion in his azure gaze made her eyes smart. Her own father hadn't bothered to ask. Unable to speak past the knot in her throat, she nodded.

"She needs to be examined by a doctor," Duncan asserted.

Albert summoned Anthony and sent him to fetch Doc Owens. "Oh, and Anthony?

Bring Reverend Monroe, as well. Tell him it's a matter of great urgency."

The gap in his teeth appeared. "Yes, sir."

The hush surrounding them was deafening. His intentions sunk in, and Caroline weaved on her feet. Surely he wouldn't force them to marry?

"If you are indeed a man of honor, Mr. McKenna, you will put to rest the speculation and give my daughter your name."

Caroline gaped at the man beside her. "You aren't going to agree to this, are you? I'm not about to marry a stable manager!"

Snickers spilled through the spectators. Duncan winced, just like he'd done on Independence Day when she'd declined his invitation to dance. Caroline wished the words unsaid.

Heaving in a breath that made his wide chest expand, he curled his hands into fists. "This may come as a shock to you, lady, but I'm no' keen on marrying a self-absorbed, shallow socialite with nothing in her head but fashion and parties. Looks like that's what I'm getting, though. You can thank your stubbornness for this debacle."

His words stung. *Shallow.* Wasn't that similar to what Theo had said? That people thought she was an empty shell with nothing of substance inside?

Twisting away, a vein ticking at his temple, he addressed her father. "I'll wed her."

The edges of her vision grew fuzzy. This couldn't be happening.

She wanted to stomp her feet and scream at the top of her lungs and make them all go away.

If she married Duncan McKenna, she wouldn't be able to leave Gatlinburg, after all. She'd be stuck here in her old, miserable life, only now she'd be known as the girl whose husband had been guilted into marrying her.

CHAPTER SIX

"Why, God?" he groaned. "Of all the women in the world, why her?"

He couldn't fathom how the Father who claimed to love him and want good things for him would shackle him to a woman like Caroline Turner. A woman who, on the inside where it counted, could be Maureen Craig's twin. He'd left Boston to escape just these sorts of people, and now he was rejoining their ranks.

The bread and jam he'd choked down earlier soured on his stomach.

In a few hours' time, he'd enter into a marriage he didn't want.

His arms full of supplies, he was about to enter Rain's stall when the man Albert had introduced as Shane Timmons strode into the stable. The light shining through the high windows glanced off the pistol at his hip.

"How can I help you, Sheriff?"

His probing gaze cataloged the scene. "Looks like you're the one who could use a hand." He came close and, spying Rain's flank wound, whistled low. "That's a doozy."

"Aye, it is." Going in, he arranged the honey jar and bandages in the corner and tried not to relive those horrible moments when he'd watched Caroline slide from the saddle and plunge to the ground. Running his hand along Rain's side, he said, "It could've been worse." For both the animal and her owner.

Shane removed his hat and, pushing his light brown hair out of his eyes, gestured to the horse. "How about I apply honey to the bandage while you clean the wound?"

Duncan didn't exactly feel like company, but he wasn't about to refuse the sheriff. Now that Gatlinburg was to be his permanent home, making allies would prove important.

"I'd appreciate it."

While he filled a container with clean water, Shane applied a generous amount of honey to the square bandage that would cover the wound. Rain was a docile patient. In a matter of minutes, they had her patched up, the bandage protecting the gash from flies and dirt getting in.

Shane surveyed their work. "Should heal

nicely. Caroline will be relieved."

Duncan twisted the lid to the honey jar. He didn't ask how well the sheriff knew her. It didn't matter.

"I realize you haven't had time to get to know many people yet," he continued. "I want you to know I'm here if you need anything."

"How about a way to turn back the clock?" he muttered, carrying the remaining bandages and honey jar to the tack room.

Shane closed the stall door and followed him. "You don't have ties here. You could refuse to marry her. Leave town."

Duncan pivoted. "Is she that bad then?"

Humor graced his mouth. "This isn't about Caroline or my opinion of what you should do. I'm trying to put myself in your shoes. I wanted you to know the whole of Gatlinburg isn't against you."

"I'd be lyin' if I said I hadn't thought of running. I've done nothing wrong in the sight of God, and neither has she."

"I believe you."

"But it's my duty to honor the McKenna name. I won't sully it by acting the coward and sowing seeds of doubt in the locals' minds."

And there was the matter of his intended bride to consider. As furious as he was with her, the thought of leaving her to bear the brunt of his rejection troubled him. *It would serve her right,* he reminded himself, recalling her adamant objection to marrying a common working man. In that moment, he'd been the object of every single man's pity within hearing distance.

The sheriff held out his hand. "I suppose this means you'll be adding to our population. Welcome to Gatlinburg, Mr. Mc-Kenna."

"Call me Duncan." They shook hands.

"I'll be praying for you and Caroline."

He blinked at the reference to them as a team. A couple. From this day forward, he'd be irrevocably linked to her.

"We'll need all the prayers we can get." Did his face bear the same grave acceptance as his tone?

After the sheriff departed, Duncan returned to his humble cabin, one that didn't even belong to him. One bright spot in this mess? The thought of watching Caroline adjust to life as a stable manager's wife.

"I can't do this."

Caroline's reflection in the mirror was nothing like how she'd imagined a bride should look. With no time to procure a proper wedding dress, Louise had chosen a ball gown from Caroline's wardrobe that she hadn't yet worn. Besides the ostentatious design, the color was wrong for her. But she hadn't had the gumption to argue with her mother, not when she'd caused Louise's dreams for her to shatter.

Crafted of fine, golden yellow silk and overlaid with white netting, the bodice was snug, the curved neckline lower than she preferred and the skirt boasted poofs of fabric that reminded her of popped corn. She ran her palms over her waist. The style certainly didn't hide the span of her hips.

Her best friend, Jane Leighton, adjusted one of the yellow paste jewels Betty had woven into her upswept hair. "You're going to get through this," she encouraged, her moss green eyes solemn. "Don't think about what next week or next month might bring. Take things one day at a time."

"He hates me."

Jane met her gaze in the mirror. One of a set of identical twin sisters Caroline had known since she was fifteen years old, Jane was practical and calm and wise. She was one of a very small handful of people Caroline trusted.

"I'm sure he's merely frustrated with the situation he finds himself in."

Caroline twisted on the low, circular seat.

"No, he truly hates me, Jane."

"Then I suggest you find ways to change his mind."

"I don't think anything I could do or say will make him forgive me."

"There were two of you on that mountain ridge. You didn't force him to accompany you." She swept a swath of her thick red hair behind her shoulder, the band on her fourth finger catching Caroline's gaze. Jane was married to the love of her life. Tom Leighton adored and respected his wife. Sadly, that was not to be the case in her own marriage.

"I haven't said 'I do' yet, and I already know my marriage is going to be a disaster."

"You can't think like that, Caroline. Focus on being friends first. The rest will come later."

Exactly what the rest was comprised of worried her. Once Louise had unleashed the brunt of her disappointment, she'd attempted to broach the subject of wifely duties. Horrified, Caroline had cut her off. Theirs wasn't the caring mother-daughter relationship that would make such a delicate conversation easy.

She comforted herself with the fact that Duncan's intense dislike would prevent him from pursuing that aspect of their relationship. She recalled the way his casual touch made her feel — jumpy and awkward and strangely empty — and prayed she was right.

Louise breezed inside the bedroom. "It's time, Caroline." She appeared to have acquired dozens more wrinkles about her mouth in the hours since that morning.

Jane gave her hand a final squeeze. "You're going to be fine. You're God's beloved child. He's allowing this for a reason."

Caroline worried over that tidbit the entire trek down the stairs, through the main floor and out into the sweltering July afternoon. The heavy air closed around her like a wool glove. The heat, combined with nerves, caused her palms to grow damp. While she considered herself a follower of Jesus Christ, she'd never felt like a beloved child of God. She'd never felt like *anyone's* beloved.

The yard was blessedly empty of most of the morning's onlookers. As she made her way into the shade of a multitude of oak and maple trees, her gaze swept those in attendance. Their out-of-town guests, including Isaiah and Theo, congregated on her left. Theo's expression was inscrutable, his light eyes intent on her. The group on her right was comprised of her friends and their husbands. Tom was there waiting for Jane to rejoin him. Shane stood with his arm around Allison, his wife, who shot her a reassuring smile. Caroline's gaze fell to Allison's unmistakable pregnancy, and she stumbled. Panic clawed its way to the surface.

"Miss Caroline." Wendell stood shyly off to the side, wearing his finest clothes, his wispy black hair slicked off his face. He held out a bouquet of white and yellow blossoms plucked from the gardens. "For you."

Her fingers closing around the stems, she brought the flowers to her nose, hoping the rush of emotion would pass.

"How thoughtful of you, Wendell," she murmured. "Thank you."

He dipped his head. The affection in his brown-black eyes made her want to weep. Since the day they'd arrived in Tennessee, the older man had taken a shine to her. He'd been kind. He'd invited her to help him with the flowers, and she'd accepted, mostly because she'd known Louise wouldn't approve. But then she'd started to enjoy his company and the work, and an unlikely friendship had flourished. He'd become like a benevolent grandfather.

Unable to linger, she took a single step and encountered the reverend standing with a striking, somewhat forbidding stranger. Caroline halted. She scanned the manicured lawns. Where was Duncan?

She peered at the stranger a second time. His expression had gone grimmer than before, his familiar cobalt gaze searing her like a branding iron. She hadn't recognized him at first. His auburn hair had been cut military short on the sides and back, the top locks left slightly longer to spill over his forehead. The beard was gone. The planes and angles of his face were uncovered for her inspection. His jaw was square and firm, his chin unyielding, his full, sculpted mouth softening the noble beauty of his features. His tan was uneven, but a few days in the sun would fix that.

Caroline's lungs squeezed every last drop of air out. In his crisp black suit and snowy white shirt, her husband-to-be was elegant and refined, his bearing that of a king assured of his subjects' loyalty. His new appearance couldn't hide the untamed part of him that fascinated her, however, and she knew then and there she was in big trouble.

"Please join hands."

Duncan automatically obeyed the reverend's directive, reaching for Caroline's and enclosing them in his. Her skin was smooth and cool, the opposite of his work-worn hands. He thought his heart might fail him.

As the words rolled from the older man's lips, Duncan stared at the woman who was about to pledge to love, honor and obey him. She didn't love him. Didn't respect him. As for heeding his wishes? He doubted she'd do that without a fight.

She didn't look like any bride he'd ever seen. Brides were supposed to wear flowing white gowns and appear serenely happy as they met their groom at the altar. Caroline may as well have been attending a costume ball or an opera. And she didn't look serene in the slightest. Gone was the haughty disdain. She looked as if a single tap of his finger would shatter her into a thousand pieces. Not an auspicious start to any union.

Unfortunately, the garish ensemble didn't lessen her outward appeal . . . an appeal he would have to fight against. He'd seen her reaction to his polished appearance. He'd assumed, wrongly, that she'd prefer him shorn and shaved. But the moment she'd spied him, she'd glanced about for a way of escape. He repulsed her.

She wouldn't even meet his gaze. Her luminous blue eyes, dark and tumultuous, were fastened on his collar. Every few seconds, she'd moisten her lips and pull in slivers of air. Because her hair had been pulled into a tight roll at the back of her head, he could see the rapid pulse in the curve of her neck. Duncan had the inane urge to place his fingertips there, to soothe her anxiety, to make her feel better about what was happening.

Who was he kidding? She wouldn't welcome his touch.

"Do you, Duncan McKenna, take this woman, Caroline Turner, to be your lawfully wedded wife?"

He didn't speak. All he could think was that his parents and his brothers were missing the most momentous day of his life. He pictured his kilt hanging in his wardrobe and his great-grandmother's ring that had been kept in the family safe for his future bride. This wasn't the way it was supposed to have gone.

At his prolonged silence, Caroline finally lifted her eyes to search his. The whirlwind of emotions there punched him in the gut.

"Aye."

Her throat worked, and in that moment, her disquiet was palpable.

"Do you, Caroline Turner, take this man, Duncan McKenna, to be your lawfully wedded husband?"

"I . . ." Her hands were trembling now. "I do."

Her lids slid down, blocking his view.

"By the power vested in me, I now pronounce you husband and wife. You may kiss the bride."

Duncan stood there, numb to the core. He was locked in a marriage he hadn't asked for, all because of this woman's willful behavior. A fresh shock of anger pulsed through him.

He released her hands and adopted a casual air. "We can skip that part, Reverend. We all know *'tisna* a love match."

Several of the women gasped. Louise, his new mother-in-law, latched on to Albert's arm. The reverend frowned, uncertain how to proceed. Caroline kept her gaze on the grass at their feet. Was she paler than she'd been a few moments ago? Did that mean she was relieved at having been spared his attentions or was she merely annoyed at his rude behavior? At the moment, he couldn't find the energy to care.

His father-in-law saved the day. Lifting a hand above his head, he invited everyone to join the bride and groom in the parlor, where refreshments had been set out to mark the momentous occasion. Conversation joined the birds' song as a few came over to offer awkward congratulations. A dark-haired man approached Caroline, and she edged closer to Duncan.

"Theo. Meet Duncan McKenna."

He shook hands and murmured the proper pleasantries, but his eyes were hard and his smile predatory. Disregarding Duncan's presence, Theo rested his hands on Caroline's shoulders and bent his head.

"Congratulations, Caroline," he murmured. Then he pressed a prolonged kiss on the corner of her mouth.

Possessiveness caught him unawares. Duncan shifted closer and curled an arm around her waist, forcing Theo to remove his hands. She stiffened.

"If you'll excuse us," Duncan purred, "cake and lemonade await."

Theo's gaze snapped with annoyance, but he bowed deeply and stepped aside. As Duncan guided her across the lawn, his hold on her unrelenting, she said, "I'm not in the mood for cake and false pleasantries."

"Can't say that I am, either, but it's expected of us."

"I didn't figure you for a man who acted to appease others' expectations."

They'd reached the base of the porch stairs. Glancing about to ensure no one was watching, he guided her to the corner of the house.

"What are you doing?" The tremor of unease in her voice prodded his pride.

Pulling away, he snapped, "Never fear, sweet lass, I've no intention of forcing my attentions on you."

The way she kicked up her chin was at odds with how she wrapped her arms around herself in a defensive gesture. The storm of emotions in her eyes were too jumbled to measure. "That's a relief."

The jealousy that had been doing a slow burn through his veins surged. He crowded her space. Her eyes went wide and her lips parted. "Let me make something perfectly clear, my wife. I *willnae* tolerate infidelity. This may no' be a true marriage of our hearts and minds, but in the eyes of the law and this town, we're husband and wife. Whatever's been goin' on between you and that businessman can no' continue. I *willnae* allow it."

"Nothing has been *going on* between us."

"He's the man your parents wished you to marry, is he no'?"

"There are a number of men my parents considered for me."

"Forget them."

The breath whooshed out of her. "You're impossible."

He blocked her retreat, unsure why he was persisting but unwilling to drop the matter. "I mean it, Caroline. You have my complete and utter loyalty, and I expect yours in return. Do I have your word?"

Anguish flashed. "I understand you don't want me, and you don't want anyone else to, either." Her face shuttered as the starch went out of her. "Never fear, Duncan. I promise to be true to our vows."

She entered the house without him, leaving him to wonder why he suddenly cared.

CHAPTER SEVEN

She'd thought her life couldn't get any worse. She'd been wrong.

As she stood in the midst of what could only be dubbed a glorified shanty, her former complaints struck Caroline as trivial. The weight of the plain gold band on her finger felt strange. Twisting it round and round, she pondered her new identity as Duncan rearranged her trunks in an effort to make enough space to walk. He'd shed his suit coat and rolled up the sleeves of his white shirt. The muscles of his shoulders and upper back rippled with his efforts. His forearms were thick and strong, his wrists compact, his hands large and tan, his nails short and clean. This space magnified his size, increasing her awareness of their isolation.

She still smarted from his refusal to seal their vows with the traditional kiss. His obvious disdain as he'd pulled her aside and grilled her about Theo cut deep. Like many others in this town, he didn't like her. Only, he didn't try to hide it.

"There are too many," he announced, his palms slapping his outer thighs. "You'll have to get rid of all but one. Since you *willnae* be needin' your fancy clothes any longer —" he eyed her popped-corn dress askance "— I suggest you donate them."

"Of course I need them. I'm the second in charge of the Gatlinburg Benevolent Society. I host ladies' functions. I organize and direct town-wide events such as the Independence Day celebration. I must dress the part."

He planted his hands on his hips. He wore a gold band that matched hers, and she was struck by the fact that, just as she belonged to him, he belonged to her. A familiar longing took root inside . . . the longing to be close to someone, to love and be loved, to share the deepest parts of her with someone in complete trust and acceptance.

"You're going to have to cope with the fact that you're no longer the pampered daughter of Gatlinburg's wealthiest man. You're a common laborer's wife now." His beautiful, bright blue eyes rimmed with spiky auburn lashes taunted her.

"Surely you don't expect me to give up

my charitable endeavors?"

"You *willnae* have time for such things. You'll be too busy cooking my meals." Patting his taut midsection, he said, "I warn you, I have a hearty appetite. I like meat and lots of it. Then there's the matter of my clothing. My socks will need darning, my pants patched and my shirts and handkerchiefs ironed. You'll also be tending the pigs and chickens, as well as the vegetable garden. I also like fresh fruits and vegetables. Tomatoes are my favorite."

Horrified by the images passing through her mind, she said, "I don't know how to do any of that!"

He shrugged. "I'll teach you."

"I have money. I'll hire someone. That way, I can continue my charitable work. Nothing has to change."

With someone else to perform all those chores he'd listed, she could spend most of her time in the main house. She wouldn't be forced to spend every day, all day, in his company. *Just the nights.* Anxiety congealed in her stomach. No need to worry about that. He viewed her as a worm in the soil.

Gesturing to their surroundings, he said, "Look around, Caroline. *Everything* has changed. This is your home and I'm your husband. As such, your money is now mine to use as I see fit. And we're not hiring someone else to do what's your place to do."

Fear left an acrid taste in her mouth. If Duncan garnered control of her money, how would she meet the blackmailer's demands?

Running a hand through his shortened locks, he sighed. "I have work to do. Go through your things and pick out the clothes you wish to keep. Choose sensible items you won't mind getting dirty and a couple of dresses for church. Don't bother moving anything. I'll take care of it when I get back."

Snatching up his Stetson, he left without another glance, assuming she would follow his instructions. Caroline snatched the nearest object, a cracked enamel mug, and lobbed it at the closed door. It bounced off the wood, hit the floor with a thud and rolled beneath the bed.

"I don't take orders from you, Duncan McKenna!"

Why should she give up her things simply because his home was inadequate? And why should she alter her lifestyle because he'd decided he was tired of providing for his own needs? Darn his socks, her foot. Jane was right. While it had been Caroline's decision to go for a ride with a storm approaching, she hadn't held a gun to Duncan's head. *He* was the one who'd decreed they couldn't come home until morning. She wasn't going to be the only one to make sacrifices.

But what to do about the trunks? There *were* too many, crammed as they were on the stone fireplace hearth, around the shoddy pine table and chairs and blocking the hutch and cast-iron stove. They had to have room to maneuver. However, no solution presented itself.

Exhaustion clawed at her, rendering clear thinking impossible. She'd slept very little in their mountain shelter and had been running on high emotions since their return. The bruises she'd sustained reminded her of her brush with death every time she moved. Going over to the bed that didn't appear large enough to hold two people, she gave in to her body's demand for rest. Just for a few minutes. But the moment her head found the dip in the pillow, she drifted off to blessed oblivion.

He was pretty sure he could watch Caroline sleep for hours and not get bored. Stationed beside the bed, his hands tucked in his pockets, he shied away from sorting through the confusing feelings she aroused in him. Duncan had learned many lessons throughout his twenty-six years. Allowing his heart to get tangled with a woman such as her would produce nothing but disappointment and grief.

Nestled on her side atop the faded quilt, her hands tucked beneath her cheek, she slept deeply. Between the jewels in her hair, the pearls draped about her neck and the shimmering golden fabric rippling about her still form, she looked out of place in the rustic cabin. Like a fairy-tale heroine who'd wandered far from her castle and gotten lost. Her eyebrows pulled together, forming a crevice there, and he wondered what she dreamt about. He knew very little about his wife. What he did know made him question whether or not it was possible for this union to be successful.

I still don't understand why you've allowed this, Lord. Love is out of the question. I can't see how she and I could possibly build a relationship that would satisfy either of us. I'm not even certain we can be friends.

His spirit heavy, he checked the trunks and his wardrobe. She hadn't accomplished a single thing in the hour and a half he'd been in the stables. Bombarding her earlier with the list of demands had been a petty move on his part. Irate over this entire situation, he'd found himself wanting to punish her in some small way.

"Nap time's over, lass."

She stirred, the V between her brows deepening as she burrowed deeper into his pillow. It was going to smell like her lemon verbena scent, he was sure of it. She proved difficult to rouse. When spoken commands didn't work, he reached down and gave her a gentle shake.

Caroline batted his hand away. "Leave me be, Betty," she groaned, her voice thick.

Duncan had to admit, she was adorable in this state. He would've liked to explore her cheek's soft promise. He didn't dare.

"Up with ya now," he said in a booming voice. "We've work to do."

Bolting upright, she gaped at him in confusion. "Why are you yelling at me?"

"Mayhap because it would take a fire-cracker to blast you from sleep." He tapped the nearest trunk with his boot. "I thought I made my wishes plain."

Moving her legs around and setting her feet on the floor, she shot him a scathing glare. "I'm not getting rid of my things."

He crossed his arms and counted to ten in his head. "And I say you are. Unless you wish to use the forest as your closet."

Caroline rose and faced him. Her right cheek was pink and creased from the pillow, and stray strands had escaped the tight roll at the back of her head and now skimmed her jawline. Annoyance aside, he itched to smooth them behind her ear.

"I don't recall being consulted about where we live. Why does it have to be here?" She wrinkled her nose. "You can just as easily move into the main house with me."

"Honestly, Caroline? You'd have me move into your bedroom and live under the same roof as your parents?"

Clearly aghast at that prospect, she worried her bottom lip, which brought his attention to things better left alone. He was a male, after all, and had been left to his own company for too long. Reminding himself that she'd turned his life upside down because of a silly whim, he shoved the attraction aside.

"My guess is your mother wouldn't tolerate having the man who ruined her daughter's life underfoot. Besides, I happen to like my independence and privacy. For now, we stay put, which means this stuff has to go."

Hefting the nearest one in his arms, he carried it out to the wagon. When he returned inside, she looked disconcerted. More stunned than when he'd listed off the tasks in store for her. She found her tongue after the second trip.

"Where are you taking my things?"

"The church. Reverend Munroe will know who to donate it to."

She trailed him onto the porch. "You can't do this!"

"Trust me, you'll soon get used to living with less. You don't need hordes of material goods to be happy."

"That's easy for you to say," she exclaimed hotly. "You've no idea what it's like to live in comfort."

He brushed past her, disappointed by her attitude. He knew exactly what it was like to live in comfort, but he didn't want that life anymore. Maureen's tirade had sounded similar. He wouldn't soon forget that day he'd gone to her and explained his reasons for breaking off their engagement.

"I may be poor in your eyes, but I'm rich in what truly matters."

As his wife, she was assuming a less prominent role in society, one she'd disdained in front of half the town. Getting rid of her excessive belongings was a huge step in forcing her to face that fact.

Outrage churned in her heavily-lashed eyes. "You'll regret this."

When she realized he was intent on his task, she hurried to open the remaining trunks and began to pile articles of clothing on the bed. By the time he got the cabin cleared out and the wagon loaded, his anger had cooled, and his conscience warned him he was making a mistake. He couldn't relent at this point, however. She'd never respect him.

Rolling into the reverend's yard long minutes later, Duncan halted the team and experienced a twinge of unease. His temper had gotten him into fixes before and unpleasant consequences had followed. Something told him this wasn't going to end well. While the older man was surprised by Duncan's visit, he expressed his gratitude over Caroline's generosity. There were plenty of needy families in these mountain coves, he said, and promised to return the empty trunks within the week.

The ride back to the cabin passed in a blur. Now that he'd had time to think it through, Duncan was convinced he'd made a grave error in judgment. He could've easily stored her clothes in the barn's hayloft. Or returned some of them to the main house for temporary storage. But he'd let his feelings about being forced into marriage get the best of him.

Not the smartest way to start out your marriage, McKenna.

He was going to have to apologize, he realized. More important, he was going to have to forgive her for her part in this forced union and take responsibility for his own role.

Words of humility were forming in his mind when he halted the team at the edge of the profuse forest surrounding the cabin. His throat tight, he jumped down and strode across the yard. He had one boot on the bottom step when he noticed the clothes strewn about the porch. *His* clothes.

"She wouldn't dare," he growled.

Snatching up his suit coat where it lay half in the grass, he was filled with disbelief. Gathering up an armful, he shoved the door open with such force it banged against the wall. His chest heaved and blood channeled through his veins until he felt light-headed.

Caroline calmly turned from the wardrobe. She had the audacity to smile. "There wasn't enough room for everything. You won't be needing that stuff, right?"

CHAPTER EIGHT

He was going to explode.

Caroline's pasted-on smile slipped. Perhaps tossing his clothes out had been an extreme, not to mention immature, act of retaliation. But she was still so very upset with him. He had no right to do what he'd done.

A muscle in his jaw throbbed. His glare bore the heat of a hundred campfires. "You are fortunate I'm a God-fearing man."

He prowled toward her. She leapt out of the way. Not looking at her, he proceeded to rehang his clothes in the scant inches available in the hulking furniture. The tension in the room made her feel as if it were filling with water and she had maybe a minute's span of oxygen left. She didn't know whether to stay or leave.

The sound of feminine chatter passed through the windows and, moments later, a knock resounded through the space. Duncan froze.

"I'll get it." Caroline rushed to greet the visitors, grateful for the intrusion. "Jane. Jessica. What are you doing here?" The twins both held baskets, the contents obscured by blue-and-white-checked fabric. "I — I mean, what can I do for you?"

"Sorry for stopping by unannounced, but we couldn't let the day go by without presenting the newlyweds with a gift." Jessica, the more spirited sister, didn't look the least bit apologetic. Curiosity brightened her eyes as she peered past Caroline. "I'm sorry I wasn't able to attend the ceremony."

Jane's gaze bore the weight of concern. "Um, did you know there are articles of clothing out here?"

Behind Caroline, Duncan snorted. Her face flushed. "Um, yes. Thank you, Jane. We're still sorting through everything. Won't you come in?"

As the sisters deposited the baskets on the table, Caroline looked everywhere except at Duncan. She listened with half an ear as they unpacked their wares, chattering about baked goods and preserves.

"Aren't you going to introduce me to your husband?" Jessica's innocent request brought Caroline's whirling thoughts to a standstill.

"Of course." Smoothing her hands over her skirts, she made the introductions, risking a glance at him as he greeted the twins. He'd managed to school his handsome, aristocratic features into a mask of polite civility. When his gaze punched hers and his mouth tightened, she almost wished Jane and Jessica could stick around. He'd have no opportunity to unleash his displeasure.

"My husband, Grant, and I would love to have you over for dinner sometime." Jessica's smile was welcoming. "You're an official resident now."

Duncan nodded. "I'd like that."

"And after that, you're invited to our house," Jane added. "Tom mentioned he'd like to hear about Scotland."

Caroline found herself wondering about Duncan's homeland, as well. His background was a complete mystery to her. He'd mentioned having been engaged. Why hadn't it worked out?

All too soon they were taking their leave, and Caroline lingered in the doorway watching them stroll down the dirt trail, the setting sun throwing long shadows over them. They were returning to their happy homes, to husbands who'd welcome them with affection.

Take me with you, she was tempted to call out.

"Caroline."

She jumped at the nearness of his rumbling voice. Spinning, she latched onto the doorjamb for support.

"It's getting late. Neither one of us got much rest last night. We should eat and prepare for bed."

"Bed?" Her fingers dug into the wood. Maybe she should've had that talk with her mother, after all.

Frowning, he massaged the back of his neck and studied the floor. "I meant what I said. You've no need to worry on that score." Turning on his heel, he went to the hutch, removed a set of plates and began to fill them with the savory items the girls had brought.

Relief swept through her, at odds with the twinge of despair. That her husband had no wish to be close to her troubled her more than she thought possible.

You're being ridiculous, she scolded herself. Between the lack of sleep, the soreness in her ribs and muscles and the surreal events of the day, she was overwrought. She had no desire to be close to him, either.

She advanced to the middle of the room. "There's only one bed."

115

Duncan paused in his movements, his gaze touching hers and sliding away. "I'll get another one tomorrow and hang quilts from the ceiling. We'll need privacy for dressing, anyway."

"What about tonight? Where will you sleep?"

He laughed, a brief, humorless sound. "It's my cabin. Where do you expect me to sleep?"

"A gentleman would let me have the bed."

"A rolled-up quilt will act as a proper barrier. If you don't like it, sleep on the floor." He shrugged and bit off a slice of ham. "There may be mice, though."

Upset again, battling an onslaught of loneliness that pushed her to the edge of despair, she curled her hands into fists. "I'd take the mice over you any day."

His face was a blank mask. "Fine. More space for me."

Infuriating, callous man! "What can I use to make a pallet?"

With a sigh, he ceased eating and gathered a pair of wool blankets, a pillow and a quilt from a cedar chest at the foot of the bed. He pushed them into her arms. "Here you go. Sleep well, lass."

Not bothering with a lantern, Duncan

stalked out of the cabin. Caroline didn't require his presence as she got ready for bed. A separate bedroom sure would've come in handy. He was going to have to talk to Albert about expanding. The one-room structure might've been fine for a couple of love-struck newlyweds. Not for them. They would need enough space to give each other a break. Something as expansive as his parents' estate would've meant they wouldn't cross paths unless they wished to.

A sense of loss invaded him. The dream he'd cherished of a genuine, loving relationship was out of reach. Impossible.

Walking past dark woods and tranquil fields to the main house, he entered the stables and was surprised to see Wendell standing at Rain's stall.

"Evenin'," he said, coming alongside. "How's she doing?"

"She's her usual content self."

"Good to hear." The mare butted her head against his shoulder. Chuckling, he petted her face. "You're a fortunate one, that you are."

He sensed Wendell's gaze on him. The black pools were sorrowful.

"What's on your mind?" Duncan said, although he had a pretty good idea. He'd seen the fondness on Wendell's face that afternoon as he'd presented Caroline with the flowers.

"You didn't wish to marry her."

"Everyone's aware of that," he said drily. "She didn't want this, either."

"She deserves a man who will cherish her."

Duncan bit the inside of his cheek. *Cherish* and *Caroline* didn't fit in the same sentence.

"You will give her a chance?" Wendell persisted. "Get to know the woman behind the mask?"

"This sounds like a speech I should be getting from her father."

"Exactly." He nodded. "But you didn't get that from Mr. Albert, did you?"

He patted Rain's neck. "No, I didn't. Why is that?"

"I don't know. I'm not inside that house. But I see her unhappiness. I see Mr. Albert busy with his work and his friends. He has no time for his daughter." Crow's-feet appeared at the corners of his eyes. "I had a daughter once."

"What happened to her?"

"She became ill and died. She was eighteen. Beautiful. Kindhearted."

"I'm sorry for your loss."

"She's been gone many moons." He got a

faraway look.

Duncan began to understand Wendell's attachment to Caroline. He viewed her as a substitute daughter. "Do you have other children?"

"Two strong sons and many grand-children. Make my wife and me proud." He smiled then. "You and Caroline will have fine, strapping children."

"I can't think about that right now." Ruth-lessly banning images of blond-haired babies with his wife's stunning blue eyes, he pushed off the stall door. "I should go back."

"Think about what I said."

"Good night, Wendell."

Duncan chose the exit that was closer to the barn. As he passed the smokehouse, he heard voices. One of the barn's doors was open, and low light from inside illuminated the figures of a man and woman. He recog-nized Theo Marsh at once. The woman's back was to him, so he couldn't make out her features. The hair escaping her bonnet was light brown, and she was small and thin and dressed in what appeared to be a uniform. Their furious whispers indicated they were arguing.

Not wanting to intrude, he veered to the left and followed the paddock's fence line until he'd left the outbuildings behind. Who was Theo meeting in the late evening hours out of sight of the Turners? And why?

The pop and sizzle of frying bacon teased her awake. Caroline burrowed farther into the soft ticking, her aching body's protests shredding the last remnants of sleep. Opening her eyes, she stared at the rafters from which dried herbs and garlic bulbs hung suspended. To her left, the clink of utensils against cookware was interspersed with the creak of floorboards as Duncan moved about the kitchen. Slowly shifting her head on the pillow, she searched for the pallet on which she'd started the night. It was gone.

Her scraped-in breath was audible. How had she gotten from the dirty, rock-hard floor to the bed? Her mind raced with possibilities.

The floor creaked and suddenly Duncan was there in her line of sight, dressed for the day in tan trousers and a pine green shirt, his short hair damp and shiny and his manner grim.

"You're awake. How do you feel?"

Confused. Nervous. "Okay."

"You were asleep when I returned from the stables last night. I moved you to the bed and I slept on the pallet." Spoon in hand, he gestured to the stove. "You hungry?

Breakfast is almost ready."

Sitting up, she held the quilt to her throat. "Why would you do that?"

His brows lifted. "You *didnae* eat supper. I figured you'd be ravenous this morning."

"No, I mean why didn't you leave me down there."

"Ah." His lashes swept down. "After the injuries you sustained, you deserved the soft bedding. Besides, my mother's training has stuck with me long after leaving the schoolroom."

Caroline blushed thinking how he must've carried her. "Do I really snore?"

His gaze shot to hers, and his slow, lopsided smile infused her with wonder. "Now that's information I'm no' ready to divulge."

Rattled by his smile's effect, she studied the quilt's design.

"Caroline?"

"Yes?"

"I'm sorry."

The sincere humility in his voice brought her head up. He looked uncomfortable, and she got the sense he didn't often apologize for his actions. He was a proud, complicated man.

"I shouldn't have acted the way I did. After breakfast, I'm going to the Monroes' house. I'll explain what happened and hope-

121

fully get your clothes back."

Astonishment zinged through her. "I don't think that's a good idea. It will only make an embarrassing situation worse."

"Are you certain?"

"Yes."

His troubled expression lingered. Unused to this side of him, she said, "I'm sorry, too. For reacting the way I did."

When he advanced to her side and held out his hand, her mouth went dry. Without the beard obscuring his face, his princely features were on full display. The cedar scent clinging to his shirt mingled with a hint of soap that had her wanting to get closer.

"Truce?" he said huskily.

Letting the quilt slip free, she placed her hand in his and nearly gasped when his strong, lean fingers closed around hers. "Truce."

His cobalt gaze, framed by slashes of auburn brows, took on surprising warmth as it roamed her face and the hair spilling past her shoulders. Their isolation left her feeling vulnerable and exposed.

His brow knitted. Releasing her, he returned to the stove. "I'll have this ready in a few minutes."

While he was occupied, she hopped up

and rifled through the single remaining trunk for her dressing gown. Once she'd donned the snow-white article and fastened every button, she used the cracked, dusty mirror hanging from a nail beside the wardrobe to tie her hair back with a ribbon. She wasn't accustomed to anyone besides the household staff seeing her at less than her best.

"Do you prefer milk? Coffee? Tea?"

"Milk will be fine."

His expression remained unreadable as he poured her a glass of milk and set it at her place setting. He waited for her to sit before taking the chair opposite.

"I'll say grace." When Duncan extended his hands across the table, palms up, she hesitated. "Force of habit," he explained. "Whenever we shared a meal, my family joined hands around the table for prayer. I've eaten most of my meals alone since I left."

He started to pull back. On impulse, Caroline placed hers atop his. His eyes widened.

"I-It's a nice tradition," she said breathily.

Displays of affection hadn't been part of her upbringing. The physical connection felt good. More than good, actually. As Duncan applied light pressure, his hold gentle, she closed her eyes and opened up to the heady sensations cascading through her. If such a simple gesture made her feel like she was soaring above the clouds, how would a hug from him make her feel? Or, dare she imagine it, a kiss?

"Heavenly Father above, we thank You for Your provisions. We ask that You guide us forward on this path You've set us upon. Grant us wisdom. Grant us compassion." He paused. "Forbearance would come in handy, too. In Jesus's name, amen."

The prayer's beauty was in its simplicity. Her father's prayers didn't sound anything like this. Once Duncan was finished, she lamented the loss of his touch, a sign she was more vulnerable than she'd realized. She'd do well to remember that her husband wasn't interested in any sort of relationship with her.

Picking up her spoon, she dipped it in the bowl of oatmeal. Melted butter and cinnamon pooled on top. "Tell me about your family?"

He stabbed a forkful of fried egg and chewed. "My grandfather immigrated to this country fifteen years ago. Five years after that, my parents decided to join him. They packed the four of us boys up, along with about half our worldly possessions, and secured tickets aboard a ship. We settled in Boston and, while we miss our extended friends and family, we consider ourselves Americans now."

"I would've liked to have a sibling. Are you the oldest? Youngest?"

"Second oldest." He filled the bottom of his teacup with milk, then added tea the color of molasses from a tin kettle. "Ian is the oldest. He's thirty. Works with my father. He's married to his first love and is papa to three wee bairns. Alistair is twenty-four. He's a law professor. Still single, last I heard. And Bram is far behind at nineteen. He's studying to be a lawyer."

Cupping the china in both hands, he lifted it to his lips and tested the liquid. Clearly satisfied, he took a long sip.

"Four sons. That must've been a handful. My father had wanted a son." She lowered her gaze before he could decipher betraying emotions. Albert's disappointment that she was a girl had never waned. Seemed like any normal father would be happy to have a healthy child. Not hers.

"Did your parents want more children?" he asked.

"I think my father gave up after I came along." Reluctant to pursue the topic, she said, "Don't you miss them?"

"I do." His expression grew guarded. "I had planned to go to Boston sometime this year."

"Don't let an unasked-for bride stop you."

"There's plenty of time to discuss a trip home."

Caroline doubted he'd invite her to join him and told herself it didn't matter.

This wasn't a love match. Or a union based on mutual needs. They were a pair of strangers, pushed together to protect the Turner name. She'd given her money to save her father from embarrassment. And now she'd given her freedom.

"How long were you going to play the part of nomad?"

His gaze became hooded. "Until I found a place I liked enough to settle down, I suppose."

"It seems I've messed up your life in more ways than one. For better or worse, you're stuck with me and this town." She laid her spoon down, unable to eat any more. Her husband was going to resent her, just like her father resented her for not being what he wanted. The hope she'd nourished of a different future evaporated. "Thank you for breakfast."

Carrying her barely touched plate to the long counter hinged to the log wall, she fought for equanimity.

Still seated, Duncan said, "I like what I've seen so far of this area."

"That's one consolation." She strove for a nonchalant tone.

His chair scraped the floor, and his footsteps were measured as he approached. "I've got to get to the stables. The Lightwoods are leaving today. Would you mind cleaning the dishes?"

He'd asked instead of demanded, she noticed. "Okay, but don't expect me to cook the noon meal. I have no idea how to work that thing." She pointed to the ancient stove.

His smile was polite. Impersonal. "Can you manage a cold lunch?"

She couldn't bear to witness his disappointment. "I'll see what I can scrounge up."

After he'd slipped outside, Caroline went to the window. His hat pulled low, he walked with purpose and confidence past the tiny vegetable garden.

Duncan may like Tennessee, but there was no guarantee he'd ever like her.

CHAPTER NINE

"What are you saying? That I can't access my own money?"

Dread congealed in her bones.

The clerk wore a smarmy smirk. "We must have your husband's signature before you withdraw any amount above what's stated on the documents."

A paltry amount that wouldn't meet a single demand her blackmailer made. So far, she'd received two missives per month. It was mid-July. If his routine remained unchanged, she would receive another one soon.

"Did Duncan come in here today?"

"No. Mr. Turner made the arrangements." Flicking a glance at the queue of customers waiting inside the door, he said, "Is there anything else, Mrs. McKenna?"

Caroline twisted the wedding band on her finger. Mrs. McKenna. It would take time to get used to her new name. "Since you won't grant me access to my own money, I guess not."

Shoulders stiff and head high, she marched outside into the sunshine. What had her father been thinking? That he hadn't consulted her smarted. He might've given her the courtesy of alerting her, thus saving her the embarrassment of being denied.

The boardwalk was bustling this Monday morning. She passed the post office crowded with people and Josh O'Malley's furniture store. He saw her through the window and waved. A flash of poppy red across the way caught her eye. Walking to the street's edge, she observed the girl emerging from the mercantile. The brunette was a longtime resident who rarely left her isolated farm higher in the mountains. The stylish dress she wore looked like an exact copy of the one Louise had ordered from Paris, France, one Caroline had been saving to wear to the annual tea she and her mother hosted each August.

The girl laughed with her companion, strolling along without a care in the world, drawing attention from everyone who passed by. And why not? It was a magnificent design, the fabric crafted by the best seamstresses money could buy.

Caroline couldn't breathe. That was *her* dress.

Indignation overtook her. She stepped into the dusty street, intent on action. A holler on her left registered, and she leapt out of the way as a horse and rider pulled up hard. The horse tossed his head and pranced to the side. The rider glowered at her.

Whirling about, she left Main Street by way of a deserted alley between two buildings. *This isn't fair, Lord. I had plans! I was going to alter the course of my life. This marriage has ruined everything.*

She still had her travel bag. If things between her and Duncan became unbearable, she'd use it, marriage certificate or no.

At home, she headed straight for her father's study. He was seated behind his massive desk, bent over a sheaf of papers, and didn't welcome her with the paternal affection she'd witnessed in other families.

Impatience tightened his eyes. "Caroline, I'm afraid I don't have time to chat. There's a problem in our Northside factory that requires my attention."

Her thoughts went straight to the blackmailer's accusations. "What kind of problem?"

"Nothing you need to worry about." He

scratched his fountain pen across the utmost paper and, frowning, gave it a little shake. "Out of ink." He set it down and searched for another in his drawer.

"I don't mind business talk, Father." Perhaps she could ferret out the truth without having to outright broach the subject. "I'm particularly interested in how our soaps are made. As your only offspring, I should be apprised of the inner workings of our factories."

Head bent, he gave a dismissive flick of his hand. "You're a married woman now. You have plenty to occupy your time."

Perching on the edge of a leather chair facing the desk, she folded her hands in her lap. "Speaking of that, I was at the bank just now. Was it necessary to put restrictions on my account?"

"As head of your household, Duncan needs to have the ability to act on your behalf."

"Adding his name is one thing. Why put restrictions on my withdrawals?"

Snapping the drawer shut, he looked down his hawk nose at her. "Did you think I wouldn't hear of your recent habits, Caroline? I don't want to know what trinkets you thought you needed to add to your collection, but I refuse to stand by and watch you squander your inheritance. With this constraint in place, I won't have to worry. Besides, Duncan strikes me as a levelheaded sort. I've informed him of the new arrangement. He'll make sure you're taken care of while making certain you don't go bankrupt."

She curled her fingers inward until the nails bit into her palms. What did her father truly care about her well-being? To him, she was a responsibility, nothing more.

"Albert, I've instructed Sylvia to pack enough clothes for two weeks." Louise swept into the room, belatedly noticing Caroline. Her eyes welled with tears. "Look at you." She put a trembling hand to her mouth. "What have you done to your hair? Did you go to town like that?"

"I didn't have Betty to assist me, did I?" she retorted.

Caroline touched a self-conscious hand to her hair. All she'd been able to manage without an adequate mirror and supplies was an uneven braid tied off with a ribbon. She'd forgone a corset beneath the royal purple outfit, one of only a handful of acceptable dresses she'd saved from Duncan's raid.

Louise turned to her husband and threw up her hands. "You see why I must accompany you to Charleston?"

Caroline popped up. "You're leaving? When?"

"I must pay a visit to Northside. Your mother is accompanying me. After what's happened, she could use a change of scenery."

Heat rushed through her veins. "*She* could use a change of scenery?" Her voice rose an octave. "I'm the one whose life has been turned upside down! Of course she'd make this about her."

Louise's mouth formed an O.

Albert's brows descended. "Mind your tone, young lady."

Closing her eyes, she battled for control. "What about our tea party? I thought we were going to begin planning for this year's menu and entertainment."

"I'm not certain we should host it this year. Everyone will be whispering about your night alone with that man. And your farce of a wedding." She clutched the brooch on her collar. "I had such high expectations for you, Caroline. You could've married Theo and lived excellently. You would've been the darling of Charleston society. The wedding we could've had for you . . ."

Caroline tried to imagine pledging her life

to the suave, irreverent Marsh heir. Her skin crawled just thinking about it. Oddly enough, Duncan didn't have the same effect.

"You can't cancel the tea, Mother. It's one of the most anticipated events of the year. Think how people will react if we don't have it. There'll be even more gossip."

If she was going to survive this marriage, she needed to stay busy with the things that defined her. She couldn't let go of that, else she would lose herself entirely.

"I'll consider it," Louise said at last.

Albert stood and tugged on his sleeves' cuffs. "We're leaving in the morning. Duncan will be in charge of the property in my absence."

Unease settled in the pit of her stomach. "And what about your guests?"

"The Lightwoods already left. Isaiah is traveling with your mother and me."

"What about Theo?"

"He's got other plans. He said something about exploring the west end of the state. Possibly visiting Nashville since he has a friend there."

She was going to be left alone with Duncan and the staff. That was the least of her worries, however. Coming up with money for the next demand was her top priority. If the truth leaked, her father's reputation wasn't the only thing at stake. He could be accused of criminal activity and taken to court. Maybe even wind up in jail. Sometimes, when she was tempted to tell him what she'd been doing to protect him, she reminded herself it wouldn't raise his estimation of her. Nothing would give her value in his eyes, and that was something she was going to have to accept.

Duncan couldn't find Caroline anywhere. His frustration was exaggerated because it was a quarter past noon and he'd worked up quite the appetite. She'd agreed to prepare the meal. It bothered him when others failed to fulfill their promises. He could afford to be understanding, provided she had a valid excuse.

"Duncan, a word." Albert descended the house's rear porch steps.

Tamping down his impatience, he went to meet his boss. Er, father-in-law. The exact nature of their relationship had become muddied. Albert hadn't treated him any differently since he'd joined the family ranks. Would he change his tune if he learned of Duncan's background?

"Aye, sir?"

"Louise and I are taking a trip to Charleston in the morning. We expect to be away for two weeks, but it could prove to be longer. I'd like for you to see to the running of things." He gave him a detailed set of instructions. "I'll leave a written list on my desk."

When he made to turn away, Duncan blurted, "And what about your daughter?"

"What about her?"

He hadn't been able to get her comments from breakfast out of his head. Or Wendell's. "I realize we were married just yesterday, but I've been expecting a lecture. The typical speech a bride's father gives her new husband."

"Caroline is no longer my responsibility. She's yours." His lips thinned. "If you're seeking insight as to how to handle her, speak to my wife. Louise has far more intimate knowledge of her personality than I."

"I *dinnae* need tips on how to handle my wife," he said incredulously. "I assumed that, seeing as she's your only daughter, you'd be keen to deliver a warning to her new husband. Something along the lines of facing your wrath if I *dinnae* treat her right."

"As you don't have children yet, Mr. Mc-Kenna, you wouldn't understand. Fathers and daughters have little in common. Pray

136

Caroline bears you many sons. Now, if you'll excuse me, I have pressing tasks to tend to." With that, he spun on his heel and stalked toward the house.

Stunned, Duncan watched his retreat. That was not the response of a caring father. He experienced a pang of sympathy for his wife. How would living with this cool detachment affect a person? Then there was Louise. While she appeared to bestow Caroline with more attention, it wasn't the positive kind. She nitpicked and criticized. His own parents weren't perfect by any means, but he was assured of their love and approval no matter what.

His stomach rumbled, reminding him of his mission. Waving away a pesky mosquito, he strode for the stables. He spotted Wendell at the opposite end, leaving the room Caroline had said was used for personal storage.

Duncan hailed him. Surprise puckered his wrinkles. Shifting a bulging sack behind his back, Wendell waited without speaking.

"Have you seen Caroline? I've been searching everywhere —"

The door opened scant inches and Caroline slipped out sideways, hurriedly shutting and locking it behind her. "Duncan." Pocketing the key in a khaki-colored apron tied about her slim waist, she greeted him with lifted brows. "What a surprise to see you here."

"A surprise? Most of my work is in this building." Suspicions aroused, he let his gaze linger on a tiny orange feather clinging to her sleeve. "It's past noon."

For a moment, she looked perplexed. Then her expression cleared, and she nibbled on her lip. "Oh, I forgot. I was supposed to fix your lunch, wasn't I?"

Her casual manner put his hackles up. But then he remembered his conversation with Albert, as well as the fact this situation was as new to her as it was to him. "*Our* lunch. Aren't you hungry?"

"I could eat."

Wendell sidled toward the entrance. "I'll be in the barn if anyone needs me."

She tucked a wayward strand of hair behind her ear, drawing his attention to her unadorned earlobes. His gaze trailed lower to the dress's scooped neckline. Her usual cameo choker was absent. Her wrists didn't glitter with diamonds. In fact, the only piece of jewelry she wore was the wedding band he'd placed on her finger. Her hair looked different, too. Instead of her usual sophisticated style, the light blond tresses had been woven into a braid. Her typical polish had lost its shine. The result was a warmer, softer version of the socialite he'd met at the Independence Day celebration a few short weeks ago.

"I'm sure Cook would give us plates of whatever meal she prepared for my parents. It's her habit to fix extra in case visitors drop in unannounced."

While tempted to agree, he didn't want to begin a pattern of sponging off her parents. Caroline had to learn to be a proper housewife. Who knew if they'd remain on the Turners' property? They might decide to build elsewhere in town or move away from Tennessee altogether.

"Let's go to the cabin and eat. I neglected to show you where the supplies are kept, anyhow." Reaching out, he plucked the feather from her sleeve and held it out to her. "Was Wendell helping you sort feather boas?"

Forehead knitting in consternation, she took the feather and joined it with the key in her pocket. "Not exactly."

"Hmm."

Settling his hand low on her back, he guided her outside. They fell into step together and, although they didn't converse, he had to admit it felt nice to have company. In Boston, he'd rarely been alone. So in those first couple of months following his departure, he hadn't minded the solitude. As the weeks had worn on, he'd begun to crave more companionship than his fellow workers were willing to provide. At the churches he'd attended in various towns, the congregants had been friendly but unwilling to seek deep friendships when he'd made it plain he wasn't sticking around. He'd started seeking God's counsel in the matter of marriage and had gone so far as to ask Him to provide a chosen bride. Glancing at the woman beside him, he was convinced God's plan had gotten bungled.

When they left the fields behind and entered the wooded route to the cabin, she burst out, "Aren't you going to demand answers?"

Duncan didn't have to ask to what she referred. "Are you doing something illegal in that room?"

"What? Of course not."

"Then I'm not going to press the matter. You'll share when you feel comfortable."

A glance at her revealed that she was stewing over his answer. He directed her to the smokehouse and told her to wait while he fetched a knife. Returning, he lifted her hand and slapped the handle into it. "Smoked pork makes fine sandwiches." Bending to avoid hitting his head on the

140

low door frame, he straightened inside the cramped space. "Since it's just the two of us, we *dinnae* need a large portion."

She followed him inside, blinking to gain her bearings, the knife held at an awkward angle. "I'd rather you cut it."

"You learn best by doing." Wrapping his hand around hers, he lifted the knife to the slab hanging from the ceiling hook and set the blade at the preferred spot. "Start here and work your way down."

Her shoulder butted against his chest. Where their arms aligned, her coconut-scented skin — she must've switched soaps — was smooth and still warm from the sun. His gaze zeroed in on her profile, following the line of her brow, her nose, her mouth.

She angled her face his direction. "What if I don't cut it like you want?"

Duncan's thoughts drifted to yesterday's ceremony and missed opportunities. She was his wife. He was allowed to kiss her.

He cleared his throat. "I don't care how it's cut, Caroline."

Edging away until he bumped into another slab, he tried to calm his rapid pulse. Kissing her would complicate matters, not to mention make it difficult to maintain objectivity. They had to get to know each other. Decide how this relationship was going to work before moving into intimate territory.

When she'd finished, he praised her efforts. She didn't seem inclined to accept his compliment, however. He led her to the toolshed where the previous owner had stashed a dozen or so jarred vegetables and preserves.

"Do you like pickled okra?" he said.

"Too slimy."

"What about beets?"

She took the jar from him, her fingertips fluttering over his. "This one's mine. You can have the okra."

"You're not used to sharing, are you?"

She was so easy to tease.

Her somber gaze landed on his. "I never had to. Only child."

"You're never too old to learn." He snatched it back and, chuckling at the protest brewing on her features, sauntered into the light and discovered a familiar woman peeking into the cabin windows. "What is she doing here?"

CHAPTER TEN

"Vivian, hello." Caroline attempted to mask her dismay. Being gossiped about was bad enough. The last thing she wanted was for her friends and acquaintances to witness firsthand how far she'd sunk. "If I'd known you were dropping by, I would've met you at the main house. We're not equipped to entertain guests here."

Standing closer to the steps, Duncan cast her a sharp glance. She ignored it. A rundown cabin may be good enough for him, but it didn't meet her standards.

Not ashamed in the least at having been caught peering into their windows, Vivian waved away her concern. Caroline couldn't help but notice how her dress, crafted of fine rose fabric, enhanced her milk-white complexion. Beneath the dainty hat perched upon her head, the coils of her chocolate hair held a rich sheen.

A disturbing thought struck her. Did

Duncan have a preference for any one hair color? Did he even like fair-haired women like herself? Or did he like other hues more . . . say brunette? She had always admired raven-haired men and hadn't given a thought to auburn until Duncan. Now, she couldn't imagine anything more beautiful than his fire-kissed locks. Not that she'd ever tell him that. His ego was healthy enough as it was.

Hips swaying as she joined them in the yard, Vivian cooed, "I heard the dreadful news this morning and decided to stop and express my condolences. I can't imagine how horrible this must be for you both." She tucked her gloved hand into the crook of Duncan's arm. "Is there nothing anyone can do? An annulment could be had, I'm sure."

Vivian batted her eyelashes and pressed her generous curves against his side. Caroline felt ill. While the other woman possessed a pure heart and meant no harm, she had the tendency to flirt with any man in her vicinity. It had never bothered her until this moment.

Duncan's brows pulled together. "What's done is done. There's no going back."

"What a shame." She made a tutting noise. "I had hoped . . ." Her smoky gaze skittered to Caroline and she gave a tittering laugh. "Forgive me, I'm being rude. I'm just so overwhelmed to learn of your nuptials."

Caroline was reminded of how they'd looked dancing together at the celebration, Vivian's dark-haired beauty a perfect foil for the Scotsman's cinnamon-tinted complexion and auburn hair. Studying his face more closely, she tried to ascertain if he was as disappointed at their lost opportunity as Vivian seemed to be.

Jiggling the jar in his hand, he said, "We're getting ready to eat. Would you like to join us?"

She gave a flirty toss of her head. "I'd love that. Unless Caroline would rather keep you all to herself."

The pair regarded her with expectancy. She couldn't refuse, especially since Duncan had issued the invitation.

"Of course you must join us." Sweeping past them, she went inside and plopped the hunk of meat on the counter. "This certainly won't match Cook's standards. I hope you won't be disappointed."

"I'm sure Vivian doesn't expect a seven-course meal," he intervened.

Oh, they were on first-name terms, were they? Had they spent time together besides that one dance? Her gaze fell on the bed, and she rejoiced that he hadn't yet gotten the second one. No way did she want that tidbit bandied about town.

The brunette's smile bordered on worshipful. "It doesn't take much to impress me."

His gaze brightened with approval. "I've learned to find value in simple things."

"Oh, yes, I know what you mean," she gushed. "It's like that verse the apostle Paul wrote about being content no matter what your circumstances."

At his murmur of surprised pleasure, Caroline turned away, the feeling of sickness intensifying. She told herself it didn't matter. His opinion of her didn't matter. His admiration for Vivian didn't matter. He wasn't what she wanted in a husband, either.

"Caroline? Will you set the table?"

Turning, she thought she caught a smirk on the other woman's face but couldn't be sure. Duncan's exasperation was clear, however. He'd opened the beets and started slicing the meat. Beside him, Vivian was carving up a loaf of bread.

The meal was one of the most excruciating in recent memory. The worst part was the prayer. Duncan reached for her hand and then, in a moment of awkward uncertainty, also took Vivian's. Caroline didn't recognize the turmoil bubbling up inside her. Afterward, she remained mostly silent while the other woman regaled him with local gossip. Duncan did attempt to draw Caroline into the conversation, but she was too upset.

By the time Vivian had taken her leave, Caroline was desperate for escape. She yearned to ride into the hills atop her beloved horse and leave reality behind for a while. But Rain was far from healed. And Caroline wasn't sure she deserved to ride any horse after endangering Rain.

"I thought you liked Vivian."

His accented voice jolted her out of her thoughts.

"I do. She's not someone I'd confide my closest secrets to, but I've known her for years."

He stacked the plates and carried them to the counter. "Is there some reason you didn't want her here?" Balancing a hip against the edge, he crossed his arms. "Are you ashamed of our home?"

She couldn't admit the more humiliating truth — that her husband's obvious admiration for another woman made her feel more inadequate than usual. His already low opinion of her would suffer.

"Our home?" She snorted in an unlady-like fashion. "This doesn't feel like a proper home. For the past decade or more, it's been the abode of an unkempt, elderly bachelor." Executing a complete circle, she held out her hands. "This is nothing like what I pictured my future home would be."

"Let me ask you something. Did living in the lap of luxury make you happy?"

"Excuse me?"

"It's not a difficult question," he said patiently. "Did wearing stylish dresses and being surrounded by expensive furnishings make you happy?"

His words sliced to the heart. She couldn't recall ever being truly content. She'd been too busy striving to earn her parents' approval. "Wealth isn't wrong except to those who don't possess it."

"It's a matter of perspective and learning to be grateful for the little things. For the time being, this is our home. Could use a bit of sprucing up, 'tis true, but it keeps the elements and critters out. Not everyone can say the same. I've seen a lot during my travels. Things that would make you weep."

Caroline's conscience prodded her. She wasn't ignorant. She'd seen poverty in her own town. Take the young woman wearing her dress — that was probably the first new dress she'd owned in her entire life. One example of why Caroline was dedicated to her charity work.

Going to the window, he ran a finger across the glass, leaving a streak in its wake. "With a bit of hard work, you could turn this cabin into a cozy space."

"My idea of work is organizing the table seating for a formal dinner or gathering donations for Christmas baskets. Not scrubbing floors."

"Your ideas are going to have to change." Settling his Stetson on his head, he angled his chin toward the kitchen. "Starting with those dishes."

The chore did not appeal in the slightest. "Things would be easier if you'd agree to let me hire someone."

"And deprive you of the satisfaction of a job well done?" A twinkle entered his eyes. "I can't do that. What I can do is help you with supper. I'll be done between five and six o'clock. You'll be here, right?"

She grimly nodded. "Where else would I be?"

"I'm not putting my hand near that brooding hen."

A smile creased Duncan's face. "Are you always this pleasant in the mornings?"

Her glare didn't have the usual effect. How could it when her clothing was rumpled and her blond hair still in the long, messy braid she'd slept in?

"Until two days ago, I was awoken every day by the gentle rays of the sun and the sweet smell of hot cocoa on my bedside stand."

He let loose a low whistle. "Cossetted lady."

"You can understand why my mood isn't the best right now."

"Like I said, you're slow to wake up, and we have a lot to accomplish today. I couldn't wait an hour for you to decide to open your pretty eyes."

Surprise softened her mouth. He hadn't meant to let that slip. If she sensed his attraction, she'd wield it to her advantage just like Maureen had.

Having separate sleeping areas was for the best. He'd procured a second bed frame and feather-filled mattress yesterday afternoon and positioned it on the opposite wall from his. To ensure her privacy, he'd hung a quilt from the ceiling, obscuring her bed from the rest of the cabin. That morning, he'd called her name several times from the outside of that barrier. When that didn't work, he'd ducked under the quilt and, setting the lamp on the floor, jostled her shoulder. Muttering her displeasure, she'd pushed his hand away and turned on her side toward the wall. As a last resort, he'd whipped off the covers and started tickling her feet. He grinned again thinking about how she'd scrambled off that bed in a flash, her disorientation quickly turning to irritability.

Her gaze sliding away, she observed the hen atop its nest with concern. "If I put my hand there, she'll bite me."

Around their feet, most of the hens pecked at the bits of stale bread scattered on the ground. He had gathered four eggs. It was Caroline's turn. "If you don't want to use your hand, use a stick."

Leaving the pen, he found a slim twig in the grass and brought it to her.

"How about I watch you this time?" she said.

"I don't think so, because tomorrow you're doing this on your own." Like he had with the knife, he placed the twig in her hand and, with his hand guiding her, showed her how to gently prod the chicken out of the box.

With a disgruntled squawk and flurry of wings, the hen abandoned its haven. Caroline jumped back, knocking into Duncan.

His arms came up to steady her. "Whoa, lassie. No need to be frightened."

His lips caught in her hair. Beneath his hands, her blouse was smooth cotton and her arms were slender yet strong. He was reminded of that long, uncomfortable ride on Jet's back. Then, she'd been an intriguing, annoying complication. Days later, she was Caroline McKenna, his wife. No matter how many times he registered that fact, it never failed to surprise him.

She shifted out of his reach. Disappointment flooded him, and he longed to pull her back.

Taking the basket from the coop's roof, he reached in the nest and transferred the remaining four eggs. "I forgot to mention that if the eggs are dirty, the hens have worms. Tell me if that happens and I'll treat them."

Her nose wrinkled. "That's disgusting."

"You may live in a fancy house, but this is rural country. You can't be ignorant about farm life."

"I choose to focus my interests elsewhere and let the paid workers do the less appealing work."

"You mean *chose*. You no longer have that luxury."

Planting her hands on her hips, she

groused, "You really know how to start the day off right, don't you?"

Settling a hand on her shoulder, he turned her toward the entrance. "Come on," he coaxed. "I'm sure you'll feel better once you've milked Lulabelle."

"I thought we were eating breakfast." She dug in her heels. "If you'd set aside your pride, we could sit down to a scrumptious meal right now. Remember how much you like Cook's flapjacks?"

"With practice, you can make them as good or better than hers."

Duncan worked to keep his amusement hidden as he instructed her in the art of milking. He had to hand it to her, she didn't complain often. But she did tend to give up easily. Her confidence was surprisingly low. Good thing he was a patient man.

After fifteen solid minutes of trying and failing, and getting whacked in the face with a cow tail, he sensed she was nearing the end of her frustration. He touched her arm.

"Let me take over. We'll try again tomorrow morning."

"Oh, joy," she muttered, pushing a hank of hair out of her eyes. Her eyes looked suspiciously bright.

"Hey." Cupping her shoulders, he dipped his head to capture her gaze. "It's okay if you don't get it right on the first try."

She didn't look convinced. He almost told her about his background and how he'd had to learn a lot of new things once he struck out on his own. He decided against it.

His stomach rumbled. She arched a single brow as if to remind him what was available a short walk away.

Letting his hands slip free, he walked around her and lowered himself onto the stool. "I'll have this done in a few minutes if you want to take those eggs inside. How does an omelette sound? I can grab a green pepper and tomato from the garden."

"I think it sounds like an upscale dish for a traveling Scotsman."

"You meet people from different backgrounds and ethnicities when you travel." Leaning his shoulder into Lulabelle's side, he began to direct streams of milk into the pail. "So? Does that sound agreeable?"

"It does." He heard her move toward the doorway. "I'll get the vegetables if you want. Since you're busy."

He paused to look over his shoulder. "I'd appreciate that."

"It doesn't take skill to separate a vegetable from the vine," she quipped before slipping out.

His curiosity about Caroline deepened.

He mulled over the scant facts he'd gleaned during their short acquaintance and found himself hungry for more. What was her greatest disappointment in life? Her deepest hurt? What made her laugh? What were her favorite things to do? He had no clue if she'd been in love or had her heart broken. He wasn't privy to her political views. While he had to be careful to guard his feelings, it was important to get to know the woman he'd married.

CHAPTER ELEVEN

Taking refuge in her private sanctuary later that morning, Caroline guided the tweezers to the papier-mâché half mask and carefully set the aquamarine feather in place among the others. The precision required to decorate a mask worked to calm her tumultuous emotions and help her forget her problems for a while. Duncan wouldn't be happy to know she was here instead of picking the cucumbers he'd said would rot if left on the vine another day. But she'd thought of a way to earn money to satisfy the blackmailer. Neither Duncan nor her father would have to know.

She lifted her bird-themed creation and examined it for flaws. Masquerade balls were a popular pastime in Charleston. She could use her family's business connections and arrange to sell them in stores there. Some customers might even want them to display in their homes. Of course, mask making was delicate work. In order to free up her time, she would use a small portion of what money she did have to pay Sylvia to do the menial chores Duncan expected her to do. Good thing she had stocked up on supplies recently and wouldn't need to purchase any in the foreseeable future.

If only her workroom wasn't in the stables. When Caroline had first decided to try her hand at masks, she'd chosen to pursue her new hobby in a place her mother didn't frequent. Old George hadn't bothered her here, and of course her father didn't concern himself with her pursuits. Duncan was another story. She would have to be sneaky in order to avoid his detection.

The prospect bothered her. The rugged Scot was turning out to be the opposite of what she'd first assumed. Oh, he was still infuriating. He still made her want to stomp her feet and howl in frustration sometimes. But he had good qualities, too.

He'd been a remarkably patient instructor. She'd never admit it, but cooking with him — both last evening and this morning — hadn't been the tortuous activity she'd thought it would be. He doled out encouragement like it was penny candy and hadn't complained when she'd burned the corn bread to a crisp. Cleaning up the mess afterward wasn't as tedious with him beside her.

Scrutinizing the many masks hung on the slat walls, she wondered what he'd think about her hobby. This was the one thing she was truly good at, yet no one besides Wendell knew about it. That Duncan hadn't demanded she show him astonished her.

Activity on the other side of the door alerted her to someone's presence. The deep, slick voice didn't belong to Duncan. The feminine voice was too muffled to identify.

Caroline replaced her tools in the container and untied her apron. She checked her muslin dress for stray feathers and smoothed her hair, ensuring the proper bun was tidy in the mirror. She was glad she hadn't glimpsed herself that morning. Fresh embarrassment stung her cheeks. Over the years, she'd perfected her beauty routine and didn't emerge from her bedroom until her stylish armor was in place. No one besides her mother and Betty had ever seen her at less than her best. And now Duncan had seen her with her hair resembling a bird's nest and her skin crying out for moisture-rich lotion.

Out in the stables, the conversation ceased. She pressed her ear to the wood for long moments. Reassured, she left the workroom and hurriedly locked it. Turning, she yelped at the sight of Theo's suit-clad chest.

"What are you doing here, Theo? I thought you'd left already."

"I had planned to, but my horse was favoring his front leg and had to postpone. Your husband promised to tend him."

That meant he'd be sticking around a while longer. Wonderful. "Well, I hope Thunder recovers quickly. Good day, Theo."

He grasped her hand. "There's no need to rush off, is there? We haven't had a chance to talk since the ceremony."

"What is there to talk about?"

He tugged her closer. "Marriage agrees with you, Caroline. There's something different about you." His gaze roamed her features in frank admiration.

"I'm the same woman I was the night of the party."

"No, I don't believe you are." The pressure of his hand intensified. "I was crass that night. And foolish. I apologize."

"Release me, Theo."

"I regret not scooping you up when I had the chance."

This was the sort of scene that would evoke her husband's ire. The last time Theo had bestowed his attentions on her — nearly kissing her full on the lips! — Duncan's temper had spilled over and it had not been pleasant.

"You and I would not have made a pleasing match."

He arched a sardonic brow. "And you and that Scotsman do? Forgive me for being blunt, but neither of you seem happy with your current circumstances."

A scraping noise on the cobblestones sent alarm skittering over her nerves. "Someone's coming. Let me go."

He did as she requested, to her relief. Spinning around, she glimpsed the telltale gray-and-white uniform.

"Sylvia!" Caroline pursued her into the yard, catching up to her at the kitchen stoop. "Sylvia, I require a minute of your time."

The spindly young woman had her hand on the doorknob. Tendrils of her brown hair had slipped from beneath her white cap to curl around her stiff collar. She faced Caroline and clasped her hands at her waist. While not classically pretty, Sylvia Leonard was attractive in a unique sense — her large, yellowish-brown eyes, pointy nose and diminutive mouth having put Caroline in mind of a cat. "Yes, miss? How may I be of service?"

Entering the shade thrown by the trees on this side of the house, she noted the hyacinth bushes were blooming at last and the bee balm was nearly taking over the garden beds.

"I have a proposition for you," Caroline explained. "Would you be interested in earning extra wages?"

Her nose appeared to twitch. "Extra wages? I believe I would, miss. Doing what?"

"Odd jobs. I wouldn't need you every day, of course."

Sylvia stroked the skin above her upper lip. "My mother has been ill these past months and unable to work. Any additional income would be helpful."

Caroline hid a cringe. She hadn't known. And she should have.

"Here's what I need for you to do today." She gave her instructions. "Oh, and Sylvia? Let's keep this between us."

"Understood, miss."

With a sigh of satisfaction, she returned to her masks. She now had the entire afternoon to use as she wished.

He was going to throttle her.

Feeling bad about Caroline's frustrating morning, Duncan had decided to pay her a visit midafternoon and offer his assistance with the chores. He hadn't gotten around to giving the dilapidated cabin a thorough scrubbing since his arrival, and he could imagine how overwhelmed she must be at the long list of tasks to tackle. At first, he'd thought the figure crouched in the garden was her. But then he'd hailed her, and the skinny maid named Sylvia had bolted to her feet in surprise. She'd been reluctant to provide him with answers, no doubt urged to secrecy by Caroline.

Nearing his boiling point, he stalked along Main Street in search of her statuesque form. Ten minutes in, his gaze was drawn to the post office entrance and the beautiful, not-completely-put-together blonde exiting. His long strides eating up the dirt, he halted her progress with his bark, drawing curious stares from onlookers, as well.

"Duncan." Her forehead creased. "What's the matter?"

Taking her elbow, he propelled her into the alley between buildings. The shade did little to assuage the heat tightening his skin and the sweat beading on his temples.

"You deliberately defied my wishes."

She shot a sideways glance at the people passing on the boardwalk several yards away. "Lower your voice." She spoke through clenched teeth. "Do you wish to add to the gossip already swirling about us?"

"We agreed we wouldn't pay others to do what we ourselves are capable of doing."

Her navy eyes swirled like the ocean deep in the grips of a hurricane. "You have a faulty memory, sir. We did not agree to any such thing. You decreed your opinion as if it were law. Am I not allowed to think for myself? Must I come to you with every decision for approval?"

His shirt was damp and sticky. Pulling the material away from his skin, he fanned it in a vain search for relief. "The household is your domain. You have responsibilities. Sooner or later, you're going to figure out that the woman you were before you met me is gone. You are no longer Caroline Turner, heiress to piles of money and co-ordinator of formal dinners. Your world is no longer about the latest in European fashion and the juiciest bits of gossip shared over tea and pastries. You're a farmwife now, like thousands of other women across this great nation."

His chest heaving with the force of his speech, he belatedly noticed her growing pallor, her pinched features and the hurt in her eyes.

"Look, maybe I *didnae* word that right —"

"Oh, I believe you said exactly what was on your mind." Her voice was shaky. "Not surprising, considering you're only concerned with what *you* think and how *you* view the world."

Head high, arms stiff at her sides, she marched in the opposite direction of Main Street.

"Caroline!"

She didn't break stride. Once again, they were at odds, and he hated it.

"Mr. McKenna? Everything okay?"

Mopping his face with his handkerchief, Duncan greeted the deputy. "I'm no' sure if anythin' will be okay again."

Coming alongside him, Ben MacGregor squinted in the direction Caroline had fled. "Would you like to talk about it?"

"*Willnae* help."

"There's something you should know about me." Grinning, Ben thumbed the brim of his Stetson up. "I'm acquainted with a great number of women. For whatever reason, they're drawn to me."

Duncan couldn't stop a small smile at the younger man's boast. "Is that so?"

"Yep. One thing I'm sure of is women like to be courted. They like to be romanced.

You don't have to spend a fortune on them, either. A bouquet of wildflowers has the same impact as a box of expensive chocolates. It's the thought that counts. They want to know you've put some effort into pleasing them." He paused. "You didn't have a chance to court Caroline, did you?"

"You already know the answer."

"Apparently you needed me to point it out."

Duncan heaved a sigh. "Apparently."

Ben's green eyes twinkled as he clapped Duncan's back. "I missed lunch. Let me buy you a bowl of chicken noodle soup at the Plum Café."

"I heard eating there's a waste of hard-earned money."

He nodded. "It is if you don't know the menu. Stay away from the meat loaf and fried chicken. The pork chops aren't bad if you've a sturdy set of teeth. Now, the chicken noodle soup is downright tasty. Just have to add a touch of salt."

Duncan hesitated.

"We don't have to talk about Caroline. You can tell me about your travels, and I'll answer any questions you have about the town."

"Do they serve cold drinks?"

"Lemonade."

"Sold."

The Plum Café had a dingy, abandoned feel to it. The woodwork around the fireplace was dull and coated with dust, the mirror above it cracked and the maroon tablecloths threadbare. The young waitress wore an expression of boredom. Only two of the tables were occupied.

Choosing a corner table with four chairs, Ben set his hat on the empty seat between them and gave their order to the girl who looked to be around the same age as his youngest brother, Bram.

"Sure you don't want dessert?" he asked Duncan. "The spice cake's not bad. Right, Sally?" Tilting his head to one side, he grinned up at her and was rewarded with a stammering blush.

"That's right, Deputy."

"I'll pass this time," Duncan said.

The waitress promised coffee and ambled toward the kitchen door. A dark-haired man emerged and waylaid her. Lean to the point of thinness and unkempt, he didn't look well.

"Is that the cook?"

"That's Alexander Copeland. He owns this place." Sinking against the chair slats and crossing his arms, Ben eyed the man with curiosity. "I'm surprised to see him.

166

He bought the café a few years ago from the previous owner, Mrs. Greene. We all assumed he'd maintain her high standards. Unfortunately, that didn't turn out to be the case. He spends most of his time locked away in his office and doesn't seem to care about the decline in business. Lets his employees do as they please. He avoids interacting with the locals."

"Do you know anything about his past? Why he came to Gatlinburg in the first place?"

"The sheriff and I did some poking around, with little success. He didn't meet our inquiries with enthusiasm, to say the least. Only thing we can do is monitor his actions and keep an eye on the wanted posters on the off chance he's been involved in shady dealings."

Duncan fiddled with the silverware. "So tell me, if you're a connoisseur of women, why haven't you chosen one to settle down with?"

A laugh burst out of Ben. "I grew up with four younger sisters who made it their mission to torture me. Flirting is fun and harmless. Actually taking on a female who I'd be responsible for for the rest of my days? No, thank you." Leaning forward, he said, "Let's talk about something more interesting. Like how you're going to go about wooing your wife?"

"I thought we weren't going to discuss her."

"You know, if you were a local, I'd be a lot less optimistic about your success. But there's something about you that makes me think you'll be able to win her heart."

Duncan gazed out the window, his mind in turmoil. He didn't wish to win Caroline's heart. He simply wanted peace in his home.

Caroline rolled a stray cucumber away from the counter edge and closer to the mound in the middle. The pint jars were lined up in a straight row, shiny and clean, the necessary pickling ingredients beside them. She read the instructions for the third time.

The door opened and, at the glimpse of a facial structure Michelangelo would've paid handsomely to carve, she braced herself for another row. If there was one thing they were good at, it was making each other boiling mad. At least he hadn't showed up a few minutes earlier and seen the package of masks she'd shipped to Charleston. He would've demanded answers and that would've unraveled everything.

His cobalt gaze wary, he left his hat and a

crinkly brown sack on the table. "What's this?"

"I don't think we can manage to eat all these cucumbers before they rot, do you?"

"I don't like them enough to risk a bellyache, no."

Coming to stand beside her, he bent and peered at the large open tome she'd borrowed from Cook's kitchen. Her gaze ate up the strong planes of his face, the hint of stubble along his jaw and the curve of his eyelashes. His shaving soap wafted up to her, and she inhaled the pleasing scent before she could stop herself.

He picked up the packet of dill seed. "Do you know how to preserve them?"

Still upset over his high-handed attitude, she snapped, "I'm a reasonably intelligent woman. I can figure it out."

He slowly straightened. "I'm sure you can do just about anything you set your mind to."

The air seemed to shimmer with leftover frustration from their encounter in town. Duncan was staring at her like a sailor contemplating uncharted waters. His direct gaze made her feel self-conscious about her creased blouse and less-than-perfect hair. With him more than anyone else, it was imperative she keep her guard in place, not easy when she no longer had a personal maid or an extensive wardrobe.

"The instructions are forthright," she said to splinter the silence. "I sterilize the jars and lids first. Once the cucumbers are cut and placed in the jars, I'll boil the brine that goes inside. At the end, I'll boil the entire jars in order to seal them."

He replaced the dill seed with the garlic bulbs. "Doesn't sound too complicated."

"No, it doesn't."

With an exaggerated grimace, he ran a hand through his hair. "Caroline, I'm sorry for making a spectacle earlier. My stance *hasnae* changed, but you had a solid point. I've been on my own for a long while now. I'll have to learn how to compromise."

Caroline's lips parted. Her proud husband was apologizing? She couldn't think of a single sane response. Not once had she heard her father eat humble pie.

Clearing his throat, he retrieved the sack. "I brought you a gift."

Her astonishment deepening, she unrolled the top and lifted out a thick bundle of fabric. "Um, it's pretty."

"You can use it to make curtains. Maybe a tablecloth."

The vulnerable light in his eyes suppressed the retort forming on her lips. Her idea of an exceptional gift was a piece of jewelry or a scarf. A sentimental trinket or a unique, edible treat from a distant locale.

This wasn't a gift. It was a project.

Lowering her gaze, she tested the fabric's sturdiness with her fingers. "Thank you, Duncan."

Outside the window, a woodpecker drilled into a nearby tree.

"You don't say my name very often," he said quietly.

"I — I don't?"

His expression solemn, he took a step closer. "I like hearing you say it."

Lifting his hand, he righted the edge of her collar, the feather-like sweep of his fingertips showering her with shimmery tingles.

In that moment, Caroline didn't see him as the enemy. The destroyer of dreams. He was merely a human being with faults and strengths, hopes and fears like everyone else. Since learning of their impending vows, she'd been so busy feeling sorry for herself that she'd rarely considered how he must be feeling. Her defenses cracked.

Father God, I'm so lost. I don't have the slightest clue how to be this man's wife. Before her life became entangled with Duncan's, she'd handled everything on her own. Why bother God with manageable problems, she'd thought. She'd prayed for other peoples' issues — illnesses, farming disasters, families grieving for a deceased loved one, couples worried about impending births. But this marriage was showing her how wrong such thinking had been. She needed the Lord's strength and guidance in the mundane tasks *and* the big, overwhelming, obviously-too-much-for-her difficulties. *Help me, God, please.*

"I should've discussed my plan with you before hiring Sylvia. Seeing as you feel so strongly about it, I won't enlist her help in the future."

The words weren't easy to say, but she felt better for having said them.

"Thank you, Caroline. We'll make this work somehow," he said with determination.

She hoped he was right, but she couldn't help the doubts pelting her.

CHAPTER TWELVE

Duncan had plenty to occupy his time. He wasn't a lovesick newlywed who couldn't bear to leave his bride's side. And yet he found himself offering to help her. Maybe it was her obvious trepidation at trying something new. He had to admit he found her current state adorable, the way she nibbled on her lip as she reread the directions, her fine brows tugging together in concentration.

He knew she didn't feel presentable. She kept reaching up to check her braid, her fingers exploring the interwoven strands at the back of her head and riding the thick, shining length that fell over her shoulder. She smoothed her blouse, ensuring it was tucked into her skirt's waistline. Duncan was tempted to blurt the truth — that he preferred her this way, her harsh, hands-off elegance softened to lush, touchable femininity.

Caroline wasn't interested in what he thought about her, so he kept mum.

Choosing a knife from the hutch drawer, he picked up a cucumber. "How would you like these? In coins or spears?"

A look of confusion stole over her features. "Don't you have things to do?"

"On the farm, there's always something to do." He waggled the vegetable. "So?"

"I guess spears."

"Spears it is."

He set to slicing. When she didn't move, he paused. "What?"

"Why are you helping me?" she said softly. "Is it because you think I'll mess something up?"

"What if I said it's because I want to spend time with my wife?"

Her eyes grew round, the initial surge of wonder eclipsed by suspicion. Concern filled him. Why would she doubt him? The wounds of her upbringing must be more serious than he'd thought. Right then and there, he prayed for wisdom in how to proceed. If they were ever going to reach a state of mutual respect and, dare he hope, affection, they had to build a foundation of trust.

"I don't know much about you. I'd like to remedy that."

Her wariness lingering, she pulled the garlic to her and began to peel the papery skin from the cloves. "What do you wish to know?" she said, her attention on her work.

Since he'd yet to see a sincere smile, he said, "What gives you joy?"

"Joy?"

"My *maither* used to ask us that when we were young. For her, it was needlework. She worked on her samplers every spare moment she got."

"What did she do with them all?"

"Shared them with friends and neighbors. She gave me and my brothers some for our future wives. Mine are at home in storage." Like his grandmother's ring. He'd thought to bestow it on the woman who captured his heart. He could ask his mother to send it, but giving it to Caroline seemed wrong.

With a start, he realized he'd neglected to contact his family. They knew he had come to Tennessee for work. They had no idea he was a married man.

"You didn't answer my question," he said.

"I like to plan and organize."

"Organize what, exactly?"

"Items. Events. People."

He recalled her role at the Independence Day's event, how she'd appeared to be in charge of the vendors.

"You're a natural leader and problem solver."

"In certain areas, I suppose." She pushed a cleaned clove aside and started on another. "I enjoy the outdoors. I like helping Wendell with the flowers. Before him, I didn't know a chrysanthemum from a pansy."

"I caught you snoozing in the lake with a book. You're a reader."

"I was not snoozing or snoring." She waved her paring knife for emphasis. "My eyes had grown heavy, so I decided to daydream for a bit."

"If you say so."

Her forehead creased. "I don't really snore, do I?"

"Tell me what you do in that secret room of yours, and I'll answer that."

Resistance was written across her face. "You'll think it's silly."

"You've made it clear you don't care about a humble stable manager's opinion," he countered, then wished he hadn't. "Forget I said —"

"I like to create things," she blurted. "Things no one besides Wendell has seen."

Duncan stared at her. Remembering the feather, he said, "Hats?"

"No." Finished with the garlic, she wiped her hands on a towel. "Maybe someday I'll show you."

"I hope you will."

Duncan hoped for more than that, he realized. He longed to know her, this woman who'd invaded his home and life, to know how she thought and reacted and felt, to know what she liked and what she didn't, what frightened her and what made her laugh with abandon. He wanted to see what happiness looked like on Caroline. The prospect unsettled him a little. Instinct warned that if she ever let herself dismiss others' expectations and relax enough to enjoy life on her own terms, she'd be impossible not to fall in love with. Loving a woman who embodied the very life he'd turned his back on would lead to misery for both of them.

Farm life was exhausting. Caroline's upper back and arms were sore, and her feet cried out for a hot salt soak. She would've retired for the night if she thought sleep would claim her. Pacing from the window on the east wall that had a view of the barn and chicken coop to the one beside the main door, she watched as fireflies blinked on and off above the garden rows. Dusk lent a yellow haze to the pastoral scene. Among the thickness of trees, shadows lengthened and nocturnal animals stirred.

The whisper of pages turning ceased. "Something on your mind?"

Duncan lounged at the table, a thick book open before him. Locks of fire-kissed hair slid over his forehead. He'd unfastened the top buttons of his shirt, revealing the strong column of his throat and a V of firm, suntanned skin. He fit here in this rustic cabin. It wasn't a stretch to picture him in more refined surroundings, however. He may have the appearance of a common laborer, but his manners told a different story. From his speech and reading habits, she could tell he was an educated man.

"What are you reading?" She countered his question with one of her own.

Picking up the book edges, he showed her the cover. "Robert Burns. Many consider him to be Scotland's national poet."

"Didn't he write 'Auld Lang Syne'?"

Smiling, he nodded. "Among other things. My father's favorite Burns quote is 'There is no such uncertainty as a sure thing.' "

"Your father is an educated man?"

He blinked and shifted in the chair. "Aye, he is that."

"Did you attend university?"

"I did."

"University isn't cheap. Your brothers at-

178

tended, as well?"

"Yes, they did." His gaze faltered. "It was important to my grandfather that we go. He made it happen."

It was suddenly imperative she learn more about her husband. "Where did you attend? What did you study?"

Inhaling deeply, he aligned the attached ribbon to hold his place and closed the book. "Boston University. I earned a degree in business."

Why wasn't he putting his education to good use? Before she could voice the question, he stood and retrieved a long, skinny stick from the corner beside the wardrobe.

"Would you like to go for a walk?"

She glanced outside. "Right now?"

He chose a kerosene lamp from the kitchen shelf and handed it to her. "Nighttime's the best for fishing. If we hurry, we can get there in time to dig up a few worms to use as bait."

"You want me to go fishing?"

"You've been actin' like a caged animal this hour past. The fresh air will do you good." Lifting the lid of his cedar chest, he took out an old, tattered wool blanket. "You *willnae* have to worry about pesky insects thanks to the bats."

Wendell had built homes for them on tall

posts surrounding the pond for that purpose.

"Bats are active at night," she pointed out.

Humor graced his mouth, and she noticed he had a nice smile. Whenever he smiled, his blue eyes danced with mirth. "Never fear, fair lass, I'll protect you."

Flustered, Caroline preceded him onto the porch. Would he really go out of his way to keep her safe? Had he gotten over his anger at her? She wondered sometimes if he'd resent her for the rest of their lives. The thought saddened her.

As they headed for the main property and the pond, Duncan shortened his stride to match hers. "Did you attend university?"

"I wanted to. Mother considered it a waste of time and resources, considering I was to apply myself in securing an advantageous marriage. To that end, she hired a qualified tutor to teach me until I was eighteen, my own personal schoolteacher."

He glanced over at her. "You didn't go to school with other kids your age?"

A dry laugh escaped. That was one of many childhood dreams that had been dashed. "Not once."

When they'd moved to Gatlinburg, she'd asked if she could go to the one-room schoolhouse. She could still see Louise's horrified expression. *Attend school with rustics?* she'd exclaimed. *We may live among them, Caroline, but we will never be like them. People with simple upbringings have simple minds. They couldn't possibly relate to us. Why, you have more knowledge inside your head than I suspect their teacher does.*

"It must've been difficult to make friends. New to town. Isolated from the locals."

"I wasn't completely isolated. My parents and I have been faithful church members. Once they appointed Mother the head of the benevolence society, we began to interact more with the other ladies and their daughters."

Emerging from the wooded lane into the wide, open pastures, they walked past the paddocks. The last fingers of sun gilded each blade of grass with gold. Several horses were out grazing, their tails swishing from side to side. Summer was her favorite season. She loved the long days and the comforting heat that seeped deep into her skin. To her creative senses, the world came alive with inspiration . . . lush forests and fields teeming with wildlife and intricate plants.

A pair of blue-black butterflies flittered ahead of them. She'd never made a butterfly mask before. She'd have to remedy that.

"Is that how you became friends with the twins? Through church work?"

"We knew of each other, of course. Gatlinburg's too small not to know everyone's name, except for the more reclusive residents who stick to their hidden coves. Anyway, Jane and I sort of wandered into each other's paths a time or two. I rode almost every day. She took contemplative walks and wrote profound thoughts in her journal. After running into each other a couple of times, she invited me to stop and talk. We started planning our meetings and a friendship was born."

At the pond's edge, he arranged the blanket on the bank and gave her the stick to hold.

"Is she someone you can count on?"

"Absolutely."

"Everyone needs someone like that in their life."

As he crouched to scout for worms in the mucky soil, the sunlight slanting through the trees hit his close-cropped hair and made it shine like red-tinted gold. She stood off to the side and observed him, strange, wondrous feelings blossoming to life inside. This gorgeous, compelling, good-hearted man was her husband. *Hers.* In the past few days, she'd spent more time with him than she had any other man. He'd seen her at her worst — had witnessed frustration and ill moods and ineptitude — and was still talking to her.

He doesn't exactly have a choice, does he? He's spending time with you because he's shackled to you against his will.

Taking a seat on the blanket, tucking her legs to the side and arranging her skirt, she ceased soaking him in to gaze over the mirrorlike water. Cattails stood tall along the oblong perimeter. Water lilies joined bits of algae on the surface. Her father had had this dug out shortly after they moved here. Next to her preferred mountain riding trails, this was her second favorite spot on the property. Her parents seldom came out here and only to appease their guests.

Duncan settled on the blanket beside her, his hip wedged against hers and long legs stretched out in front of him. The blood in her veins turned to thick syrup. She became attuned to his movements, sucking in air each time his upper arm brushed hers. Folding her hands tightly in her lap, she called herself a fool. He wasn't interested in her that way. He'd refused to kiss her on their wedding day. She was grateful he hadn't pressed her into intimacy she wasn't ready for, of course. But the more time she spent in his company, the greater her yearning for at least a token of affection from him.

He glanced over and caught her staring. He flashed a smile that made her heart trip over itself. "Want to try hooking a worm?"

Her answering smile felt tight. "No, thanks."

Duncan shrugged, completely unaffected by her proximity. "You *dinnae* know what you're missin'."

When he had the line affixed to his pole and the bait ready, he lobbed it in the water. "Now we wait. Anthony said your father keeps it stocked. Let's see if he's right."

The sounds of crickets chirping and cicadas buzzing pulsed through the evening. Minutes passed without a word spoken. It wasn't uneasy, exactly. Or tense, which was good. Still, her restlessness increased the longer they sat there.

"It's getting dark," she said.

"You can light the lamp if you'd like."

After lighting the wick and setting the lamp in the grass, she resumed her seat and was imagining how to construct a butterfly mask when his deep, accented voice startled her.

"Caroline, would you mind if I asked you a personal question?"

"What about?"

"Something occurred to me just now," he said, not looking at her. "Have you ever had a serious suitor?"

"Are you asking if I've ever been in love?"

He transferred the pole to his other hand. "Have you?" His tone was serious. "I'd hate to think this marriage prevented you from being with someone you already admired."

"There's no one else."

There never had been. A couple of the Charleston bachelors who'd visited over the years had expressed interest. She'd rebuffed them because she'd been holding out for an elusive, impossible dream.

"You were engaged once. What happened?"

"We didn't want the same things. Don't get me wrong, Maureen's a vibrant, engaging woman. She fascinated me from the moment I laid eyes on her at the Winstons' Christmas ball the year I turned twenty-three."

Uncomfortable with his glowing remarks about his former fiancée, Caroline regretted opening the subject. She could all too easily picture the pair meeting and falling in love at the function they were both working. Had Maureen been a kitchen helper? Or a maid?

"What did she look like?" She despised the weakness that allowed the question to pass her lips.

"Oddly enough, she's a redhead like me. Fairer skin, of course, because she shields herself from too much sun. And her eyes are green like those lily pads there."

"I see." Caroline quelled further questions. The answers only brought her grief.

"She had scores of admirers. Even so, I decided I had to have her. I pursued her. She relished the game. I don't think she took me seriously until the night I proposed."

Disquiet arrowing through her, Caroline scrambled to her feet and walked farther down the bank. She couldn't listen to this, not so soon after their awkward, stilted vows. The muscles between her shoulders were so tense they ached. Reaching up, she kneaded the area and a slight groan escaped.

Muffled movement warned her of his approach. "Are you okay?"

"Of course." Although her features were likely as shadowed as his, she faked a smile. "My legs were getting stiff."

His gleaming gaze caught her feeble efforts to ease her discomfort. "How are you recovering from your fall? Are the bruises fading? Should you see Doc —"

"I'm fine," she interrupted, lowering her arm to her side. She didn't like to be reminded of her reckless stupidity. "Much improved."

He edged behind her and gingerly settled his hands atop her shoulders, his thumbs aligned on either side of her spine. The weight and warmth of him seared through her thin cotton blouse.

"What are you doing?" When she would've turned, his hold tightened, preventing her.

"You've been doing chores you're not accustomed to." His mouth was close enough that his breath stirred the tendrils on her nape. "And so soon after being bucked off a horse. You're bound to be stiff."

At the first gentle pressure of his fingers on her poor muscles, Caroline closed her eyes and blew out a long breath. Languid warmth flowed through her. *Bliss.* That's what this was. The knots gradually melted away beneath his careful ministrations. She had to fight to remain upright instead of sagging against his chest.

She almost protested aloud when he stopped.

He bent his head close. "All better now?"

Awareness roared to life. Caroline envisioned him sliding his arms around her waist and pulling her back against him, maybe even nuzzling her cheek.

"Caroline?" he prompted, his voice thicker

than usual.

She started. "Yes! Yes, I'm fine. If I was any better, I'd be a puddle at your feet."

His hands fell away, and she bit her lip. Wrong thing to say?

Turning, she searched his features for a sign he felt something other than repulsion. His expression was frustratingly blank.

"Thank you, Duncan."

"Glad I could help." He gestured to the blanket. "Shall we stay and try for a fish? Or would you rather leave?"

Caroline wanted to stay. She craved his company, ironic considering how she'd initially felt about him. But he didn't truly want hers. So she strove for an excuse to give him some time alone.

"Actually, I need to stop in the house and get something from my old bedroom."

Nodding, he bent to retrieve the lamp. "I'll walk with you."

"No."

He looked up sharply.

"I mean, it's not necessary. Stay. Enjoy your hobby for a while longer."

"All right." When he handed her the lamp, their fingers tangled, and his laugh had a self-conscious ring to it. "Don't get lost."

With a quick, perfunctory smile, she left

him there, her heart clamoring for the impossible.

CHAPTER THIRTEEN

Duncan was struggling with growing dissatisfaction, and it was centered around the woman at his side. Collective voices lifting in song resonated through the church building. Caroline possessed a fine, clear voice. His gaze was drawn to her for what seemed the hundredth time since she'd met him at the wagon, ready for services. Outfitted in the audacious dress she'd worn for their wedding, she'd left her hair loose. It spilled down her back like a silken waterfall. He sorely wished to curve his arm around her shoulders and caress the length of it. A hairpin was tucked above her left ear, exposing the shell pink lobe and the creamy skin of her nape. Not so long ago, he'd come close to pressing kisses in that exact spot.

Ripping his gaze away and refocusing on the reverend, he tried to expel the memory of their time at the pond and how a straightforward offer to alleviate her discomfort had transformed into something else entirely. The intense need to hold her had almost obliterated his decision to maintain his distance. They were finally making progress, sharing parts of themselves and their histories. He didn't want to slow the process or, worse, halt it altogether.

The piano music trailed away and, bidding the congregation to sit, the reverend shared important announcements. Duncan's gaze wandered to the pews on their right and snagged on a familiar arrogant profile. A slow burn set up in his gut. Theo Marsh was up to something. Why else would he be inventing excuses to linger on the Turners' property? First it had been flimsy concerns about his horse. Then it had been a digestive issue.

He looked over at Caroline and was absurdly relieved to find her attention on the reverend. While Duncan hadn't seen any evidence that she harbored feelings for the other man, he couldn't be certain Theo had accepted she was out of reach. What other draw was there in Gatlinburg besides Caroline? At the thought of their history, which was unknown to him, jealousy crept up, catching him unawares. He bunched his fists. *You're being unreasonable, McKenna. She's wearing your ring, not his.*

A late arrival entered the church, heels clacking on the polished floorboards. Beside him, Caroline stiffened as Vivian strolled past, a vision in canary yellow, and assumed the empty space beside Theo. The two exchanged polite greetings. Then Theo glanced over his shoulder, his gray gaze seeking Caroline, smoldering with unnamed emotion.

Duncan was about to come out of his seat when the sound of Caroline's name snatched him out of his ruminations.

Reverend Munroe was staring straight at them. "Don't be shy, Caroline. Come on up here. I'd like to say a brief word."

The congregants twisted in their seats, open speculation on their faces. A sense of foreboding swept over him. Glancing at her, he noted her sudden pallor.

Staring straight ahead, she slowly gained her feet and walked to the front. She faced the crowd as if they were about to lob raw eggs at her. Oblivious, the reverend beamed with paternal pride, his smile stretched from ear to ear.

Duncan gripped the pew seat on either side of his legs, the desire to create a diversion and spare her seizing him. Time seemed to slow. The rainbow-hued light from the stained-glass windows blurred in his peripheral vision.

"Ladies and gentlemen, I've asked Miss Turner up here —"

Someone interrupted with a muffled comment Duncan couldn't hear.

The older man laughed and patted Caroline's shoulder. "Forgive me, young lady. I'm still getting used to the fact you're a married woman. I've asked Mrs. McKenna up here today to publicly thank her for her awe-inspiring generosity. As you know, Caroline and her mother have long been involved in charitable works. But she recently went above and beyond what was expected of her. For those of you who don't know, Mrs. McKenna donated nearly an entire wardrobe to be distributed to the needy in our community."

Caroline's gaze hit the floor. Shoulders curved inward, she was the picture of abject humiliation.

Whispers and gasps of surprise filtered through the space. Duncan wanted to snatch her out of the church and take her far away. This was his fault.

"As a congregation, we thank you, Caroline. You are a true example of God's commands regarding the care of those less fortunate. The rest of us would be wise to take note."

Hearty clapping erupted, punctuated with cheers and whistles, and she cringed. With a clipped nod at the reverend, she walked with her head held high and resumed her seat. She was trembling. Duncan ached to offer her comfort. But would she accept it from him?

The moment the noise died down and the preaching commenced, he slipped his arm through hers and found her hand. He wove their fingers together and waited. She didn't resist. Didn't pull away. But nor did she react.

Bringing their joined hands onto his knee, he used his free hand to press heat into her cold flesh. Once again, he wished he could undo his actions. Caroline was a private woman who'd taken pride in her position in the community. Whether or not he agreed with that, he'd been unfair to act as he had.

At the closing of the service, she made a beeline for the exit. He had to dodge several people to catch up and, when he did, a pair of matronly ladies blocked their path.

Caroline stopped short, the need to escape written across her face. "Excuse me, Mrs. Smith. Mrs. Plumley. I can't tarry today."

"We won't keep you, Caroline," the plump, bushy-haired one cooed. "We wanted to express how proud we are of you.

Your heart is truly the most generous we've encountered in a long while."

Caroline began to blink rapidly. Her throat worked. The obvious cracks in her composure became apparent. Placing a hand on her back, Duncan nodded to the ladies. "You're very kind. I'm afraid we're in a bit of a rush to get home. Perhaps you can pay my wife a visit later on in the week?"

Out of the corner of his eye, he caught her sharp side glance.

"That would be lovely." The second woman whose figure resembled a barrel clutched her hankie to her chest. "We actually have a family who's suffered an extended illness and is in dire need of assistance. We wondered if Caroline could enlist donations."

They both looked to Caroline, who quipped, "I'd be happy to help. However, you'll have to get my husband's permission first."

The barrel lady's mouth formed an O. The bushy one's eyebrows disappeared beneath her bangs.

Duncan smiled and curved his arm around her waist. "Of course you don't need my permission for such a noble cause."

Not meeting his gaze, she edged away from his side and worked out a time for the women to meet her at Albert and Louise's house. She marched to the wagon and climbed onto the seat without his assistance. Boarding on his side, he released the brake and guided the team out of the churchyard. He waited until they left Main Street behind to speak.

"Caroline —"

"I don't wish to discuss it."

Her body was angled away from him, but he didn't need to see her expression to know how upset she was. The tone in her voice was a mix of stern warning and shaky uncertainty. Praying for wisdom, he remained quiet the remainder of the brief trip. The conveyance rolled to a stop before the barn. She scrambled down. Duncan wrapped the reins around the brake and jumped to the ground, hurrying to catch up to her.

"Caroline, please hear me out."

"What's there to say?" she called over her shoulder. Her skirts raised to avoid soiling the hem, she marched through the ankle-high grass.

"I'm sorry."

Abruptly pivoting to face him, she demanded, "For what? Giving away my belongings? For forbidding me to continue my charitable work and then changing your mind without telling me? Or are you sorry that you ever met me?"

The last one threw him for a loop. He couldn't answer that. His feelings about her and this marriage were too confused to sort through.

"I'm sorry I've bungled things," he said at last. "I had no idea what the repercussions would be. I certainly never thought the reverend would make a public spectacle of it." Snatching off his hat, he tunneled his fingers through his hair. "I didn't consider how seeing other women wearing your clothes would make you feel."

Her eyes darkened to midnight blue, the only pinpoints of color in her ashen face. Her lips quivered. Releasing her skirts and turning her back to him, she wrapped her arms around her middle. Her forlorn stance carved a deep fissure in his heart. With a flash of insight, he realized she'd been alone for most of her life. Alone in that grand house with parents who didn't see her true worth and servants who were there just for the money. Alone with her trinkets and shoes and dresses.

Duncan smoothed his hand down her back, registering the slide of satiny fabric and even softer hair.

"I'm sorry my actions hurt you," he

murmured. "I don't like to see you upset."

"I'm a selfish person," she said on a sob. "I *wish* donating my clothes to the needy had been my idea. You were right. I — I attached importance to things that don't matter."

Taking gentle hold of her arm, he urged her around. The sight of her damp cheeks clamped his chest in a vise. This wasn't a ploy to make him feel sorry for her. He'd seen Maureen's performances enough to know the difference.

Brushing the curtain of hair behind her shoulder, he ran his hand up and down her arm in reassuring strokes. "You aren't selfish, lass. A selfish person *disnae* give of their time and energy to help others. The problem here is I *didnae* give you a choice. I *willnae* make the same mistake again."

Caroline gazed at him with huge, stormy eyes, indecision stamped all over her. Then she did something he never would've expected. She stepped into his arms and buried her face in his chest. Floored that she'd seek solace from him, he didn't immediately react. A second later he snapped into action and he held her securely against him, stroking her long, fine hair while she cried.

He sensed her hurt had less to do with

the clothes and more to do with burdens she carried deep inside. Duncan's protective instincts flared to life. He hadn't pursued this union, but Caroline was his wife, his to protect and support. *And cherish. Don't forget that.*

Holding her like this, he didn't find the prospect of cherishing her as daunting as he once had.

"Mr. McKenna?"

At the sound of Anthony's voice, Caroline went rigid in his arms. Duncan lifted his head and directed an impatient stare at the lad. He'd been so wrapped up in her, he hadn't been aware of anyone approaching.

"Yes, Anthony?"

His face the hue of a ripe tomato, Anthony crumpled his hat in his hands. "I apologize for intruding like this, sir. Mr. Marsh is preparing to depart and insists on seeing you."

Caroline pulled out of his arms and, keeping her back to the lad, dashed the wetness from her cheeks. Duncan fished a handkerchief from his pocket and handed it to her, then moved to stand so that Anthony didn't have a clear view.

"Did he say why?"

"No, sir."

"Tell him I'll be along in five minutes."

Anthony cast a curious glance toward Caroline, then touched his forelock. "Yes, sir." He dashed back the way he'd come.

Duncan turned around. "I have to go and see what he wants."

She shrugged. "It's fine."

"It's no' fine. When I return, we'll talk, all right?"

He thought she might dismiss the matter altogether. But then her watery gaze met his and she nodded. "All right."

Duncan hated to leave her. On impulse, he tipped up her chin and dropped a kiss on her cool, smooth cheek, catching a whiff of a fruity scent. "I'll hurry. The stew should be ready. If you're hungry, go ahead and eat without me."

"I'll wait for you."

He pondered her wide-eyed wonder during the walk to the stables. How would she have reacted if he'd kissed her lips? Would she welcome his touch?

The sight of Theo in the stable yard drove such thoughts from his mind. He was glad to be rid of the man.

"Mr. McKenna." Stepping away from his horse, which was already prepped for travel, Theo greeted him with a smug smile. "Thank you for coming. I regret intruding upon your private time with Caroline, but I couldn't leave town without apologizing."

Unconvinced of the man's sincerity, Duncan diverted his attention to the horse, scrubbing the spot between his ears. "I *cannae* imagine what you have to apologize for."

"I'm afraid I'm partially to blame for your hasty nuptials." His attempt at remorse fell short.

Misgivings filtered through Duncan. "I *dinnae* follow."

"You see, I'm the reason Caroline fled the party in such a heightened state of emotion. She rode out against your wishes because she was embarrassed. Our families have been friends for many years. She's long nursed an infatuation for me. I'm certain Louise put it in her head that she and I would make a match." His clear, gray gaze held Duncan's. "On my honor, I didn't give her false hope. I've been honest from the beginning that I was only interested in friendship. You know how stubborn Caroline can be."

The tender feelings evoked by their embrace evaporated. He felt sick. Thinking back to that night, he recalled how she'd burst from the house and whipped into the stables, so upset she'd ignored his warnings. She hadn't been thinking clearly, that much

201

was obvious. And it had been due to dashed hopes?

Had she lied about her feelings for Theo to avoid angering him? After all, what woman would admit to her new husband that she harbored feelings for another man?

"That night in the parlor, she pressed the issue," Theo continued. "She wanted a commitment that I was unwilling to give. Needless to say, she wasn't happy. Some of the guests overheard. That's why she was in the state she was in."

"I see." He stared at a point in the distance, his mouth felt full of sawdust.

"I wanted you to know that she doesn't carry the entire blame for your unfortunate circumstances."

Duncan couldn't think straight. He kept picturing her in her fancy gown atop Rain, drenched and miserable. Because of Theo.

He must've gotten everything backward. It wasn't Theo who had unrequited feelings.

Remembering his manners, he stuck out his hand. "I bid you safe travels, Mr. Marsh."

"I'm sure we'll meet again."

Duncan watched him mount and ride down the lane toward town, his eagerness to return to Caroline gone.

CHAPTER FOURTEEN

Hope was a fragile thing. Caroline was afraid to nurture the feeling inside her, but she'd experienced this sort of contentment so seldom that she couldn't resist. After setting out the dishes and spoons, along with the platter of corn bread Duncan had helped her make that morning before church, she hurried to splash the residual tears from her face and check that her hair was neat and the pin straight. In the cracked mirror's reflection, she realized her eyes, though a tad red, were brighter than usual.

Turning to Duncan for comfort had been a huge risk for her. Her mother wasn't a sentimental woman and hadn't reacted well to Caroline's expressions of sadness. She'd become conditioned to keeping her feelings hidden. But witnessing her breakdown hadn't offended Duncan. He'd offered sympathy and understanding and a haven she would've liked to linger in far longer than she had.

He'd been so sweet and attentive. And then he'd kissed her! On the cheek, granted, but it still counted. The look in his brilliant blue eyes said he cared that she was unhappy, which meant he might possibly care about *her.*

Her stomach rumbled. She looked at the mantel clock. He'd been gone thirty minutes. Going to the window, she felt relief at the sight of his commanding figure striding past the trees.

She waited for him beside the table, eager to see what he had planned for the afternoon. Jane and Tom usually took their kids to the local fishing spot and spent hours exploring the stream banks and tossing a ball around. Jessica and her husband, Grant, rode into nearby Maryville and passed the time playing their instruments with fellow musicians. She liked the idea of starting a tradition with him.

When he entered, his expression no longer bore patience and concern. His jaw was tight and grooves bracketed his mouth. His enigmatic gaze roved over her and the table's contents.

"I wish you hadn't waited." He strode to the corner and picked up his fishing pole.

Confusion arrowed through her. "I told

you I would."

"I'm not hungry. I've got a bit of a head-ache." Pole in hand, he strode to the kitchen and drank from the water dipper.

Caroline wasn't sure what was happening. He wouldn't look at her. His voice had that cold detachment she recognized from before their wedding. It sent shivers of foreboding along her skin.

"Perhaps you'd feel better after you ate something," she ventured.

He circled around the opposite side of the table and snagged a triangle of corn bread. "I'm going fishing for a few hours."

"That sounds nice."

The hint of hope in her voice must've registered because he finally looked at her a second time, his gaze penetrating . . . looking for what? "I'll be back in time to rustle up dinner."

And then he was gone, no explanation for what had changed.

She spent the afternoon sewing curtains and fretting over the situation. His mood hadn't improved by the time he returned with three hefty fish. The atmosphere during supper was fraught with tension, and afterward he spent the bulk of the evening in the barn. Still nursing hope, she attributed it to his headache. But the next day, his distant manner continued. By the time Friday rolled around, Caroline couldn't deny the truth — *she* was the cause.

He must've mulled over everything that had passed between them and decided she wasn't worthy of his compassion. Angry at herself for believing this marriage had a chance of becoming more than a stilted merger between strangers, she left the cabin midmorning with the intention of confronting him. No more guessing. No more sulking silences. She was going to insist he admit the truth.

Entering the stable yard, she was on the lookout for him when Sylvia ceased her sweeping and intercepted her.

"Miss Caroline," she called from the veranda. "I have something for you."

Caroline's mouth went dry as she approached the stairs. "What is it, Sylvia?"

Reaching into her apron pocket, she pulled out an envelope. "You've had another letter. I discovered it about an hour ago."

She accepted the envelope with trembling fingers. Her name was written across the front in the characteristic bold script. "It was slipped under the front door?"

Her brows pulled together in concern. "Yes, miss. The same as the others."

"You didn't see who delivered it?"

"I'm afraid not." She paused. "Can I help in some way?"

Caroline braved a smile. Sylvia had sensed something was amiss, and that would not do. "No, thank you."

Her confrontation with Duncan would have to wait. Returning to the cabin, she carried the missive to her makeshift bedroom and, sinking on the bed, ripped it open. The thin parchment looked like the others, only this time the demanded amount was twice what it had been before. The paper fluttered to the floor. She had little more than twenty-four hours, and without Duncan's signature, there was no way for her to access the money. Even if she were to ask his consent, he'd want to know why. She couldn't confide the truth. Her family's reputation meant nothing to him. And as for their financial status, he cared even less.

She'd mailed three masks to Charleston, but she hadn't heard whether or not they'd sold. There simply hadn't been enough time.

There was no other recourse but to explain the situation and ask for an extension. She hoped the blackguard's common sense outweighed his greed.

Gray smoke billowed out of the cabin's

open door. Alarm punched him square in the chest.

"Caroline!"

Duncan sprinted through the yard, his heart hammering against his rib cage as he imagined her unconscious on the floor. *Lord, please let her be all right.* His boots thundered on the porch. Inside, he sucked in the acrid smoke and commenced choking. No flames were visible. As he moved closer to the kitchen, the air cleared, allowing him to see her. She was unhurt.

Relief crashed over him, soured by the weight of disillusionment he'd been carrying around all week.

"What happened?" he demanded between coughs.

As she fanned the air with a towel, her frown turned into a scowl. "I scorched our meal."

After opening the windows, he returned to the stove and eyed the still-smoking lumps in the skillet. "What was that?"

"Pork from the smokehouse."

She passed a weary hand over her damp forehead, and he saw that one of her fingers was wrapped in cloth strips. He reached for her hand. He'd gone out of his way to avoid physical contact since their embrace. The renewed connection made him want to dismiss Theo's claims.

"Did you burn yourself?"

"It's a small cut, that's all." She tugged free.

"You have to be careful, Caroline. There are hundreds of ways to get hurt on a farm. Even a small cut can be dangerous if infection sets in. Be sure to keep that clean and dry."

Her eyes flashing fire, she crossed her arms. "Don't pretend to care, Duncan. Admit it. You'd be pleased as punch to be rid of me."

His jaw sagged.

"What? Have I shocked you by speaking the truth?" she retorted. "You can't stand to be in the same room with me! You hardly look at me. You make up excuses to spend evenings in the barn."

"That's no' true," he denied halfheartedly, calling himself a fool. She wasn't clueless. Of course she'd figure out something wasn't right. He should've been honest with her instead of giving his wounded pride free rein.

A light breeze swept through the windows, carrying some of the smoke out. Her apron was streaked with soot. The woman he'd met on Independence Day wouldn't have deigned to attempt to cook lunch for him.

She was changing in subtle ways, and he doubted she even noticed.

"Let's go outside and talk. The stench is overpowering in here."

With reluctance, she folded the towel and set it aside. In the shade of the porch overhang, he gripped the post and leveled his gaze at her.

"I spoke with Theo before he left," he said. "He's under the impression he's partly responsible for our marriage."

Duncan watched her reaction closely. Her brow furrowed and wariness clouded her gaze.

"Is that so?"

"He said the reason you were desperate to get away from the party was because he made his lack of interest plain."

A harsh, disbelieving laugh escaped her. Scorn curled her lip, and Duncan instantly realized his error. This wasn't the look of a woman suffering from unrequited love. He'd bungled things again. Would he never learn?

"And you took him at his word? A stranger who baited you by kissing your bride when you wouldn't?" Fresh hurt gave her a wounded look about her eyes. She was upset and angry, and rightly so. "You don't know me well, but you know me better than you

210

know Theo. You could've asked me about it. Instead, you chose to believe the worst."

He released the post and took a single step forward. "Caroline, I'm —"

"Sorry. I know." Her bitter, little-girl-lost tone gutted him. "Lunch is ruined. If I were you, I'd ask Cook for a plate. Or go to the Plum."

She made to enter the cabin. He intercepted her.

"I *dinnae* deserve an answer, but I'll ask anyway. What really happened between you and him?"

Caroline's gaze delved into his for long, uncomfortable moments. "He suggested I agree to a meaningless dalliance."

Duncan's gut clenched with shame. "I should've questioned his motives."

"Yes, you should have."

"What did he say exactly?"

"Nothing worth repeating."

She averted her gaze, but not before he glimpsed pain mixed with a heavy dose of self-doubt. The anger he'd felt the past few days turned inward. After that scene at the church, she'd needed him, and he'd failed her. One fact he couldn't dispute? He was relieved that she didn't have feelings for the Charleston businessman.

"I also should've come to you right away

211

and talked this out. I was overwrought by the thought of my wife in love with another man." It pained him to admit the truth. "I was so jealous I couldn't think straight."

"Y-You were?"

"He has a history with you that I know nothing about. I let my imagination take me places I shouldn't have."

"Our families are connected by business. Our fathers are friends. Theo has been in my life for many years, both in Charleston and here. I wouldn't classify us as friends, however. There's something about him that I simply don't trust."

"This is a mistake I *willnae* be repeating. You have my word. Let me make it up to you," he urged. "Give me fifteen minutes to clean the mess and assemble a cold lunch."

After some hesitation, she nodded. "All right."

He felt like doing a jig. Instead, he directed her to the rocking chair and then went to work. Before long, they were heading to the pond. Caroline carried the basket of food and he carried a metal pail and gigging pole. Fat clouds floated in an azure sky. The late-July heat was offset by the occasional breeze.

Threading her hair off her forehead, she slanted him a glance. "What's that pitchfork thing?"

"This? It's a gigging pole. We're going to use it to gig for frogs."

She stopped and stared at him. "Why would we want to do that?"

"Haven't you ever tasted fried frog legs?"

"This is your idea of making up for this past week of boyish behavior?" She planted her free hand on her hip. "You're going to teach me to thrust those prongs into a slimy, slippery frog?"

"It's a valuable life skill, I assure you." He couldn't wipe the smile from his face, he was so relieved to be talking to her again. "And you didn't answer my question."

"Our ideas of what constitutes valuable life skills are not the same. And no, I haven't had them. Nor do I wish to."

"How do you know you don't like frog legs if you've never tried them?"

Her nose wrinkled. "Now you sound like Jane when she's trying to convince her kids to eat collard greens."

"Be adventurous." He tilted his head in the direction of the pond. "Try something new."

Rolling her eyes, she flounced ahead. He began to whistle a jaunty Scottish tune.

The pond was deserted. Smoothing out the quilt beneath the shade of a massive oak tree, he said, "Next time we'll gig at night.

It's easier to see them because the light shines on their eyes."

She sank onto her knees and started unpacking the snacks. "Next time? You're awfully confident, Duncan McKenna. I'm not sure if that's due to arrogance or naive optimism."

"A wee bit of both, I suppose."

Her reticence lingering, she merely shook her head and popped a bite-sized tomato in her mouth. Appreciation hummed in her throat. "There's nothing like a sunwarmed tomato fresh from the vine."

Leaning over, he took one for himself. "Agreed. And just think, you picked them yourself."

She shot him a dry look. "They would taste the same if you'd picked them."

"Aye, I suppose they would."

They ate in silence, the whisper of the leaves overhead mingling with the repetitive warbles of the birds.

"How did your meeting go with Mrs. Smith and Mrs. Plumley?"

She looked surprised. "We compiled a list of items the Murrays could use. Between the three of us, we've been able to gather everything on the list, with a few extras thrown in."

While Duncan had avoided being alone

with his wife, he'd kept tabs of her where-
abouts. She'd met with the ladies in her
parents' home Tuesday morning, and every
day since she'd been knocking on doors
eliciting donations.

"When will you deliver everything?"

"Anthony is going to help me load the
wagon in the morning."

"Are you going alone?"

"I'm sure Anthony will accompany me if
you can spare him."

"I'll go. There's no one around to require
my assistance. I have to patch up the fence
in the far paddock, but I can get that done
before nine, if that's agreeable. Besides, I'd
like to see the benevolence society in action."

She shrugged. "It that's what you want."

"You've pitched in around the farm. It's
my turn to help you."

"You're a patient teacher." Pink suffused
her skin. "Did you not consider becoming
one? Like your brother?"

"No. I prefer being outside where I can
feel the sun on my face and the rain on my
skin. I like planting a seed and watching it
flourish. I like working with horses."

"You've taken excellent care of Rain, and
I thank you for that."

Caroline had been to see her horse every

day since the accident. They were both pleased with her recovery.

Shucking off his boots and socks, he rolled his pant legs to just below his knees. Then he stood and extended his hand. "Time for your next lesson."

She wiped the crumbs from her lap and allowed him to assist her.

Snatching up the pole, he told her, "I'll do the first one. Then it's your turn."

Caroline wore a dubious expression. She watched from the bank as he ventured into the shallow water. The cool mud squishing between his toes felt good. As he'd done since he was a boy, he scoured the lake edge for his prey, pole uplifted and muscles primed to spring. He caught one on the first try.

If he thought that would impress his wife, he was wrong. And when he informed her she needed to lose her boots and stockings and tie up her skirt hem, she balked.

"There's no one around to see," he reasoned, aware that others' opinions mattered to her.

"Look at yourself." She waggled her fingers at the mud streaking his calves. "You're a mess."

"It's not difficult to wash off. What's the matter? You afraid you *cannae* catch as

216

many as me?"

She lifted her chin. "I'm not going to accept a challenge for something you've obviously been doing your entire life."

"Fine. We *willnae* make this a competition. But you ken I can be as stubborn as you, lass. I'm no' going to stop pestering you."

"You're insufferable."

He grinned. "I've heard that a time or two."

Caroline removed her boots. When she started to tie up her skirts, she ordered him to be a gentleman and turn around.

"All right. Let's get this over with."

Deliberately not peeking at the white pantaloons he knew were visible below her knees, he took her hand and guided her into the lake.

"It's icky. And squishy," she complained, her fingers clutching at his.

"You get used to it. The water feels nice, though, right?"

Her navy eyes thoughtful, she nodded.

"Have you never gone swimming?" With reluctance, he let go of her hand and gave her the pole.

She arched a brow. "Do you think Louise Moore Turner would approve?"

"You're a married woman now. You no

longer have to live to please her. You can splash around to your heart's content."

Staring out across the lake's surface, she contemplated that for long moments. Ribbons of sunlight streaming through the lofty branches overhead set her hair to shining like a luminous pearl. Today she'd tied the mass back with a patterned ribbon. It didn't matter whether her hair style was elegant or simple, her clothing stitched in Paris or in a Tennessee cabin — her beauty didn't change. The disturbing loneliness in her eyes didn't change. The sadness around her mouth didn't change.

Duncan's heart pounded with the need to make things better for her, to make her forget the expectations and pressures of life. But all the while his mind was sounding an alarm. *Let's not forget she doesn't share the same values. Her outlook on the world is defined by different parameters, one I understand but no longer adhere to.*

Behind him, he heard a plop in the water. He pointed out the target and urged her to try. Her first few attempts were halfhearted. Gradually, though, she loosened up and began to put effort into it. The frogs were fast. It was impossible to predict which direction they'd jump in. Each time she missed, splashing water on the both of

218

them, her laughter danced on the breeze. The curve of her lips against perfect white teeth, the crinkles at the corners of her almond-shaped eyes, mesmerized him.

Muttering a sound of determination, Caroline leapt forward and brought the pole down with such force it splattered bits of mud over the front of his pants. She clapped her hand over her mouth to try and stifle a giggle.

"You think this is funny, do you?"

He bent to scoop a palmful of mud from the lake bottom and straightened, dirty water streaming down his arm to his elbow. Grinning like a fool, he advanced.

Her eyes rounded. "You wouldn't dare."

Seizing her arm, he held her long enough to swipe the muck across her shoulder and exposed skin above the blouse's scooped collar.

"Duncan!" She squealed and wriggled out of reach. For a moment, she simply stared at him, and he couldn't decide if she was going to march off in a huff or tackle him.

She did neither. In a matter of seconds, she'd scooped up her own ammunition and came after him. Laughter rumbling in his chest, he dodged her. Caroline splashed after him and managed to get his back wet and dirty.

"Oh, this is war," he promised.

By the time she called for a cease-fire, they were more wet than dry and far dirtier than when they'd arrived. Her hair hung in disarray past her shoulders. Flecks of drying mud dotted her face and arms. Like him, she'd be digging dirt from beneath her fingernails that night.

Breathing hard, one hand pressed against her stomach, she pointed to the pail. "We've managed to catch only one. It's going to be a light meal tonight, I'm afraid."

A carefree smile animated her features.

"I *dinnae* care about that."

"No? I thought that was the point."

Quickly rinsing his hands, he shook off the excess water and waded over to her. He didn't stop until he stood right in front of her. Her smile slipped and a groove appeared between her brows.

"Did you enjoy yourself?" he murmured.

Looking down, she assessed the damage. "I'm not going to relish cleaning these clothes, but I admit it was fun."

"That was the point. To make you laugh and forget what an idiot your husband can be."

"You're not an idiot." Her opaque gaze locked onto his. "At least, not every day," she amended with a smile that, on Caroline, could be considered saucy.

The water lapped their thighs. Around her, the material of her skirt floated, air bubbles trapped beneath it. Duncan gingerly raked her hair away from her face, trailing the silken strands to their ends, reveling in the sensations she wrought in him. She became very still while he caressed her cheek.

"I'm a mess," she whispered.

"A beautiful mess," he countered.

Inch by inch, he lowered his head, giving her time to push him away. She didn't, and he inwardly rejoiced. He'd been waiting for this moment since their wedding day. He'd just pressed his lips to hers and settled his hand at her waist when her hands came up and, framing his face, broke contact.

"Caroline?"

"Don't kiss me because it's convenient or because you're curious." She swallowed hard, her expression pleading. "Don't kiss me if you don't like me."

He understood then how crucial it was to proceed with care. By her own admission, she hadn't ever been courted in earnest. Her heart was untried and fragile. He'd hurt her if he wasn't careful. Duncan wouldn't love her. She wasn't the type of woman he'd allow himself to love. But they could develop a deep fondness for each other that included respect and trust.

"I like you, Caroline," he said truthfully. "Very much. That's why the thought of you having feelings for another man bothered me."

"Oh." Her hands migrated to his chest. "I — I like you, too."

He smiled, confident they could be affectionate without crossing into dangerous emotional territory.

Spanning her waist, he tugged her against him. "May I kiss you now, fair lass?"

"Please."

When their mouths met a second time, hers tentative and sweet with the blueberry preserves she'd eaten earlier, Duncan could only think how happy he was that they hadn't kissed in front of their wedding guests. As her knees buckled and her fingers curled into his shirt, he felt off balance. He was acutely aware of the differences in their heights, the way her softness molded to him as she snuggled closer, her rose scent mingling with earth and grass. A rush of delight spun through him, catching him off guard. It didn't take long for the embrace to speed from manageable to intense.

He had to pull back before the haze enveloping his mind completely obliterated his common sense. Regret filling him, Duncan lifted his head and did his best to affect a lazy, unaffected smile.

"I think we've established we like each other."

Her features were soft and unguarded, her manner shy. "I want to show you something."

"What? Now?"

"If you'd rather not . . ."

He cut her off with a quick, firm kiss. "Lead the way, woman."

As they climbed onto the bank, Duncan was afraid he would follow her anywhere. All she had to do was ask.

CHAPTER FIFTEEN

Caroline was positive she wasn't making a mistake. Still basking in the wonder of Duncan's embrace, she unlocked the door to her private sanctuary and allowed him to enter. They'd left the pond and come straight here. He'd washed his feet as best he could before donning his socks and boots and rolling down his pants. Although disheveled, he was unbearably handsome, his features now as familiar to her as her own. His hair was tousled and dark copper in spots where it was still damp. Looking at his mouth made her feel funny inside, like she'd discovered a secret no one else was privy to. What they'd shared together, no other experience in her whole life could compare.

Standing in the middle of the room, she moved in a circle in accordance with his movements, anxiously gauging his reaction.

The room was a predictable box shape,

about half the size of their cabin, the thick log walls barely visible behind neat rows of hanging masks. The masks were comprised of every shade of the rainbow and created a kaleidoscope of color, cheering the space. On the wall opposite the door, sunlight sought to breach the thick crimson curtain covering the window.

Duncan looked awestruck. She couldn't decide whether that was good or bad.

He wandered slowly around the room, reaching out to touch an elephant's trunk, peering closer at a lion's mane crafted of golden threads, frowning at the one stark white, unadorned face mask tucked in one corner. When he reached her workbench, he bent to survey the neat arrangement of supplies and tools. With reverence, he picked up the undecorated butterfly mask she'd started this week and held it in both hands.

Finally, his astonished gaze sought hers. "You made all of these?"

Hands clasped tightly behind her back, she nodded.

"They're magnificent." His gaze roamed the room again. "You're very talented, Caroline."

Pleasure unfurled inside, and she felt like she could breathe again. "Wendell knows about my work because I needed a window and asked him to cut it out for me." It was high enough on the wall to prevent anyone from peeking in while she was working, and she kept the curtains closed when she wasn't. "You're the only other person I've brought here."

He replaced the mask in progress and sank his hands in his pockets. "There are quite a number of them. How long have you been doing this? Did someone teach you?"

"I'm self-taught. I'd had some art instruction from my tutors, of course. Mostly sketching, painting on canvas and clay sculpting. The summer I turned eighteen, my mother decided to host a masquerade party — we don't have the space for a grand ball — and invite friends from Charleston. Masquerade balls are a yearly event there, and an unofficial competition exists between the attendees to outdo each other. Skilled mask makers are paid handsomely for their work."

"And this party sparked your interest?"

She smiled, remembering the fun she'd had coming up with ideas for her own mask. She'd corresponded with Alberto Senetti, a well-known artist in Charleston, who'd brought her vision to life. "My mother gave me the freedom to work with a famous mask maker. It was the most beautiful mask I'd ever seen. My gown was ivory satin studded with seed pearls. My mask covered half of my face and was crafted of white owl feathers, ribbons and pearls to match my gown."

"You must've been a vision." The admiration in his gaze warmed her. "I'd like to see it."

"I'm afraid that's not possible," she told him with regret. "My mother and I got in an argument after the guests left. She was upset. She said I hadn't applied myself to capturing some young man's fancy. I forget now who he was." She did remember the anger and disappointment she'd felt. "Up until that point, I'd actually enjoyed myself, spending most of my time with Jane, Jessica and their sisters. My mother hadn't been keen on inviting locals, but I begged her."

Duncan looked annoyed. From the start of his employment, his disapproval of Louise had been obvious. At least to Caroline. "I'm sorry you had to endure that."

"I'm used to it."

His brows descended. "What happened to the mask?"

"I pitched a childish fit and ripped it to shreds before her eyes. I'd intended to anger her. I only ended up hurting myself. I regretted my actions immediately."

Glancing around again, he said, "And so

you decided to remake it? Where is the copy?"

"There isn't one. I couldn't hope to re-create Mr. Senetti's craftsmanship."

"You should give it a try." He ran his fingertip along the edge of a rounded griz-zly bear mask. "May I?"

She smiled in answer.

He gingerly lifted it from the nail it was perched on and held it up to his face. Only his eyes were visible. "Well?" his voice was muffled.

"Nice." She sidestepped him and chose a sleek black, elegant leopard. "But I think this one would look better."

They exchanged masks, his eyes dancing and his smile relaxed. If only he'd remain like this forever . . . Happy in her company.

After hanging up the bear, she took hold of Duncan's shoulders and directed him to the mirror suspended above the workbench. Standing beside him, she watched as he studied his reflection.

"I can picture you at a masquerade wear-ing a three-piece suit in solid black," she said. "Every man would wish they could be like you, and every woman would want to know your name."

He chuckled and set the mask aside. "I *widnae* mind attending a masquerade if only to give your talent a chance to shine. These creations shouldn't be hidden in a stable, Caroline. People should be able to enjoy them."

Three empty spots seemed to scream her secret. Maybe people would get a chance to do just that, though not of her own free will. She'd crafted the letter asking for leniency and planned to deliver it in the morning while Duncan mended the fence.

"I wanted to do something just for me." Picking up the jaguar, she returned it to its spot. "Without the pressure of trying to impress anyone."

"Understandable. But it's clear you have talent. The proof's on these walls."

She prayed the owner of Lambert's Curiosities and Antiquities agreed with Duncan. Otherwise, her family's livelihood and reputation could suffer.

Something was bothering his wife, and he had no idea what it was. Duncan didn't think it had anything to do with him. After cleaning up from their mud fight yesterday, they'd prepared fried chicken and roasted potatoes — she'd declined to observe how to kill said chicken — and conversed more about her hobby over a leisurely meal. He was in awe of her ability and humbled that she'd revealed that part of herself to him. A private person, Caroline was accustomed to presenting a facade to others, one that masked her true self. The more he glimpsed of that strong, smart, sweet woman, the more invested he became in this marriage.

After dinner, he'd hung the completed curtains. Her blushing pleasure at his praise lingered in his mind. He'd longed to hold her again. Knowing he had to proceed with caution, he'd fought against it and had paid with an interminable night of tossing and turning in his lonely bed.

"Turn left up ahead." Beside him on the wagon seat, Caroline pointed to a grouping of dogwood trees. "The Murrays are the only inhabitants of this cove."

She was radiant in her fitted, tangerine-hued blouse tucked into a navy skirt. The vivid color complemented her complexion and offset her dark blue irises. The effect was marred by the worry at the back of her eyes. She'd been skittish the entire morning, ever since he'd intercepted her on his return from fixing the fence. When he'd asked where she'd been, she'd spluttered something about wanting fresh air. She was a terrible liar.

So what could she have been up to?

Duncan prayed it wasn't something that

would shatter the tenuous harmony they'd achieved. He liked spending time with her. He liked discovering new things about her. He wanted — no, he *needed* — her to trust him, to continue to open up to him. Thinking too hard about the reason for that was something he refused to do.

Maybe it had been an innocent jaunt in the forest. It was possible she thought he'd be angry if he discovered her taking a break from chores.

Guiding the team onto the lane, he glanced at her profile. "You know, I don't expect you to work from dawn to dusk. I don't mind if you take walks or spend time in your art room."

Her features became pinched. "I'm glad you feel that way, because I'm not used to being responsible for every aspect of household management."

"You're trying. That's what matters."

Was she the finest cook he'd encountered? No, but she was still learning, and he was enjoying teaching her. She'd made peace with Lulabelle and gathering eggs no longer spooked her. She'd proved to be an accomplished seamstress and anyone could sweep and mop a floor.

The Murrays' two-story cabin was in good shape, but the vegetable patch was overgrown with weeds and the barn had multiple boards that needed to be replaced.

With a quiet command, Duncan guided the team to a stop. Free-roaming chickens squawked and scuttled out of the way. Behind the cabin, the steep hillside housed hunting dogs that had commenced furious barking the moment he and Caroline arrived.

"Fletcher Murray has been ill for almost a year," Caroline explained above the racket. "He suffers from a blood disorder that leaves him weak. The older kids pitch in with the farmwork, but it's been a struggle to make ends meet."

Coming around to her side, he placed his hands on either side of her waist and swung her down. "It's kind of you to help them."

"I can't take credit for the idea."

"No, but you executed it." Following her to the rear of the wagon bed, he added, "You solicited donations, and you're taking the time to come here personally. You could've delegated those tasks."

Her response was cut short as the door banged open and a passel of chattering kids spilled out, greeting Caroline with shy smiles and regarding him with open curiosity. Her smile reappearing, she introduced him. They ranged in age from three to fourteen and, though their clothing was threadbare and several were barefoot, their faces were clean and their hair neat. Each one pitched in to carry the crates and baskets inside. Excitement shone in the younger ones' eyes. The older children recognized it for what it was — handouts from caring neighbors — and so their enthusiasm was muted.

Duncan didn't get to meet Fletcher because he was asleep upstairs. Willa Murray repeatedly expressed her thanks, tears of joy sliding down her cheeks as she soaked in the volume of donations. Caroline took charge, enlisting the children's help in distributing the goods while Willa rocked an infant to sleep before the fireplace. In chatting with the woman, Duncan heard about other families Caroline had helped.

"My neighbor to the west, Lenora Griffin, she's not too fond of Miss Turner." She blinked. "Sorry, I'm used to calling her that."

"We *havnae* been married long." He smiled to ease her self-consciousness. "Sometimes I get a glimpse of my wedding ring and forget why it's there," he teased.

That brought a bloom to her cheeks. "Lenora thinks she's uppity. Says she thinks she's better than everyone else. I disagree.

She's quiet, that's all. Mrs. McKenna's not one to wear her emotions on her sleeve, if you know what I mean. Her kindness has benefitted many hurting people in this town."

The infant began to fuss. Duncan was put in mind of his own nephews, and homesickness coiled inside him. "May I?"

"Certainly." She lifted the bundle. "He's a picky one. Likes to be coddled."

Duncan cradled the infant against his chest and talked to him in a funny voice he'd used with his brother's bairns. He'd missed out on a year of their lives. Would they even remember their uncle? He wondered if it would be a wise idea to take Caroline home to Boston for a visit, then remembered the pesky detail of his background and her assumption he'd been raised poor as a church mouse.

"You're a natural," Willa said. "You and the missus will have fine-looking children someday."

At the faltering footstep to his left, he looked up and straight into Caroline's arrested gaze. She busied herself with another task, and the moment passed.

Before they left, Willa took Caroline's hand. "You're an answer to prayer, Mrs. McKenna."

"We're fortunate to have neighbors with generous hearts, aren't we?" She gracefully deflected the praise.

During the ride home, Duncan mulled over the visit and, in particular, Willa's comment. When he'd situated the horses, he found Caroline planting pretty purple towerlike flowers around the porch's base. A straw hat shielded her from the sun's unrelenting rays, and gloves protected her hands.

"Those are going to spruce up the place. What are they?"

"Purple fringe orchids. I took some from the main house gardens."

He knelt beside her, his knees balanced against the cool earth. "Mind if I help?"

She handed him a trowel. "Not at all."

After a few minutes of working side by side, he voiced his thoughts. "We haven't talked about children."

She froze, her face hidden by the hat's brim. "I'm not ready."

"To talk about it? It's an awkward subject, I know, but a necessary one."

"No, not that." She covered the plant's roots with loose soil. "To be a mother. I'm not ready."

He sought to understand. "Is it the responsibility? Or do you not wish to have children?"

Duncan steeled himself for her answer.

Sitting back, she wiped her forehead with the back of her glove and looked at him. "The prospect of motherhood scares me. I grew up in a home devoid of warmth and affection. I seriously doubt my parents like each other, let alone love each other. You and I, we didn't choose this. We were compelled to be together, to build a life with each other. I won't bring an innocent child into a battle zone or worse, an unfriendly alliance."

Duncan stroked her cheek, dislodging a speck of dirt. "We're friends, aren't we?"

Her eyes darkened with uncertainty. "I'd like to think so. We've been married for more than two weeks, yet it feels like my world still hasn't righted itself."

"I feel the same way," he ruefully confessed. He moved in and gently kissed her. She welcomed his touch, her lips trembling beneath his. Divesting herself of the gloves, she cupped the back of his neck, her fingers delving into his hair in tentative exploration. His wife was a heady mix of innocence and captivating allure. Ending the kiss was torture. Duncan wanted nothing more than to remain locked in her arms the rest of the day. That wasn't what she needed, though.

Him, either.

If he allowed emotion to overrule logic, they'd both get burned.

CHAPTER SIXTEEN

Caroline was not a good actress. She knew Duncan suspected something wasn't right. How was she supposed to relax when the blackmailer had yet to respond to her request? Forty-eight hours had passed since she'd left the note. The suspense was killing her. Was he sending those documents to the newspapers or to her father's business associates? Or was he merely making her sweat it out before demanding an even higher amount?

If only the blackmailer didn't exist, if the documents he'd allowed her to see hadn't looked authentic, then she would be cautiously optimistic. This new phase of her and Duncan's relationship filled her with joy. His approval was almost as potent as his kisses. But the secret she carried cast a shadow over the progress they'd made. And the idea she was entertaining — namely, forging Duncan's signature on the bank slip

— would shatter the trust they'd built. Losing his good opinion would devastate her.

Deeply troubled, Caroline had brewed a pot of tea and opened her Bible, starting in Psalms for comfort and in Ephesians for instruction on how to be a good wife. Of course, she didn't need to read the verses to know God didn't condone lying to one's husband.

The door unexpectedly swung open. Duncan poked his head inside and beckoned with his hand. "Can you spare a moment, lass?"

She closed the large book. "Is something the matter? I thought you and Anthony were cleaning out the tack room this morning."

"I told him to take a break. I've brought you a gift. Come see."

As she followed him past the garden, Caroline had the feeling that, like the curtain fabric, this gift didn't come in a shiny box with a pretty bow. Still, curiosity hummed through her. He led her to the far side of the barn where a small paddock was used to let the cow graze.

He walked up to the fence and rested his arms on the top slat. "Well? What do you think?"

She glanced into the paddock. "That's my gift?"

"Yep." He looked extremely satisfied with himself.

"It's a goat."

"A nanny goat."

"We already have a cow." A cantankerous one that liked to swat Caroline's face. Interested in the grass, the gray goat ignored them. Did Duncan think she'd be happy to have a second animal to milk?

"You said goat cheese was your favorite," he persisted.

"When did I say that?"

"At that first dinner party I attended, when you tried to kick me out." He arched a brow, but his blue eyes danced with mirth. "Did you not mean what you said?"

"I meant it. I'm simply surprised you remembered a minor detail about me, especially considering I tried to kick you out."

His gaze heated. "I may not have let on, but I was fascinated by you from the moment you refused to dance with me."

Caroline fought the urge to flee. She'd been dreadful. "I don't believe I ever apologized for my boorish behavior. I'm sorry."

Chuckling, he ran his knuckles along her cheek, making her nerve endings shiver with pleasure. "I *didnae* bring it up to make you feel bad." He turned and nodded at the goat. "Back to the matter at hand. Since the mercantile doesn't sell goat cheese, I thought why not enlist Tammy's help?"

"Who's Tammy?"

"The goat." His grin widened. "She gives you milk. You make the cheese. I'm sure that book you borrowed from Cook contains a recipe."

"You're right, the mercantile doesn't sell it. However, multiple women in these mountains do. I can purchase it from them."

"Think about the satisfaction you'll gain from learning a new skill. Besides, I'm convinced your cheese will taste better than theirs."

Caroline couldn't resist the boyish appeal in his eyes. She burst out laughing. "Do you ever give presents that don't require work?"

"Occasionally." His voice dropped in timbre, and her insides went mushy. She was beginning to recognize that look. He was going to kiss her again.

He settled his hands about her waist. Feeling daring, she slowly slid her hands up the contours of his firm chest and over his broad shoulders before locking her arms around his neck. His breathing quickened and his heavy gaze probed hers. Anticipation tingled along her skin.

"I love being close to you," she whispered,

caressing the smooth strip of skin above his collar.

Her husband was strong and fearless, handsome and thoughtful. In his arms, she felt like nothing could hurt her, like the loneliness she'd lived with her whole life could be conquered. She felt like a different woman, one who was capable and desirable.

His smile held a tender, almost wistful quality she hadn't witnessed before. "I love being close to you, too."

As he dipped his head to claim her mouth, she wondered if he'd ever say words similar to these. He'd said he liked her. And he obviously enjoyed kissing her. But would he ever *love* her, faults and all?

Caroline couldn't be sure how to quantify her feelings for him, and that made her vulnerable. If her heart succumbed and he later decided she wasn't good enough, that he wanted nothing more than friendship, she'd be crushed.

Duncan eased away, his brow knitting. "Is something the matter?"

"I'm fine."

Disquiet swirled in his gaze, and he shifted uneasily. "Caroline, there's something I *havnae* told you."

Apprehension slithered through her. Unlocking her arms from around his neck, she stepped out of his hold. "What is it?"

"Our visit to the Murrays reminded me how long it's been since I've seen my family. My nephews are getting bigger by the day. I'd like to introduce you to my parents and my brothers someday soon. But before I can do that, I have to tell you the truth."

That he wished to introduce her to his family meant a lot. It was overshadowed by the worry his words caused. Who could have guessed she wasn't the only one keeping secrets?

"Just say it, Duncan."

"I'm no' a pauper, Caroline. I'm a *verra* wealthy man."

Thinking back to the night of his arrival and his mountain man appearance, she rejected the idea. "A wealthy man doesn't travel around the countryside changing jobs every few months, a single bag of possessions to his name."

"I'm speaking the truth," he said gravely. "I could purchase your house and property three times over and still have money left."

The sound of swarms of angry bees buzzed in her ears. The clues had been there from the beginning, hadn't they? His authoritative bearing, like that of a man accustomed to being revered and even obeyed, was not the marker of a subservient employee. He'd treated her as a social equal. Humility wasn't a quality that sat easily on Duncan McKenna. In fact, she'd encountered his arrogance on more than one occasion. He was obviously an influential member of Boston's elite citizens.

Mind whirling, she drifted away from the paddock, her gaze snagging on the rough cabin tucked amid verdant forest. What game was he playing?

Behind her, he spoke. "The McKennas are a prominent family in Scotland. When my grandfather traveled to America, he already had the capital to expand our business. God blessed his endeavors. The time came when he needed my father's direct assistance. Corresponding with each other across the great Atlantic no longer cut it. No' long after we arrived, he purchased a prime piece of property, complete with a sprawling estate, and moved us in."

She'd been a blind idiot. Stepping out of the path of a hornet zipping past, she wrapped her arms around her middle. "I can only imagine the amusement you've had at my expense. You must think us a batch of country bumpkins." A harsh sound escaped. "Serves me right for acting the way I did."

"No, Caroline." As he came around to stand in front of her, his distress was palpable. "That's no' how it was. I should've been honest with you. At first, I simply *didnae* feel the need. You and I were nothing more than unfriendly acquaintances. And later, I was angry about our night in the storm and the aftermath."

Guilt clawed its way to the surface. How could she be upset with him when she was harboring a secret of her own?

"Tell me something. Why would you give up a life of ease and success for this?" She gestured to the rural scene.

His mouth pulled into an unhappy frown. "I woke up one day and discovered I *didnae* like the man I'd become." Pushing his fingers through his auburn locks, he studied their surroundings instead of meeting her gaze. "I bought the lie that material wealth, social standing and education determined my worth. Deep inside, I knew there was something missing. I *didnae* have peace. The thrill of new accomplishments, new acquisitions — whether it be a prized stallion, the latest in weaponry, a valuable antique — never lasted. True contentment was elusive."

Caroline understood all too well. A squirrel darted between the porch and the nearest tree, winding through the colorful blooms she'd planted. Those flowers represented a kind of freedom. Although humble, this was her home to fix up however she liked. The vegetables she tended provided sustenance for her and Duncan. Feeding the chickens, tossing corncobs to the free-roaming hogs, milking the cow — those tasks benefitted her household. While scrubbing floors wasn't an enjoyable activity, it was *her* floor. Hers and Duncan's. No one critiqued her appearance or her work.

Being a farmer's wife wasn't glamorous or easy, but there were rewards she couldn't measure in money or accolades. Caroline hadn't believed it to be true until recently.

"So you woke up one day, packed a bag and left?"

"Not exactly." He grimaced, and remorse flooded his gaze. "I resisted the truth for a long time, until one day, my selfishness blinded me to a man's plight. A man died needlessly because of me."

"What happened?"

"Edwin Naughton was my valet. He was in charge of making sure I walked out the door looking like the lord of the manor that I was." He paused, lost in thought. "He accompanied me on a hunting trip, along with several of my closest friends. Caught up in the revelry, I ignored the obvious signs of his illness. He was a stoic man. I *cannae* recall him uttering a single complaint until that trip. Instead of sending for a doctor, I told him to retire for the night and sleep it off. One of the other servants found him dead in his bed the following morning."

"Oh, Duncan." Caroline enfolded his hand in hers, drawing his troubled gaze to her face. "You can't blame yourself."

"As his employer, I was responsible for him."

"Did he ask to see a doctor and you refused?"

"No, but —"

"The outcome may have been the same even if you'd acted differently."

"I *cannae* be sure, can I?"

"Is that what drove you from your home and family?"

"Aye, his death was the catalyst. No' long after, I attended a worship service and answered the call to follow Jesus and to live according to God's Word. I finally found that peace I'd been chasing in temporary things. Suddenly the clothes, the parties, the excess . . . it meant nothing. When I tried to explain my decision to leave, Maureen didn't understand. Neither did my family. It took months of exchanging letters for them to accept that I *wasnae* ever returning to my old life."

At the mention of his former fiancée,

jealousy resurrected the multitude of doubts she harbored about herself and this relationship. She released his hand and tucked hers in the folds of her skirt. "Did you ask her to come with you?"

He hesitated. "I did."

Caroline nodded her understanding, confused by the riot of emotions inside. A few short weeks ago, she would've railed at how one woman's rejection had ultimately sent Duncan into her life, ruining it. Now, she could only feel relief.

"D-Did you love her?" She rubbed her boot against the grass and uttered a self-conscious laugh. "Stupid question. Of course you did. You proposed to her."

"I proposed to her while entrenched in my former life." Gently tipping up her chin, he said, "The man I am today would never have chosen her."

"You didn't choose me, either. You were saddled with me."

"And you with me," he challenged softly. "I have the same doubts as you, Caroline. You *didnae* have the opportunity to mull over a proposal from me and accept it."

Caroline suspected her answer would've been surprising to most, especially herself.

He cocked his head to one side. "You aren't angry that I *didnae* tell you?"

"I'm not thrilled." She couldn't muster outrage, not when she was withholding information from him.

"Caroline, I —" He stopped and, turning his head, put distance between them. "Good afternoon, Sylvia. To what do we owe this visit?"

Beneath her mobcap, her yellowish-brown eyes were big and watchful. "I've a missive for Miss Caroline."

At the sight of the slim, ivory envelope, her stomach dropped to her toes. Her feet felt leaden as she forced her legs to carry her forward.

"Who sent it?" she managed in a raw whisper.

Concern etched Sylvia's features. "I don't know, miss."

"Thank you."

She stared at the script and prayed he'd been merciful.

Duncan waited until Sylvia was out of earshot to question Caroline. A simple piece of mail shouldn't have this effect.

"Are you expecting bad news?" he said, noting her trembling fingers.

"What?" She tore her gaze from the envelope to look at him, distraction clouding the navy depths. "No, of course not. I'm sure you have things to do. I'll see you at lunch?"

His gut told him she was hiding something. After his confession, it hurt that she didn't feel free to share her worries with him. Annoyed him a wee bit, too.

"I don't have to rush back. Go ahead, open it."

Brows pulling together, she swallowed hard and stared at the envelope as if it contained poison. Slowly turning it over, she read the address. Her lips parted. Her shoulders lost their tension. "It's from my mother."

Clearly, she'd expected a different sender. But who? And what reasons would she have for not wanting him to see?

She skimmed the contents. "They're delaying their return until late August."

The news wasn't unwelcome. Without Louise's hawkeyed scrutiny and ready criticism, Caroline was finally relaxing her guard. He didn't want to see her revert to the aloof woman she'd been before.

Staring unhappily into the distance, she said almost to herself, "That means no tea party."

"Tea party?"

"Every August, we host it on the lawn. The girls and ladies of Gatlinburg are all invited. Cook enlists the help of temporary assistants to prepare an elegant meal. Jessica and Jane create dozens of frosted cookies and miniature cakes. Wendell and I are in charge of the floral arrangements for each table. It's one of the highlights of the year, especially for the younger ones, who get to wear their finest summer dresses and be treated like grown-up ladies. You should see the way their faces light up."

Her disappointment was palpable. "Host it yourself," he suggested.

Astonishment rippled across her face. "Without my mother?"

"Why no'?"

"She'd be livid, for one. Believe me, she knows how to make you regret displeasing her."

"Caroline." Settling his hands on her shoulders, he said, "You are no longer under her thumb. You're a married lady in charge of your own life. Stop frettin' over her opinions and her wishes. If it's important to you, and I can see that it is, then do it."

Conflicted, she worried her bottom lip. "I don't know. It's a huge undertaking."

"You can count on my help."

"Thank you, Duncan."

The way she looked at him then, as if he was her hero, made his chest expand with warm relief. He'd expected her to nurse anger over his confession or treat him to frosty silence.

"So you're going to do it?"

A smile flickered. "I suppose I am. Let's hope we aren't nearby when she learns what we've done."

"She has to let you go sometime."

"Good afternoon." They both turned to see Jane Leighton approaching, a basket swinging from one hand and a bouquet of daisies in the other.

"Hello, Jane," Caroline greeted with a smile. "What a nice surprise."

The redhead's big green eyes shone. "I hope I'm not interrupting."

"Not at all. You're just in time to see the latest gift Duncan brought me."

Duncan caught his wife's sideways glance and the dry humor in her voice. He was going to have to rethink this wooing thing. He could've showered her with diamonds and gold necklaces like he had Maureen, but he wasn't the same man anymore. He wanted to focus on gifts with meaning, ones that wouldn't be forgotten in a drawer and brought out only on special occasions.

"I think you'll agree that Tammy is the perfect gift." He winked at Jane, who looked perplexed.

"Tammy?"

Linking arms with her friend, Caroline said, "Let me introduce you."

Duncan saw an opportunity to take his leave. His suspicion that Caroline was harboring secrets wouldn't be quelled. If she wouldn't honor his confession with one of her own, he was going to have to root out the answers himself.

CHAPTER SEVENTEEN

"Afternoon, Sheriff." Duncan stood in the jail's open door. "I'd like a word with Ben. Any idea where I can find him?"

"How are you, Duncan?" The lawman left his chair and came around to half sit on the desk ledge, arms crossed over his chest. His demeanor was welcoming, his blue gaze alert with keen assessment. "Ben's on an errand for me. He should be back within the hour. In the meantime, is there anything I can help you with?"

Duncan hesitated a moment before crossing the threshold and closing the door. The information he sought pertained to his wife. The sheriff was married. Ben, on the other hand, was a single man with the reputation as a flirt.

Shane nudged the chair in front of him with his boot tip. "Have a seat."

Without waiting for him to comply, Shane resumed his spot behind the massive, scuffed desk. Duncan tried to get comfortable, but the room was stifling and he'd forgotten what it was like to discuss private matters with another soul . . . one disadvantage of carving one's own path in life apart from family and friends.

"You've known my wife for many years," he began.

"We're acquainted with each other. I wouldn't say I have particular insight into her personality, though. What's going on?"

"My instincts are telling me she's hiding something. Whenever I ask if something's wrong, she brushes off my questions or changes the subject altogether."

Shane looked thoughtful. "It's been my experience that you either have to continue asking until you ask the right question or wait until she's ready to share. I know that in my house, I don't always get an answer on my first try."

Duncan had met the sheriff's wife, Allison, at the wedding. The friendly blonde would soon be welcoming a child into the world and, from the looks of things, she and Shane could hardly wait to meet him or her.

"How long have you been married?"

"Eighteen months."

"Does it get any easier?"

Shane laughed outright. "Marriage is

work, but it's the fun kind. Does it get easier? I'd say communication is the key to making day-to-day life run smoothly." He drummed his fingers on the wood. "What do you suspect she's hiding? And why on earth would you think Ben could help you with this? You're aware his experience with females is limited to hooking their hearts without plans to reel them in, right?"

"I had heard that. My questions are more general in nature than romantic. Are you aware of anyone in town that Caroline might've had a falling-out with? Perhaps someone who moved away?" Someone who'd send her upsetting letters?

Getting more comfortable in the chair, he stroked his chin. "No one comes to mind. While Caroline is deeply involved in local events, you might say she reigns from afar. She's friends with the O'Malley sisters, and she's become close with Allison. With everyone else, she keeps it casual."

"Can you recall any admirers she's spurned?"

"No." He narrowed his gaze. "Duncan, has someone been harassing her?"

"I don't know." He stood and started to pace. "At this point, I have no proof that anything is wrong."

He related her reaction to the letter, as

well as her edginess that day he'd intercepted her emerging from the woods.

"Sounds like cause for concern. Want me to talk to Ben about this? See if he has any insight?"

"That's a good start." Thanking him for his time, Duncan exited the jail, only to bump into a passerby.

"Excuse me," he said in apology.

He recognized the man as the café owner. Out in the daylight, Alexander Copeland looked downright sickly. His eyes were bloodshot, and he was squinting as if he hadn't seen the sun in weeks.

"Mr. Copeland, are you all right?"

One arm cradled his midsection. "If you're asking if I need a doctor, the answer's no."

Duncan recognized signs of intense discomfort, but he couldn't force him to seek medical attention. "I'm new to town. Duncan McKenna's the name."

Alexander contemplated Duncan's extended hand as if he didn't know how to respond. Finally, he shook it with a surprisingly firm grip. An older couple strolled past, their widened gazes on the businessman.

"I ate in your establishment recently," Duncan offered.

There wasn't a flicker of reaction. As if he was numb. Or didn't care about anything or anyone in the world. "It's the only one in town."

Was that why he didn't care about the quality of his food? No competition?

"Have you owned other eating establishments?"

Alexander opened his mouth to answer, then narrowed his gaze. "Where did you say you were from?"

"Originally Scotland. More recently Boston."

Pressing his hand against his stomach again, he winced. "I've got to get back."

"Pleasure to meet you."

Lips compressed in a tight line, he inclined his head and pivoted on his heel. As he strode with his head angled toward the boardwalk, his posture screamed *stay away.* He disappeared in the alleyway between the café and post office, likely seeking a rear entrance in order to avoid his customers. Duncan sensed a mystery here, but he had a more important one to solve at the moment.

"Thank you for meeting me on short notice." Caroline reached for the pencil tucked behind her ear and consulted the uppermost sheet on the stack. "We have a little less than three weeks until the party. Not a lot of time."

Had she made the right decision? Duncan's faith in her abilities had instilled her with courage that was waning the more she envisioned her mother's ire.

Seated across the table, Allison sipped tea, nibbled on a shortbread cookie and absently rubbed her rounded stomach. "If anyone can do it, you can."

"She's right," Jane chimed in, reinforcing what she'd said yesterday after meeting Tammy. "You're a professional at this sort of thing. We'll enlist any and all of the O'Malley family members to help. Just say the word."

The café's doorbell chimed, announcing the exit of the only other customers. Because it was late afternoon, the place was deserted. Not that it was ever bustling these days. Caroline wished the former owner, Mrs. Greene, had sold it to someone other than Alexander Copeland, someone who actually cared whether or not the food was edible.

Glancing at her list once more, she said, "I can count on you and Jessica to do the desserts, right?"

"Absolutely. I'll speak with Quinn and

order the oranges for the cakes. I won't need to special order any ingredients for the cookies."

"No. Don't do that." Both women looked at Caroline in surprise. "I've grown weary of the orange-spice cakes, and I'm sure my guests have, too. We've served them every year because my mother refused to contemplate alternatives."

A slow smile curved Jane's lips. "I'm in favor of a menu change. What do you have in mind?"

She experienced a thrill of excitement at being consulted on her thoughts, for a change. "I'm partial to lemon, but I'm open to suggestions."

Between the three of them, they decided on lemon cake with raspberry-preserves filling and shortbread cookies. They didn't stop there. The savory menu was revamped. The color palette, always dusky pink paired with robin's-egg blue, was switched to Caroline's favorites — lavender and royal purple against backdrops of snowy white. Bouquets of varying shades of purple and green would have splashes of yellow for contrast. By the time they had their plans cemented, anticipation flowed through her instead of the usual onerous dread.

"Is it horrible that I'm glad my mother

isn't here?"

Allison ceased chewing, no doubt taken aback. Caroline rarely shared her private struggles with anyone. "In the relatively brief time I've lived here, I've noticed she doesn't give you much input in decisions. She expects you to follow her lead without complaint. In that sense, I understand why you'd feel that way."

Jane patted her hand. "Caroline, you've always been a dutiful daughter. But now it's time for you to come into your own. Make your own decisions about things. Besides, the tea party is your unofficial birthday celebration. If you want lemon cake, you should have it."

Allison's brows drew together. "It is? How come I didn't know that?"

"Not many do," Jane quipped. "It's how Caroline wants it."

Caroline made a dismissive motion. "The date happens to coincide with my birthday, it's true. The last thing I want is for the people of this town to feel obliged to bring me a present, especially the ones struggling to make ends meet. Doing this for them *is* my present."

"You already give so much of yourself."

"Believe it or not, I enjoy the planning and preparations, especially when I have the freedom to take part in important decisions." To Allison, she said, "You won't say anything, will you?"

She made an X over her heart. "Cross my heart."

"Duncan should know your birthdate."

"I haven't told him." Thoughts of his startling revelation were never far away. She was still wrestling with the fact her initial judgment of him had been so far off the mark. "I doubt I will. He doesn't put much stock in such things." He'd probably give her another "gift" that required work. A new cast-iron skillet, perhaps. Or a gardening tool.

Turning her head, she gazed out the window and caught sight of Vivian's unmistakable figure across the street. Positioned in an alley's shadows, she was in deep conversation with a man. He shifted into the light, and Caroline gasped.

"What's the matter?" Allison asked.

"I thought he was gone," she murmured.

"Who?"

Tossing coins beside her coffee cup, she stuffed the sheaf of papers in her satchel and snatched her bonnet from the empty seat. "Theo. I thought he'd left town. At least, that's what he led me to believe."

Jane waylaid her. "Why are you so upset

to see him?"

"I'll explain later. I'm sorry to rush out, but I have to speak with him."

"I'll be over tomorrow to work on invitations," Allison called after her.

Caroline waved in acknowledgment. Theo Marsh was going to answer for his reprehensible behavior. What she couldn't figure was why he'd try to stir up trouble between her and Duncan.

As she waited impatiently for the street to clear of wagons and riders, she lost sight of the couple. Dashing to the other side, she searched the alley. It was empty. She did a complete circle on the boardwalk. They couldn't have disappeared into thin air.

Bright pink ribbons streaming behind a perky straw hat ducked behind the corner of the barbershop. Bingo. Uncaring of onlookers, Caroline jogged along the boardwalk, trying to maintain hold of her bonnet and satchel. She was out of breath by the time she rounded the building.

"Vivian! Wait!"

The other woman turned, her features schooled to politeness. "Well, if it isn't the happy newlywed. How is that delightful husband of yours?"

Irritation firing to life, she caught up to her. "Where is Theo, Vivian?"

She cocked her head to the side. "Who?"

"Don't play dumb. I saw the two of you together. Where is he?"

"Oh, you mean that suave charmer, Mr. Marsh." She waved her hand, drawing Caroline's attention to the elegant pink gloves. Vivian owned countless pairs of gloves. In fact, she couldn't recall seeing Vivian without them. "We spoke only in passing. He didn't divulge his next destination to me."

Caroline didn't believe her. "How do you know him? What were you talking about?"

"Honestly, Caroline," she drawled, her words dripping in honey, "One would think you'd be too wrapped up in your new husband to worry about any other man."

"Stop the games, Vivian," she snapped. "You don't know what he's hiding beneath that handsome exterior. Theo's cunning. Oftentimes spiteful. And as you said, he's adept at charming ladies into believing he's interested. Take care that he doesn't use you."

"It's sweet that you're concerned about me. I've always had the feeling that I wasn't your favorite person." Her gaze took on a sly innuendo. "You certainly didn't act pleased when Duncan invited me to join you for lunch."

She recalled the raw, uncomfortable feel-

264

ings that day had wrought. The mere idea of Duncan being drawn to another woman filled her with despair. A worrisome sign her heart wasn't as impenetrable as she'd thought.

"I was still struggling at finding myself suddenly married to a stranger," she said. That was true, although not the whole of it. She wasn't about to admit to being jealous. "Theo lied to Duncan. I want to know why."

"I can't answer for his actions. I hardly know the man."

"If you see him again, give him a message for me — I will figure out what he's up to."

Her eyes widened a fraction before she affected a sugary smile. "I doubt we'll cross paths again, but I'll keep your message in mind."

She flounced off, candy pink skirts bouncing in time with her short strides. When she reached the wooden bridge suspended over the Pigeon River, she stopped, ostensibly to ponder the rushing water below. Minutes passed. Then she glanced in Caroline's direction, a frown flashing before she resumed walking. The move was a telling one. Her suspicions that Vivian was more deeply involved with Theo than she let on increased. She couldn't fathom how the two had become acquainted or the exact nature of their relationship, but something told her Theo's decision to stay would yield nothing good.

Chapter Eighteen

The thundering of an approaching rider startled Caroline. About to pass through the stable entrance, she whirled around. Duncan slowed Jet to an abrupt halt a few yards away and dismounted. Sweat and dirt streaked his face. His boots showed signs of treks through mountains creeks.

Striding to her, he whipped off his hat and leaned down to kiss her cheek. She felt his fleeting touch on her elbow.

"I *dinnae* wanna get too close. I'm sweaty."

"Where have you been?" Following him into the stable's cooler interior, she watched as he dunked his handkerchief in the water barrel and wiped his face and neck. She hadn't seen him since breakfast.

"When I got here this morning, I discovered one of your father's stallions was missing."

Bending over the barrel, he cupped handfuls of water to wet his hair. Droplets dripped from the wet strands onto his pale green shirt. The bulging of his biceps beneath the thin material distracted her. She knew the wonder of having those strong arms wrapped around her.

"The signs point to theft."

Her gaze snapped to his face. "You're saying someone snuck onto our property and stole a horse?"

"Dusty's worth a fortune. All anyone has to do is take him out of these mountains and sell him to the highest bidder."

"This hasn't happened before," she said, unnerved at the thought of a thief poking around while they slept. "My father will be furious."

"I sent him a telegram as soon as I found out." His blue gaze was grim. Fatigue carved lines in his face. "I spent the day scouring the area, to no avail."

"Alone?" The thought of him chasing criminals sent alarm cascading through her.

"Ben MacGregor rode along with me."

Coming closer, his hair plastered to his head, he rubbed his hand down the length of her arm. "Caroline, I *cannae* leave the rest of these horses unprotected. I'm going to have to spend the nights here."

"For how long?"

He sighed. "Until I'm confident he's not

coming back."

"What if there's more than one?" she demanded. "They'll be armed. You can't face them alone. And there's always the possibility you'll drift off and won't hear them . . ." A shudder overtook her. When had this man's well-being become vitally important?

"Hey, there's no need to worry." He squeezed her hand. "I'll be fine, I promise."

"You can't promise that." She bit her lip. "I don't like this."

"Neither do I." He ruffled his wet hair to try and dislodge the moisture. "It's unlikely they'll return. They know we'll be prepared against further attempts."

Drifting over to Rain's stall, she greeted the mare and stroked her sleek face. "I'm thankful they didn't take more, especially Rain."

He stood close behind her. "You'll be alone in the cabin. While I have no reason to believe you're in danger, I'm going to ask Anthony to bunk outside there."

For the first time since he told her the news, she smiled. "No, thank you. I'd be the protector in that scenario."

"Wendell, then."

She turned around and was stunned by the intensity of the concern in his eyes. "I'm

269

not taking Wendell away from his family. His grandchildren wouldn't be too happy with me."

"Then sleep in the main house."

"I'd feel more secure in the cabin alone. The house has too many entrances and windows, too many places to hide. Besides, you said yourself that it's unlikely they'll return. I'll be fine."

His brow smoothed and his mouth curved. "I'll miss your snoring."

She punched his arm. He rubbed the spot and pretended to be hurt.

"Did everything go okay with your meeting today?"

Not wanting him to see her frown, she turned around again to pet Rain. "We have lots to do to prepare, but Jane offered the entire O'Malley clan's help if I need it."

"Good."

Her mind reeling with the conundrum that was Theo Marsh, she left Duncan with the excuse she had work to do in the main house. Allison was coming tomorrow to help with invitations, and Caroline had supplies to gather. He would not be pleased to learn of Theo's continued presence. She'd tell him eventually. His head had to be clear if he was going to capture thieves and stay safe doing it.

She stayed busy the rest of the evening. Duncan stopped by the cabin long enough to tend the animals and to eat a bowl of pinto beans she'd prepared. Beans were easy. Her corn bread still tended to have a crusty exterior and gummy interior, but he downed it without blinking an eye. He truly was a patient man, a character trait she appreciated.

Before he left, he instructed her not to open the door for anyone besides him. Then he dropped a kiss on her forehead and left. A prayer for his protection left her lips without conscious thought. Realizing she'd been remiss in this, she vowed to pray for him each and every day.

As night enveloped the cabin and nocturnal creatures stirred, Caroline huddled beneath her thin quilt, her earlier confidence flagging. She hadn't spent a single night alone. Not one. Every sound, both within and without the walls, became magnified. She missed the reassurance of Duncan's presence, the occasional creak of his bed and his mumbles in the midst of sleep. How long she lay there, as awake as she'd been midday, she had no idea. When a horse whinnied and a man's low command reached her, she bolted upright. Had Duncan come back?

Slipping into her housecoat, she lit her bedside lamp and carried it to the windows. A moonless night, she couldn't distinguish the shadow-draped shapes. She went outside onto the porch and held the lamp aloft.

"Duncan?"

Yards from where she stood, movement in the tree line had her swinging around. An imposing figure emerged from the shadows. Her heart leapt into her throat. *Should've stayed inside where it was safe.*

"Good evening, Caroline," a silken voice greeted. "I heard you were looking for me."

Theo stepped onto the far porch end, a hulking figure of the night.

She edged toward the open doorway. "You shouldn't be here."

"Your husband doesn't have to know I paid you a late-night visit. I saw him carrying bedding into the tack room. Seems he plans to camp out there."

A frisson of unease skittered along her spine. She hadn't feared the Charleston businessman until this moment. His intentions weren't at all clear.

He strolled toward her, the light playing over the sharp angles of his face. "While I regret the circumstances that led to the change in you, I'm glad I got the opportunity to see you like this." His gleaming gaze swept over her, and he sighed deeply. "Are you even aware of the changes, Caroline? Your whole face has been transformed. Your eyes are soft with promise, your mouth invites a man closer. You carry yourself with newfound confidence. Irresistible, really."

He lifted a hand to stroke her hair, and she flinched. "Don't touch me."

Surprise knit his brows. "I'm not going to hurt you, my dear."

"Why did you lie to Duncan about us?"

"I made a mistake the night of the party. I worded things wrong and drove you into that man's arms. Lying about what happened was my pathetic attempt to stir up trouble. I thought if I could make him leave you, I'd be here to console you."

Caroline gaped at him. "You had plenty of opportunity to court me, Theo."

"It wasn't until you were no longer available that I realized my error."

She pictured him with Vivian in the alley. He was up to something. But what? "I don't believe you."

Suddenly he was crowding her space, his cold-as-marble hands framing her cheeks. Fear froze the breath in her lungs. "Don't."

"Leave him," he implored. "Come away with me tonight. We can have this farce of a marriage annulled. Where would you like to go? Name it, and I'll make it happen. You don't have to live like this anymore."

She used her free hand to try and tug his wrist away. He was too strong.

"I am not leaving Duncan."

Her heart thundered in her chest. *Please, God, make him leave me alone.* Their isolation gave him the advantage. No one would hear her if she screamed.

Theo's head dipped, and she thought for a sick moment that he was going to kiss her. "You're saying that out of loyalty or fear of scandal or both. But you have nothing to compare him to. Trust me, I can make you happier than that bumbling Scotsman ever could."

Anger and fear twining higher inside, she pushed out, "Duncan is not who you think he is. The McKenna family is far wealthier than yours or mine. He's an educated, respected man. If you hurt me, he won't rest until you pay and pay dearly."

Her husband may not love her, and he may not be interested in pursuing an intimate relationship with her, but he wouldn't let an offense of this nature slide. He was too proud for that.

Theo stilled. "What am I doing?" Slowly, his hands slid from her face and he stepped back. "I don't know what came over me.

274

I'm having trouble accepting that you may never be mine."

"I'm taken. I won't ever be yours."

He nodded gravely. "I apologize for overstepping the bounds. I didn't intend to frighten you."

Her legs threatened to buckle. "Just go, Theo."

Bolting inside, she slammed the door and lowered the slat. Her scalp prickled with unease. She stood there, huddled behind the door, for what seemed an hour. Waiting for him to return. To bust through a window. Shove down the door.

Finally, she extinguished the light and went to bed. Not her bed. Duncan's.

Cocooned in his bedding, his pillow beneath her cheek, she inhaled his telltale scent. She drew a modicum of comfort from being among his things. She fell asleep praying.

Caroline was in his bed again.

Exhaustion riding him, Duncan sank onto the mattress edge and studied her in the early morning light, struck anew by her fair, tousled beauty. He'd worried about her during the long night, and here was proof she hadn't felt comfortable alone. The desire to stretch out beside her and sink into the oblivion of sleep was strong. Chores awaited him, however. The livestock wanted their breakfast, and so did he.

He smoothed a lock of moon-kissed hair off her forehead. She stirred beneath the covers, her face turning toward his hand, seeking his touch. Tenderness that was at once fierce and gentle invaded him. He was treading on dangerous ground. He could feel it in his bones.

Shifting, he was about to get up when her lids fluttered. He remained where he was, watching as she shed the remnants of sleep. Stretching, she blinked several times, her focus on the rafters above. Then her gaze lowered and widened. In an instant, she was in his arms, her own locked around his neck.

His smile hidden by her hair, he rubbed her lower back, glorying in her enthusiastic welcome. More and more each day, Caroline was becoming home to him. The need to make this a true marriage was becoming more and more insistent. Not only was she lovelier than the most flawless painting, her nearness awakened longing that was ever present these days. But something held him back, something he couldn't identify.

As Duncan registered her warmth and softness, he also noticed the desperate quality of her hold. "I'm here now, lass," he murmured into her shoulder. "Were you so very frightened, then?"

"I have to tell you something."

Her voice was pitched lower than usual. Gently pulling away, he tried to get a glimpse of her face. "What's the matter? Did you have a nightmare?"

"Theo was here."

He wanted to deny what she was saying, what he was seeing in her eyes. His gut burned with sudden, horrible possibilities. "Did he harm you? If he laid a finger on you —"

"I'm fine, Duncan." She shook her head. "A little rattled, but otherwise okay. He talked about foolish things and then he left."

"Did he threaten you?"

"No."

"That's why you slept in my bed. You *were* frightened. No' of sleeping alone, but of him." Pushing to his feet, he snatched the gun belt he'd taken off minutes ago and affixed it about his waist again. "I'm going to rip this town apart until I find him. When I'm through with him, he won't dare allow your name to cross his lips, let alone come around harassing you."

"Duncan, no." Hurrying over, she latched onto his arm. "Don't do this."

"If I *dinnae* warn him away, he'll think it's

okay to do as he pleases. He'll come back."

"I'm not convinced he will. Something's not adding up. Theo said he wants to be with me, but I sense he and Vivian are more than friends."

"Of course he wants to be with you. What man wouldn't?"

She looked astonished. "You remember what I told you? It's not like the men of this town were knocking down my door begging to court me."

"They *didnae* know the real you. You *dinnae* make it easy for people to get close."

"I learned early what image to project and what to keep hidden."

Witnessing the grief on her face, Duncan wanted to throttle her parents. Not only had they withheld their love and acceptance, they'd made her feel inadequate.

"Caroline, I want you to feel secure with me. I want you to be free to be yourself."

Something akin to remorse flashed over her features. "I appreciate that, Duncan. Lifelong habits are difficult to break, but I promise I'll try."

Duncan wasn't completely satisfied. He was a patient man, however, and a positive one. Before long, his wife would be so convinced of his regard that she'd come to him with any problem.

278

He headed for the door.

"Where are you going?"

"To speak to Theo." At the protest brewing on her face, he held up a hand. "Caroline, he approached you in the middle of the night, fully aware you were alone. I *cannae* let that slide. Don't worry, I *willnae* do anythin' that would land me in jail."

"You don't think he had anything to do with the stolen horse, do you? Perhaps his interest in me is a ruse."

"I *dinnae* ken the answer to that." He settled his hat on his head, "but I plan to find out."

CHAPTER NINETEEN

Duncan's temper was on a very short fuse. At the sight of his target chatting with a pair of local farmers on the boardwalk, it lit up and went boom. His surroundings faded. The sounds of passing conveyances and conversational chatter became muted. He strode up to the trio, seized fistfuls of Theo's lapels and shoved him against the barbershop wall.

"McKenna!" Theo grunted. "What's the meaning of this?"

Duncan used his greater strength to pin him in place. "I should shoot you where you stand," he growled, the impudence of this man begging for revenge. "You've done nothing but disrespect me and Caroline since I set eyes on you. I let that sorry display at the wedding slide. I chose not to confront you about your lies. But visiting my wife in the dead of night goes beyond the pale, sir, even for a snake like you."

Unease gripping his features, Theo glanced to his right and left. "Perhaps we should take this discussion somewhere less public."

"Having witnesses is a good thing. *'Twill* prevent me from unleashing the full extent of my fury."

In his peripheral vision, Duncan registered Theo's companions leaving and other passersby giving them a wide berth.

Theo tried to shift his stance and was prevented. Sweat dotted his brow. "You can release me. I promise not to flee."

He eased off the pressure. Theo sucked in a deep breath and straightened his tie. Duncan kept only spare inches between them, his hands fisted at his sides.

"Look, I apologize for my error in judgment. I shouldn't have approached her."

"You knew I'd be in the stables." He recalled her immense disquiet, hours after the event, and struggled with the desire to land the man a facer. "You frightened her."

Theo's gray eyes reflected first surprise, then remorse. "She knows me well enough to know I'd never hurt her."

"*Dinnae* put this on her," he snapped. "You're the one in the wrong here. What's your game, Marsh? You had your chance.

Caroline's a married woman, and she's loyal to me."

Whatever else was going on in their marriage, he was convinced she'd never betray him in that manner.

His brows tugged together. "I know."

"You *dinnae* act like you know." Again, memories taunted him. The memory of this man kissing his bride minutes after their vows had been said. The rift he'd intentionally caused between them.

"Trust me, I do."

"Then why put her through that?" Duncan demanded. "Are you involved with Vivian?"

"What? No! Of course not."

"Caroline believes you are."

He shook his head vigorously. "She's mistaken."

Theo's sincerity in this matter, at least, was undeniable.

"Did you have anything to do with the theft of Albert's horse?"

Lips thinning, he again shook his head. "Albert's a trusted friend of my father's. Besides, what need do I have of an extra horse?"

His denial was less forceful, and Duncan's suspicions were stirred.

"If you're lyin', I'll find out." Splaying his

hand against Theo's chest, he got in his face. "You stay away from my wife, do ya hear me? I *dinnae* care what's gone on in the past between you. Consider your friendship with her over."

Something akin to grief flitted over his face. He firmed his jaw. "Is that what Caroline wants?"

"After last night, she wants nothing to do with you."

His gaze slid past Duncan's shoulder. After long moments, he said, "I will respect her wishes."

Duncan released him. "You'd better, because next time I *willnae* be so nice."

After days of silence, her blackmailer finally contacted her. This time, instead of leaving the letter at the main house, he'd propped it against the cabin door where Duncan could've stumbled upon it. A foolish risk, because the second Duncan learned of this, he'd put a stop to it. The threat to her father's reputation and livelihood meant nothing to him. Feeling chilled despite the midsummer heat, Caroline walked along the boardwalk, limiting her interactions to polite smiles that didn't invite conversation. She had a distasteful errand to complete.

The bank's large sign loomed overhead,

and her steps slowed to a snail's pace. Her fingers bent the folded document that held Duncan's supposed signature. She reminded herself again that she had no other choice. Her blackmailer wanted double the usual amount. If she didn't bring the money to the desired spot by five o'clock the following day, all of Charleston would soon be reading about her father's alleged deception in the newspaper. Loyal customers would snub Turner soaps and other sundries and her family's name would be tarnished forever.

Slim hope resided in her. The masks she'd shipped to Charleston might appeal to buyers. If so, she could use the proceeds to offset her withdrawal. To her knowledge, Duncan didn't monitor the account he shared with her. He'd set up his own not long after his arrival. The odds of him discovering her deception were low.

Caroline wondered briefly if protecting her father was worth the risk to her relationship with her husband. She and her father weren't close, no matter how much she wished otherwise. There was the other matter of his guilt. If he'd actually done what her blackmailer insinuated and lied about the quality of ingredients in their expensive soaps, didn't he deserve to deal with the consequences?

A towheaded boy of about seven or eight bumped into her. "Excuse me, ma'am."

"It's all right."

She couldn't stand in this spot staring at the bank. People would notice.

Drawing in a bracing breath, she entered the rough-hewn building, her stomach sinking at the sight of Milton Donahue. The clerk hadn't attempted to hide his dislike of her. Above his wire-rimmed spectacles that perched low on his nose, his beady eyes met hers. His mouth puckering as if he'd tasted a persimmon, he waved her forward.

"What can I do for you, Mrs. McKenna?"

"I brought the signed document." Perching on one of two seats angled toward his desk, she handed it to him. "The amount I require is there on the top line."

He scanned the information. "Typically we'd require Mr. McKenna to come in to the bank and sign in person."

Perspiration dripped down her spine. She affixed an apologetic smile on her face. "My husband is a very busy man. I'm not sure if you've heard, but we've had a horse theft this past week. He's working throughout the day with his normal chores and keeping watch at night. He simply can't spare the time, I'm afraid."

At least that part was true. Duncan's fatigue was obvious, but he refused to risk her father's animals. His confrontation with Theo had yielded nothing of value. And since she'd yet to hear of Theo sporting a black eye or broken nose, she had to believe that what Duncan had told her was true — they'd come to an agreement without resorting to physical violence. An apologetic Theo had promised to respect their vows. That little detail niggled at her.

Theo wasn't the apologetic sort.

His reason for remaining in Gatlinburg — a newfound friendship with Vivian Lowe — validated her suspicions. And if he in fact wanted Vivian, not Caroline, what had been his purpose for visiting her the other night?

"I did hear that," Milton reluctantly admitted.

Her shoulders sagged with relief.

"However, I will have to check with Mr. Jenkins before I proceed with the transaction."

Caroline schooled her features, while inside she was railing at him. Why was he being so difficult? It was *her* money, after all!

"Of course."

While she waited, she prayed for God's forgiveness. She hoped He understood her motivations. The last thing she wanted was to deceive Duncan. Every time the bell above the door jangled announcing a new arrival, she flinched.

Milton returned after what seemed like a lifetime, accompanied by Mr. Jenkins. "Caroline, how wonderful to see you."

His smile was wide, his gaze clear. He didn't suspect a thing.

"How are your parents?"

Standing, she curled her fingers into her palms and tried not to stare at the thick envelope in Milton's grip. "Enjoying their holiday, apparently. They've decided to prolong their stay."

"My wife is practically giddy with joy that you're going ahead with the tea party."

"I'm happy to hear it."

"Well, I bid you a good day." He clapped his clerk's shoulder. "Take excellent care of Mrs. McKenna, you hear?"

Milton colored. "Yes, sir."

As Mr. Jenkins returned to his office, Milton handed her the envelope. "The amount requested."

"Thank you."

Resisting the urge to sprint through the door, Caroline pivoted.

"Mrs. McKenna?"

Tensing, she turned. "Yes?"

His look of satisfaction didn't bode well. "Next time, your husband will have to come in with you."

"I understand."

Feeling lower than low, Caroline reentered the hustle and bustle of Main Street. A rural community like Gatlinburg was comprised mainly of hardworking farmers and their families, with a handful of professionals sprinkled in. Most were honest, God-fearing people. But like in any population, there was a portion that wasn't. Who in these mountains would have the necessary knowledge of the Turner enterprise — not to mention the audacity — to coerce money from her in exchange for silence?

Before Theo's odd behavior, she hadn't given him a second thought. Now she couldn't be certain he wasn't involved. She'd heard rumblings that the Marshes' business had suffered some setbacks in the past year. As a lifelong family friend, Theo's presence in Turner factories wouldn't be cause for suspicion. He could've gained access to offices and warehouses.

Hurrying home, she detoured to her parents' house and, after greeting Cook, entered her father's study. Surely there was a piece of correspondence with Theo's handwriting in here. If she located a sample, she could compare it to the demand letters.

She started with the desk. Sinking into the leather chair, she caught a whiff of the tangy cigars her father collected but rarely smoked. The wooden box was angled on the desk corner in clear sight of anyone who entered. Albert knew Louise despised the habit, and yet he left this reminder out to taunt her.

With a sigh, she examined the drawers' contents. Twenty minutes later, she hadn't found a single piece of correspondence between the Marshes and Albert.

"Miss Caroline, I didn't know you were here." Sylvia lifted a dusting cloth, her curious gaze taking in the papers fanned out before her. "I'll come back later."

Caroline glanced about the room. "I don't see a single speck of dust. You're very conscientious, Sylvia. My father would appreciate knowing how hard you work in his absence."

"That's kind of you, miss." She smiled tremulously. "This job has been a lifesaver. I owe your parents my best effort."

"A shame not all employees share your view. How is your mother?"

"Still struggling, I'm afraid. Doc said to give the medicine time to do its job, but I . . ." Pressing a hand to her throat, she shook her head, and her mobcap trembled. "I get discouraged sometimes."

"I'm sorry to hear that. I gather you're very close."

Tears shimmered. "She's my best friend."

Caroline made a mental note to advise Cook to prepare an appropriate meal for the pair and have it delivered. "She's fortunate to have a devoted daughter like you."

"That's kind of you to say." She hesitated before gesturing to the desk. "Is there anything I can help you with, miss?"

"No, thank you." Restacking the papers, she rose to her feet. "I was searching for something I'm not sure is even here." With a shaky laugh, she pointed to the large mantel clock. "I've got lunch to prepare. A wife's duties are never done."

Funny, she didn't mind the chores as much as she used to.

"Sylvia, you weren't here in August last year, so you missed the tea party."

"That's right. I've heard it's a feast for the senses. You can count on me to do whatever needs to be done."

"Actually, I thought you might like to attend as a guest. Do you think your mother would be able to come, too?"

Sylvia's expression reflected shock. "That would be lovely, Miss Caroline. However,

I'm not sure I should. Miss Louise certainly wouldn't approve."

"My mother isn't attending this year." Slipping her reticule ribbon over her wrist, Caroline came around the desk to stand in the middle of the study. "I'm in charge, and I'd like you both to be there, if possible."

"I'd love to." A blush added much-needed color to the girl's cheeks. "Thank you."

"You're most welcome."

Caroline left then, no closer to answers than before. The extra weight in her reticule served as a reminder of the errand she had yet to complete. She may have satisfied his demands this time, but what happened next month? And the month after that? She couldn't continue like this. She had to discover who was behind the threats.

When Duncan decided to accept work in Tennessee, he couldn't have foreseen that he'd wind up with a wife not of his own choosing. Caroline hadn't been his choice. However, she was God's choice. Duncan hadn't taken Albert Turner's offer of employment lightly. He'd considered it long and hard, had prayed about the decision for weeks. In the end, he'd had peace about leaving North Carolina. He had to believe this marriage factored in with God's plan for his life.

Indeed, he and Caroline had made great strides since exchanging vows. Like a delicate bloom, she was slowly opening up to him. It was his own impatience that was causing his continuing dissatisfaction. While he didn't blame her for being cautious, Duncan was a man of action. He didn't deal well with uncertainty. He wanted the assurance that their relationship was on solid footing and was going to succeed. He wanted intimacy with his wife. And children. Both would have to wait until Caroline was completely and utterly forthcoming. Based on her recent anxious behavior, he had the feeling he'd be waiting a long while.

His thoughts running amok, he finished shoeing the horse and turned to leave the stall, almost mowing over Wendell.

"Wendell, I *didnae* hear you come in."

"Have you ever heard me come in?"

Duncan laughed. The man moved aside to let him pass, padding behind him to the tack room. "Anything in particular I can do for you?" he said.

"You're good for her." Wendell's dark eyes were probing.

"What makes you say that?"

"She's happier now that you're here."

Duncan pondered the statement. "I'd like

to take the credit, believe me. But I think it's more to do with her altered circumstances than me. She's no longer under her parents' rule. She's also learning new skills, which boosts her confidence."

Wendell's enigmatic gaze tracked Duncan's movements. "She has secrets."

Tension stiffened his neck. "You know something I don't?"

"I've been married many moons. I had a daughter. I can tell when my womenfolk are carrying big burdens." He waggled a finger. "Caroline's eyes tell a story. It's up to you to figure out the ending."

"Why don't you talk to her? She trusts you."

"I'm not her husband."

"She's no' ready to confide in me." The admission felt like a failure.

"Keep trying."

As soon as he'd left, Duncan washed his hands and went searching for his wife. She wasn't in the cabin, so he tried the main house, her command center for the party. He questioned Sylvia, who told him Caroline had expressed a desire to be alone. Concerned, he checked the pond, thinking she may have taken a book out there. The water was placid, the canoe empty. The spot reminded him of the fun they'd had frog gigging and the kiss — their first — that had flipped his world on its head. He hadn't kissed her in days. It was too difficult to be close to her, knowing she didn't trust him enough to share her deepest worries. She'd insisted she was merely preoccupied by the party planning. Duncan didn't buy it.

Returning to the stables, he checked the last place he could think of — her art room. He knocked softly. "Caroline, it's me. Are you in there?"

He heard the clink of glass, followed by her quick footsteps. The door swung inward about six inches, her body blocking the view to the room. "Duncan. Is it time for the noon meal already?"

"May I come in?"

Her brows drew together. "Um, sure." Allowing him entrance, she quickly closed the door behind him. "What's the matter?"

"Does the barn have to be on fire before I can seek out my wife's company?"

Her navy eyes darkening, she smoothed a paint-spattered hand over her upswept hair. "Of course not." Caroline went to her work area and picked up the mask, then she dipped a brush into a pot of orange paint and made controlled swipes across the surface.

Duncan was tempted to take those things

away and force her to give him her full attention. Sinking his hands into his pockets, he quietly observed her craftsmanship adorning the walls. The riot of colors lent cheer to the space. He could spend hours studying the details on each one of her creations.

"Why are these spots empty?"

The brush stilled and lifted from the papier-mâché as her head whipped up. "What spots?" she hedged.

"These." He indicated the random areas.

He sensed an internal war being waged inside her. Lowering the mask and brush to the table, she locked her hands behind her back. "I sent them to a curiosity shop in Charleston in hopes they will sell."

"Recently?"

She pulled in a deep breath. "Yes."

"Why? You have plenty of money at your disposal. Are you aiming to make a name for yourself in the art world?"

Please say the latter, he silently implored.

"I simply wished to see if they would sell."

The way she avoided his gaze told him more than mere words could.

Frustration compelled him forward. Lightly gripping her upper arms, he said, "There's something you're no' telling me. Why *dinnae* you trust me?"

Her lips parted. "I could ask the same of you. I've told you repeatedly that right now is a crazy time for me. This party is a huge undertaking. The entire town will hear about it if it's a failure. And wouldn't my mother be pleased. In the past, I was the second-in-command, a soldier following orders. That's not the case this time." Waving at her surroundings, she said, "I haven't been in here in days. I had to get away from the chaos for a bit."

He released her. "She's no' going to be in attendance, and yet you're still worried about failing her? Caroline, it's impossible to measure up to some people's standards. No matter how hard you try, no matter what you do, you *willnae* be able to please them. Focus on pleasing God in your thoughts and deeds. Do things for the pure joy of them, because *you* want to. Like these masks."

"I want to host this party."

"Then enjoy the planning and the ordering people about and the chaos. Stick to your decisions, and forget about what your mother might think."

She closed her eyes. "That's like telling me not to breathe."

"I realize how difficult it must be for you, lass, but I suspect you'll never know contentment unless you start viewing yourself through the Lord's eyes instead of your parents'."

"How am I supposed to do that?"

"Pray, then pray some more. Search the Scriptures. God's Word says you're wonderfully and fearfully made."

"Since we got married, I've read my Bible more than I ever have."

"Is that because I'm such a trial to you, lass?"

"What? No, I —"

With a wink, he seized her hand. "I'm teasing. Sort of. I ken I can be as stubborn as a mule sometimes. I'm glad you're seeking the Lord's guidance. Without it, we'll fail to pattern a godly union."

"I want us to have a good marriage," she shyly admitted.

Duncan caressed her cheek and moved closer.

Her stomach rumbled. Chuckling, he tugged her toward the door. "Come on, let's go out for the noon meal."

"Seriously?"

As a couple, they had yet to eat anywhere other than at their humble cabin. "Aye, I'm serious. Ben advised me which menu items to avoid."

"I won't turn down an opportunity to get

out of cooking." Smiling, she untied her apron and snatched her bonnet from the table. "Even if it is the Rotten Plum."

He'd heard it referred to as that a couple of times. As they strolled past the house and onto the lane leading to town, he said, "Why *disnae* someone else open up a restaurant? With a decent cook, I *cannae* see why it wouldn't be a success."

"I'm not sure." Holding her bonnet by the ribbons, she let it dangle in the folds of her skirt. The sunlight filtering through the trees overhead created patterns on her hair and clothes. "When Mrs. Greene still lived here, she paid Jessica and Jane to supply the desserts. The place did good business. No one was more surprised than the twins when Mr. Copeland canceled the agreement. The food quality went down soon after."

"I've seen Jessica's desserts on display at the mercantile."

"Maybe we can purchase something after lunch. It will be money well spent, I assure you."

"I'd like that." He glanced over. "I had a brief conversation with Alexander Copeland the other day."

"Did you?" Her eyebrows rose. "That's surprising. He's a hermit. Rarely interacts with the locals unless absolutely necessary.

Even the employees say he keeps their conversations to a minimum. What's he like?"

"Unhappy." They both paused as a pair of squirrels darted across the lane. "I believe he's suffering from an illness. He *disnae* look well."

"Perhaps that's the reason he doesn't socialize. Although, if his health isn't good, I'm not sure why he doesn't sell."

They fell into a comfortable silence, and Duncan caught her hand, threading his fingers through hers. This was nice. Being together without working on some task or another. He liked teaching her things, but he also enjoyed engaging her in conversation. She had a sharp, intuitive mind.

When they reached Main Street, they noticed a commotion outside the café.

"What's going on?" Caroline's grip tightened.

"Let's find out."

People were knotted in front of the large windows, peering through the glass and whispering in hushed tones. Duncan was about to inquire about the problem when the door opened and Ben MacGregor appeared, his arm slung around Alexander's waist as he guided him through the throng. The owner's face was pale and sweaty, his mouth twisted in pain, and he was leaning heavily on the deputy.

"Give us some room," Ben ordered, his demeanor grim.

The people parted to let them pass, their expressions more fascinated than sympathetic. Alexander groaned and clutched his stomach. His gaze lifted and met Duncan's for an instant. The torment in his eyes went far beyond any physical ailment. Duncan wondered if the man had any friends or family, anyone who cared enough to help.

The group was silent as they watched the pair hobble in the direction of Doc's office. The young waitress emerged from the café.

"Ladies and gentlemen, Mr. Copeland wanted me to relay the message that we're still open for business."

A man beside Duncan snorted. Others muttered rude remarks and left.

Caroline waylaid the girl. "Sally, is he going to be all right?"

She nodded. "Mr. Copeland suffers from a stomach ulcer. He doesn't follow Doc's instructions, so he has flare-ups from time to time. I think the cook quitting this morning sent him over the edge. I heard them yelling at each other." Clapping her hand over her mouth, she shook her head. "I shouldn't have said anything. He values his privacy."

"Who's doing the cooking?" Duncan asked.

Sally's expression turned sheepish. "I am. The other girl, Lynette, is going to wait tables."

He pulled Caroline aside. "Seems to me that Alexander Copeland could use a friend."

"What do you propose we do?"

"Between the two of us, surely we can think of something."

She was silent a moment. "I have an idea, but I doubt he'll thank us for it."

CHAPTER TWENTY

"He's going to blow his top when he finds out." Chewing on her fingernails, Sally studied Caroline's hand-drawn sign.

Sally Hatcher had started working at the café about a year ago. Caroline didn't know her well — the eighteen-year-old spent time with girls her own age — but she seemed like an earnest, hardworking sort. She certainly had a healthy dose of respect for her employer.

Duncan stood near one of a dozen square tables, his hands propped on his waist and his eyes soft with compassion. "The worst he can do is order us out of his establishment. Besides, he may surprise you."

"But closing the café for a day without his permission?"

Caroline laid the pen aside and turned, the sign in her hands. "It is necessary to close it in order to find a new cook."

Ben straightened from the fireplace mantel

and, coming alongside Sally, slung an arm around her shoulders. "Doc's keeping him for at least twenty-four hours. This flare-up's a doozy. You have time to sort things here before he returns."

Predictably, Sally flushed at the handsome deputy's nearness. Sometimes Caroline wondered if he realized the potency of his effect on females.

With a wink, he left her side. "If you'll give me that sign, I'm going to stir up interest."

She gave it to him, and he headed for the door.

"This should be interesting," Duncan murmured. "Let's go watch the show, shall we?"

The threesome followed Ben onto the boardwalk, where he waved the sign above his head.

"Ladies and gentlemen, please gather around," he called. "I have exciting news."

Across the street, beneath the mercantile's overhang, a group of elderly men left their bench. An adolescent lad poked his head inside the mercantile and relayed Ben's message. People on both sides of the street stopped what they were doing and wandered over.

"As you all have no doubt heard by now,"

Ben began, "Alexander Copeland has fallen ill. What you may not know is that his cook has quit."

Cheers and whistles erupted. Duncan shot Caroline a surprised glance, his brows lifting.

"Enough of that," Ben ordered. "The café is closed for general business today because we're going to be interviewing potential cooks. So spread the word that anyone interested in the job should stop by today with a sample of their cooking. We'll be here until eight o'clock this evening. Thank you."

"Why would anyone want to work for a man like Copeland?" a wizened farmer named John Dunham griped, spewing a stream of tobacco onto the dirt.

"Agreed," another man said, nodding vigorously. "He acts like he's too good to socialize with any of us."

Sally straightened her shoulders. "Mr. Copeland is a decent man. He has his quirks, but he's got a good heart."

"He's been part of our community for a while now," Ben said. "So he keeps to himself. He clearly has his reasons. Has any one of you attempted to befriend him?"

No one answered. They'd expected Alexander to woo them into his restaurant. When he'd ignored them, they'd returned the favor.

Pulling Duncan aside, she murmured, "I'm as guilty as the rest. I hope our plan doesn't alienate him further."

He patted her hand. "I'll go and talk to him in the morning. Explain what we're doing. Hopefully he'll understand our intentions are good."

"You're new in town. Why are you intent on helping him?"

"Remember the man I told you about? My employee that died?"

"Yes, of course."

"Alexander puts me in mind of him. I *didnae* help Edwin. My conscience won't let me stand by a second time and watch someone suffer."

"You're a good man, Duncan McKenna."

Pleasure warming the blue depths of his gaze, he bent and kissed her cheek. "Knowing you think so means the world to me."

Ben was suddenly there, grinning like a fool. "Kissing on the street in broad daylight? No time for that. We've got work to do."

Caroline rolled her eyes. She liked the deputy well enough, but sometimes she imagined what it would be like for someone to turn the tables on him. For once, she'd like to see him lovesick over a girl who refused to give him the time of day.

The four of them returned inside. Since their lunch had been thwarted, they sat down to a decent, if bland, meal of vegetable soup and day-old corn bread. Sally clearly wasn't the replacement they sought.

Their first applicant arrived an hour after Ben's announcement. More arrived throughout the day, bringing everything from venison chili to shepherd's pie to fried chicken livers. Caroline lost count of how many cobblers and cakes she sampled. By the cutoff time that evening, her stomach had had enough. After locking the door, Ben led the group in a discussion. The decision was unanimous — Ellie Jameson was by far the standout candidate. Vivacious and cheerful, the young woman had brought in stuffed quail with a side of greens in vinegar dressing, along with a blackberry cobbler that had just the right amount of sweetness. Ellie had declared that, in her mind, cooking wasn't a chore. Who better to return the Plum to its former glory than a talented young woman with a passion for cooking?

Returning to the stables, Caroline fed and petted Rain while Duncan tended the other horses.

She walked into the aisle and shut the stall door. "I wonder how Mr. Copeland will take the news that we hired a new cook without his knowledge."

Duncan exited Chestnut's stall. "He'll probably be angry at first. When he sees the people lining up to sample Ellie's food, he'll change his mind."

"That's assuming he doesn't leave the sickbed to order her off his property." Turning to the exit, they walked together into the mild summer evening.

"I *dinnae* think he's physically strong enough to do that just yet." Tilting his head to one side, he said, "Although, you've given me an idea. I believe I'll postpone my visit until after lunch tomorrow. That way, I'll go in armed with a good report."

"Do you think people will give her a chance?"

"I've learned that in towns the size of Gatlinburg, there's no such thing as trivial news. A brand-new cook at Plum's? People will come out of sheer nosiness."

She stopped when they reached the first paddock. "Are you staying in the barn again tonight?"

Despite her numerous worries, the day had been a good one. It had been nice to focus on someone else's needs, no matter that Alexander was basically a stranger. More than that, she'd enjoyed spending time with Duncan. She was reluctant to see the day end.

His expression turned somber. "I'd rather stay in the cabin with you, but I *cannae* leave the horses unattended. Your father's terse response indicated he was most displeased. *Cannae* say as I blame him."

"I understand."

"You aren't frightened, are you?"

"No." How could she explain that she found comfort in his presence? "I haven't seen more than a glimpse of Theo these past weeks."

"Good. That means he's taking my warning seriously."

"He'd be a fool not to."

His eyes darkened. "If you need anything, you know where to find me."

"I know."

Her heartbeat quickened. She wished he'd kiss her good-night. He'd kept his distance recently, and she couldn't figure out why.

"I'll miss you," she blurted, instantly regretting it when his expression reflected misgivings.

"Sweet dreams, Caroline. I'll see you in the morning."

He disappeared into the stables. Apparently he didn't share her feelings. It was as if their relationship's forward momentum had come to a screeching halt. Confused and disheartened, she went home. She'd been lonely most of her life, but never had she felt as alone as she did now.

Caroline's earnest confession remained with him throughout the long night and into the next day. He'd been about to say that he'd miss her, too — of course he would — when the issue of her continued secrecy pushed to the forefront of his mind. Duncan knew she was confused by his withdrawal. What she couldn't or wouldn't accept was that he was waiting for her to share her private pain. He was waiting for her to trust him. He refused to think what would happen if she never did.

At least this day had brought about something positive. Since choosing Ellie Jameson for the job last evening, Ben had spread the word about her kitchen skills. A line had formed outside the café a full hour before opening time. With only Sally and Lynette there to wait tables, he, Caroline and Ben had been forced to assist in order to get the food out in a timely manner. The compliments had flowed like honey. People loved Ellie's food.

Now to convince Alexander to swallow his pride and keep her.

"Mr. McKenna." Doc Owens bade him enter. His office occupied the bottom floor of a white clapboard house trimmed in sky blue. "Are you here seeking medical care?"

"I'm actually here to pay your patient a visit."

"Ah. Mr. Copeland." His brows descended. "I'm afraid he's not in the best frame of mind. As long as you're not expecting a warm welcome, you're free to go in."

"I'm hoping to cheer him up with a bit of news."

Duncan followed him past a neat, sparsely decorated parlor and a set of narrow stairs leading to the second floor. He peeked in an empty examination room while Doc rapped on the bedroom door and turned the knob.

"Mr. Copeland, you have a visitor."

When there was no response, the older man glanced at Duncan and shrugged. He entered first, his broad frame blocking Duncan's view.

"Duncan McKenna is here to see you," he said.

"Who?"

The doctor moved aside, allowing Duncan to walk to the bed. Propped up by a mound of pillows, a quilt with green, blue and white swirls pulled up to his chest, Alexander stared at him with dawning recognition. His coloring had improved, and he no longer looked to be in dire physical distress.

"Good afternoon, Mr. Copeland," he offered. "I'm glad to see you're improving."

"Why would you care?" His tone wasn't mean-spirited, merely curious. Duncan had no problem with bluntness.

Doc edged toward the hallway. "I'll leave you two to converse." He pointed at Duncan. "Not too long, okay?"

"Yes, sir." Without waiting for permission, he sat on the hard-backed chair beside the bed and balanced his hat on his knee. "I have news about the café."

Interest flickered in his distrustful gaze. "What sort of news?"

"When we learned you no longer employed a cook, Deputy Ben MacGregor organized a town-wide search for a replacement."

Alexander's jaw sagged.

Duncan continued, "It was like a tryout for a stage play, you might say, except in this case folks were trying out for a job. The four of us — Ben, Sally, Caroline and I — taste-tested meals until late last night. There was one standout. Her name is Ellie Jameson. She's a fantastic cook. Just wait until you taste her stuffed quail." His mouth watered just thinking about the succulent meat and vinegary greens she'd served.

The café owner's hands fisting in the quilt until his knuckles went white, he said through clenched teeth, "You mean to tell me that you *hired* this Ellie person? Without my approval?"

"I understand you're surprised."

"Surprised doesn't begin to explain what I'm feeling right now." Shoving the quilt to the side, he set his feet on the floorboards and searched in vain for his shoes.

"Does it help to know it was a neighborly gesture of friendship?"

"I don't have friends in this town, Mr. McKenna." His gaze was at once frosty and fire-licked. "Nor do I want any. Now where are my shoes? Doc!"

"Mr. Copeland, Ellie prepared the noon meal today. Every single table was filled. Patrons crowded the boardwalk, waiting for up to half an hour for a chance to sample her food."

"Mere curiosity," he dismissed with a glare. "Doesn't mean they'll come back."

"I *dinnae* think that's the case. Everyone I spoke to was full of compliments."

Alexander shook his head, as if reluctant to accept that his business could turn around. Or perhaps his pride prevented him from accepting Ellie's help since he wasn't involved in her hiring.

"Ben MacGregor had no right to interfere, and neither did Caroline. You're new here. They, on the other hand, are aware that I don't take kindly to meddlers. And Sally should've learned by now to keep her mouth shut."

Alexander slowly gained his feet. Gauging by the white lines carved into his cheeks, the effort cost him.

"What are you going to do?" Duncan asked quietly.

"The first thing I'm going to do is get dressed." Putting one foot in front of the other, Alexander made his way to the wardrobe in the corner. "Then I'm going to the café and inform this Ellie woman that she'll have to look for employment elsewhere."

Duncan stood. "Do you really care so little about the success of your business? Or is your pride blinding you to the fact you need her?"

Wincing, Alexander shrugged a long-sleeved shirt on over his undershirt. "I admit I can't think of a single thing that I care about in this world, Mr. McKenna."

Stunned speechless, Duncan wondered what tragedy could've befallen the man to evoke such a despondent outlook. After long moments, he found his wits.

"It's a pride problem then," he surmised. "You can't overcome the fact that you weren't in charge of hiring her."

Ignoring him, Alexander pulled a pair of trousers from a hanger. "If you don't mind, I'd like some privacy."

"Certainly."

Unhappy with the outcome of their conversation, Duncan strode to the door.

"Mr. McKenna?"

"Aye?"

"I do appreciate you taking the time to apprise me of the situation."

"Of course. Good day."

Closing the door behind him, he met the doctor coming out of his study.

"How did it go?"

"Not as well as I'd hoped, but that was to be expected. By the way, Mr. Copeland has decided to end his time here prematurely. He's getting dressed as we speak."

His eyes widened. "Oh, no, that simply won't do. Excuse me, I have a patient to corral."

Duncan let himself out, silently praying the Lord would soften the café owner's heart. Ellie had indicated that she sorely needed the income. Seemed to him that both she and Alexander would benefit from working together.

As he was passing the bank, Claude Jenkins emerged and waved him over.

"Hello, Duncan. How are you this fine day?"

"I *cannae* complain. How about you?"

They shook hands over the usual greetings.

"How's that pretty little wife of yours?" With a grin and a wink, he leaned in close. "You're wise not to curtail her spending, at least not in the beginning. Caroline's been accustomed to being in charge of her own funds. Albert should've known that putting restrictions in place at this stage would lead to problems."

Duncan nodded mutely as a cold wave of dread washed over him. What had she done?

"Some women view acquiring new things as a hobby," he ventured, hoping the banker would clue him in. Maureen had had a voracious appetite for the latest fashions — always looking to add to her already bursting closets — fans, hats, gloves, brooches, stockings, jewelry. The list was endless. Nothing she bought satisfied her for long.

" 'Tis true, my man." His gaze wandering beyond Duncan's shoulder, he said, "I've got to speak to Mr. Walters. See you later."

Duncan stared unseeing at the activity going on around him. He thought Caroline had moved beyond seeking self-worth in meaningless things. He'd been wrong. Apparently her desire for status and popularity meant so much to her that she was willing to lie to achieve it.

CHAPTER TWENTY-ONE

After the deliveryman thanked her for his tip and left, Caroline examined the tissue-wrapped bundles of silk flowers laid out on her parents' dining room table. The intricate handiwork lent the blooms, which were crafted in hues of yellow, purple and green, a lifelike appearance. They would blend perfectly with the live flowers, giving fullness to the bouquets that would grace the serving and dining tables.

Sylvia had helped Caroline unpack them and was now on the opposite side of the table, bent slightly at the waist. She extended a hand toward one, not quite touching the surface.

"Exquisite, aren't they?" Caroline smiled, pleased another detail had fallen into place. With only three days until the tea party, she was feeling the pressure to make everything perfect.

Sylvia snatched her hand back. "Yes, they

are, indeed. Did you acquire them locally?"

"Actually, my father owns three flower-making shops in the outskirts of Charleston. We ship them in each year."

Sylvia's mouth thinned and a deep wrinkle formed above her nose. "I thought your father operated soap factories."

Consulting her list of chores to complete, Caroline marked through the pertinent entry. "He started out in the artificial-flower business. When he decided to pursue different avenues, he sold off most of the shops but not all."

The slamming of the rear door reverberated through the downstairs hallway. Caroline frowned. "What on earth . . ."

"Caroline, here you are." Duncan's large form dominated the doorway, his hands biting into the frame on each side. "Sylvia, will you please excuse us?"

The maid dipped her head and exited using the other door.

Concerned, Caroline put her pen and paper down. "Is it the horses? Did the thief strike again?"

Stalking toward her, he stopped midway between the door and the spot in which she stood, crossing his arms over his chest and leveling her with a glare that spelled her doom.

"What were you doing at the bank?"

She reached out and gripped the chair beside her for support. "I take it you spoke to Milton Donahue."

"In fact, it was Claude who approached me. I had no idea what he was talking about, but I have a pretty good idea." His snarling gaze jerked to the flowers. "I'm a sensible man. I ken how important this party is to you. If you'd simply come to me and explained that you needed funds, I would've gladly given my signature."

The blood drained from her head and, for a moment, Caroline thought she might faint. "I didn't need the money for the party," she said through wooden lips. "My mother has an account set up for this sort of event."

"I see." His scowl deepened, as did the disappointment on his face. "You *didnae* need the money. You *wanted* it. And for what? To replenish the outfits I gave away?" His upper lip curled as his gaze swept her blouse and skirt. "Where are the new gowns, Caroline? Or are you still waiting for them to arrive? I recall it takes weeks to ship from Europe, slightly less if you ordered from New York."

The wounds his assumption inflicted carved a deep fissure in her heart. But she had no right to be hurt, not when she'd deliberately deceived him.

She had to release her dark secret, to unload this heavy burden.

"Let me explain."

He shook his head with force. "No explanation could make up for the fact that you obliterated my trust. You *forged* my signature, didn't you? Why else would Claude say I was wise not to curtail your spending?" With a sound of disgust, he threw his arms wide. "Were you ever plannin' on telling me? What were you going to do? Hide your purchases in this house and pull them out one by one with more lies at the ready?"

Tears blurred her vision. He was looking at her the same way he'd looked at her the night of the storm, as if she didn't have a valuable thought in her brain, as if talking to her was a waste of his precious time. She never dreamed he'd look at her that way again.

Forcing her feet forward, she gripped his arm. "Please, Duncan, hear me out. I didn't intend to anger you. I —"

Wresting free of her hold, he backed up several steps, his features shuttered, his mouth a hard line of disapproval. "I'm going to Boston."

"What?" She willed herself to keep it

together. "When?"

"I'll stay until the tea party and leave early the next morning."

She was losing him. If he returned to Boston in this state of mind, he'd be reminded of everything he'd given up. He'd see his former fiancée, the woman he'd actually proposed marriage to, and decide to cut ties to East Tennessee altogether.

"C-Can I go with you?"

His brows lifted slightly before he averted his gaze. "No."

"Will I ever see you again?"

He looked at her with a grimness that scared her. "This is to be a brief visit only. I have a responsibility to your father."

His words brought her little relief. She wasn't convinced he'd come back. "Duncan, I'm sorry —"

He held up a hand. "Stop. I *dinnae* wish to speak of this. Perhaps, when I return, we can discuss it. I'm too angry right now."

He spun on his heel and stalked out. Caroline trailed after him, hoping he'd relent and listen to her. All she needed was five minutes. Duncan may not give a fig for her father's reputation, and he certainly wouldn't approve of appeasing a blackmailer, but at least he'd know she hadn't acted out of vain selfishness.

321

But he didn't relent. He didn't even look back as he pushed through the door and descended the steps, his posture rigid and stride clipped.

Caroline went as far as the landing and clung to the post, watching until he ducked into the stables. Then she sank onto the top step and, uncaring who might see, buried her head in her arms and wept.

Three days later, Caroline opened the door of her parents' house and braced herself. She didn't fake a smile. Didn't bother to check her hair. Why should she when she hadn't even brushed it that morning?

Jane stood on the porch, resplendent in a forest green frock, her glossy red hair in a romantic, loose style. Her eyes widened.

"Are you ill?" Passing into the hallway, she felt Caroline's forehead. "You don't feel hot. Please tell me you aren't sick on your birthday!"

Caroline closed the door and led the way into the dining room and returned to her uneaten breakfast. Sinking into the chair, she sipped her cooled tea. "Have you eaten?" She indicated the platters on the server. "Help yourself. There's plenty."

Jane slipped her reticule from her wrist and set it aside. Her eyes were serious as she gazed down at her. "What's the matter? I've never seen you like this."

Unable to meet her friend's gaze, Caroline stared at the golden liquid in her cup. "I think my marriage is over."

The misery dogging her these past days welled up again, making it difficult to breathe. Knowing he hadn't wanted to talk to her, let alone see her, she'd packed a bag of essentials and stayed in her old bedroom. The one time she'd gotten a glimpse of him was when she'd been out in the side yard, directing the temporary workers where to set up the tables and chairs and poles to hang canvas from in case of rain.

Jane came around and, pulling out the chair beside Caroline, sank into it. "What's happened? Did you argue? Because every couple has disagreements now and then —"

"This is different, Jane. I did something, and he found out. He despises me." Her voice wobbled, and Jane clasped her hand.

"I don't believe that for a second. Sweetie, I've seen the way he looks at you. He cares for you more than I surmise he lets on."

"I wish that were true. I — I thought that, given time, he'd cool off. I thought he'd give me a chance to defend my actions. He hasn't. He won't." Dashing away errant tears, she said, "He's leaving tomorrow at dawn. I don't think he's coming back."

Jane gasped. "I think you need to start at the beginning."

Caroline looked into her friend's anxious gaze and found she couldn't contain the past months' turmoil a second longer. The story came pouring out. She told her about the blackmail, the money, the forgery. Everything.

"I can't believe this." Jane's hold tightened, and she leaned forward. "Caroline, you have to tell Duncan!"

"What am I supposed to do? Tie him to a chair?"

"If that's what it takes, yes!"

Hopelessness assailed her. "I've given this a lot of thought. Duncan *should* go to Boston. This isn't his home. He's unhappy here. I'm going to write a letter and release him from this marriage."

"But don't you see? This changes everything, Caroline. Do you love him?"

"Yes," she whispered, her heart aching.

"Then fight for him," she urged. "Make him understand."

"Did you know he didn't plan to stick around Gatlinburg? This wasn't the last stop on his grand tour of independence. He was going to work here for a while and move on to the next opportunity." Pushing out of her chair, she went to the mantel and stared at her reflection in the gilt-edged mirror. The woman she used to be was in there somewhere, but she was changed, altered almost beyond recognition. "Because of me, he found himself in a prison not of his own making. I won't be his jailer any longer."

"You're not his jailer! You're his *wife.*" Jane came to stand behind her. "What if he's found contentment in his new life here? With you?"

Sighing, Caroline hugged her. "Thank you for listening. You can't know how much that means to me." Easing away, she said, "Promise me you won't breathe a word of this to anyone."

"If you won't tell Duncan, you have to talk to Shane. Or Ben. You could be in danger."

"Whoever's behind this has had plenty of chances to hurt me. Greed is his crime, not violence."

"I wish you'd consider this further."

The clock chimed the hour. "The guests will be arriving in four hours. I have to put aside my troubles and be the flawless hostess they've come to expect." She touched her stringy hair. "Right now, I'm nowhere near presentable, let alone flawless."

"I'm here for you, no matter what you need."

"Thank you, friend."

What she needed was divine strength to get through this day. She was going to fall apart, but it would have to wait until after Duncan left Gatlinburg.

Duncan was spying on his wife.

Drawn by lilting violin music, happy voices and the clink of china, he'd left the stables and found a shadowy tree where he could observe the tea party's proceedings without being noticed. Females of all ages and economic status had gathered on the lawn, which under Caroline's direction had been transformed into an elegant garden retreat. Along one side, tables draped with pristine white tablecloths offered ripe berries and cream, savory dishes and desserts, jars of raspberry shrub and silver urns containing tea and coffee. The other tables were laid with expensive china dishes — purple flowers on a white background — along with polished silverware and dainty teacups atop matching saucers. Elaborate flower arrangements echoed the color scheme. Overhead, not a single cloud in the vivid blue sky marred the day. A gentle breeze occasionally passed through the property, stirring the tree leaves and teasing the ribbons on ladies' bonnets. The guests' expressions of delight meant Caroline's hard work had paid off.

His gaze sought her out, hungry for the sight of her. The sense of betrayal lingered, eating away at him. Keeping his distance that first and second day had been easy. But today, knowing he was leaving in a matter of hours, he couldn't ignore the desire to see her. At least from a distance.

He finally spotted her. Surrounded by a semicircle of women intent on her words, she appeared at ease in this environment. She was once again the graceful, stunning socialite who'd first caught his eye at the end of an arduous, over-mountain journey. Her blond hair shone like moonlight, swept to one side and pinned into a sleek twist, with a single yellow bloom tucked into the mass. Her statuesque form was on display in a blue dress . . .

Duncan stepped out of the shadows and tipped his hat brim up, squinting in the light. The dress wasn't new. It was the one Louise had spurned, the one he'd complimented her on. For an event as momentous as this one, he'd expected her to wear a dress that would inspire the admiration of the attendees.

Movement off to his side distracted him. He dragged his attention away and was surprised to see Ben ambling toward him, a huge grin on his face.

"Are you going to join the festivities, Duncan?"

"I wasn't invited, and neither were you."

Propping his hands on his hips, Ben eagerly surveyed the activity before them. "I would say all of Gatlinburg's female population is represented here today."

"I've heard it said you've courted half of them," he drawled.

Ben threw back his head and laughed, earning them curious glances from a few of the guests. Taking his arm, Duncan guided him closer to the house.

"Are you here for a reason?"

The younger man looked at him in surprise but didn't comment on his foul mood. "I came to tell you that Ellie's position is secure. At least for the time being. Thank you for putting in a good word for her."

"Alexander changed his mind?"

"When he returned from the doctor's, he was a bit taken aback by the number of customers in his dining room. He wasn't too gracious about it, but he agreed to let her stay on a trial basis. I get the feeling that if she doesn't interfere with his wish to seclude himself in his office, she'll have the job as long as she wants it."

"Good for her."

"There's another matter." Scratching his chin, his expression turned thoughtful. "Albert's horse turned up in Maryville. I was there yesterday on business and recognized the markings. The man who had him said he bought him off a fancy gent with a distinct accent. The physical description he gave matches Theo Marsh."

"He has no need to steal a horse."

Twisting slightly so that he could see Caroline, he recalled the night Theo had invaded her privacy.

"Shane and I paid him a visit last evening. He's staying with the Lowe family. Theo denies he was involved, and Vivian insists he was with her the night of the theft."

"Do you believe them?"

A sigh gusted out of him. "They acted sincere, but my gut's telling me they're up to something."

Caroline ceased her conversation and instructed everyone to take their places. Several young men dressed in black and white positioned themselves at the serving tables. She asked the reverend's wife to bless the meal. When her prayer was concluded, Duncan turned to the deputy.

"Ben, I need a favor."

"Anything."

"I'm going to be gone for a couple of weeks. I need for you to keep an eye on Caroline. I think she'll be safe in her parents' house, but I'd feel better knowing you're watching over her."

"May I ask where you're going?"

"Home. To Boston."

Questions churned in his eyes. "I see. And what or who am I supposed to be keeping Caroline safe from?"

Duncan told him about Theo's late-night visit. "He's kept his distance since then. Still, once word gets out that I'm not around . . ."

"If you're worried, why not take her with you? I'd have thought you'd like to introduce your new wife to your family."

"It's no' an option right now."

"Why —"

"Are you willing to do it or not?"

Ben snapped his mouth shut, his jaw tensing. "I'll do it."

"I owe you, Ben."

Instead of answering, the lawman nodded his head toward Caroline, who'd finally taken her seat not with her friends, but with the maid Sylvia, an elderly, frail woman who appeared to be Sylvia's mother and several

330

other women he'd never seen before. Probably reclusive women who spent a bulk of their lives in hard-to-get-to coves and rarely came to town.

"A birdie told me that today is her birthday."

"Whose?"

"Your wife's."

Surprise stole his breath. "I didn't know. She didn't tell me."

Like she hadn't told him a lot of things. Resentment mingled with hurt. She didn't trust him with much of anything, big or small. He hated to admit it, but he was quickly losing hope this marriage could last.

Chapter Twenty-Two

The tea party was a resounding success. She couldn't have asked for finer weather or more delicious food. As the musicians played their last song and one by one the ladies expressed their effusive gratitude, Caroline told the hired lads to help themselves to the leftovers before beginning the massive cleanup. Her closest friends lingered, chatting and laughing together and complaining good-naturedly about indulging in too many sweets.

Allison separated herself from the group. Shane, who'd come to escort her home, called her name and held out a white box. They exchanged tender smiles that made Caroline hurt all over. Fingers curling into her palms, she refrained from searching the grounds for Duncan. Seeing him right now would shatter the false front of contentment she'd manufactured for the sake of her guests.

"Caroline." Allison's blue eyes were bright with joy. "This wasn't the first tea I've attended, but it was by far the best. Thank you for what you did today."

"I couldn't have done it without you and Jane and countless others."

"We were happy to be involved." She wiggled the box. "I know you didn't want to advertise that it's your special day, but most everyone is gone. Happy birthday."

"You shouldn't have." Caroline slowly untied the purple ribbon and lifted the lid. She ran her fingers over a flower-and-gold-embossed journal set, complete with a fountain pen. "It's lovely, Allison. Thank you."

"I thought you might like to record your thoughts or special occasions during your first year of marriage. Something to pass on to your children or grandchildren someday."

Caroline's stomach cramped. There weren't going to be any children. The way Duncan felt about her, he'd never choose to have a family with her.

Jane and Jessica rescued her, appearing on either side of Allison and thrusting gifts at her. "Don't forget our presents," Jessica admonished with a cheeky grin. "You were supposed to wait on us, Allie." She tapped her shoulder.

"Shane's anxious to get home," Allison said by way of apology. "He says he's worried about what the twins might be getting into, but I suspect he's determined to get me off my feet." With a grimace, she rubbed her lower back. "I admit I wouldn't mind relaxing for an hour or so."

"I hope you didn't overtire yourself," Caroline said.

"I'm not fatigued, exactly." Indicating her protruding belly, she said wryly, "It's more that I can't find a way to be comfortable. This baby is very active. I think he or she is going to have double the energy the twins have."

They shared a laugh, then Jessica urged Caroline to open her gift first. "A book of recipes." Caroline's throat grew thick. Who was she supposed to cook for with Duncan gone? Who would help her measure out the cornmeal correctly and make sure she didn't start a fire? "This is so thoughtful."

"I have the same one at home. I went through and put check marks on the ones Grant raves over."

"I'll start with those." She managed to sound halfway normal.

"Now for mine." Jane clapped her hands together.

Nestled in the jewelry-sized box was a

sterling silver ring engraved in floral patterns. She traced the lines of the flowers and leaves, suddenly overcome with emotion. She was no longer that sad little girl who was expected to be perfect, like a collector's item kept on the shelf until it was time to impress people. She was a reasonable adult who no longer believed in dreams. Birthdays weren't a big deal. Why was her friends' thoughtfulness ripping apart her self-control?

"I'm blessed to have you in my life," she whispered. "All of you."

She didn't say it, but she'd need them in the coming weeks and months as she adjusted to life without Duncan.

Jane drew her into a hug, whispering in her ear, "I'm praying for you."

Caroline was about to respond when Jane stiffened and pulled away. "Caroline, did you know your parents were returning today?"

"What?" Spinning around, she watched with mounting dread as the partly-enclosed carriage pulled up the lane.

Feeling as if she were encased in rock, she stood immobile as her father disembarked and turned to assist her mother. Shaking out her skirts, Louise contemplated the scene with ill-concealed indignation. Albert hung back to speak to the driver. Caroline's friends fell silent as Louise marched their way.

Depositing her gifts on a nearby table, Caroline greeted her. "Hello, Mother. How was your trip?"

Lips pursed, Louise inventoried everything with an eagle-like gaze, from the dirty dishes to empty glasses to the musicians packing up their instruments. "You went ahead with the tea party without me, I see."

Keenly aware of their audience, Caroline kept her tone neutral. "I didn't want to disappoint everyone."

"Are you quite certain that's the reason, Caroline?" she quipped. She peered at the china and fingered a yellow bloom. "If your aim had been to maintain tradition, you wouldn't have changed the color scheme or the menu. You would've kept everything the same."

"Don't you agree the varying shades of purple are a nice change?" Caroline attempted to placate her. "You once said that it's the color of royalty."

"Purple is my favorite color," Jane piped up.

"And having the same menu every year becomes monotonous," Jessica interjected. "I was sick and tired of those orange-spice cakes." Locating an uneaten dessert on the table behind her, she held it out to Louise. "You should try this. Lemon cake with raspberry filling. Caroline's idea."

Louise's nostrils flared. "I detest lemon in desserts." Returning her attention to Caroline, she said, "No, I don't agree. The colors you chose look gaudy, as if a child picked them out. I told you we were canceling the tea, did I not? Not only did you proceed without my permission, you made a complete mess of things. What I can't comprehend is what made you think you could do something of this magnitude without me?"

"Enough."

Startled by the lash of Duncan's voice, Caroline jerked. Standing near the sheriff, he zeroed his intense blue gaze in on Louise, and he didn't look happy. She'd been too mired in embarrassment to notice his approach.

"I've had enough of the shameful way you treat your daughter."

Louise bristled. She opened her mouth to respond, but he didn't give her the chance.

"Do you think God is pleased with you? He blessed you with a precious child, and you act as if she's a burden. Have you considered how that makes her feel?"

Amazement arced through Caroline. While

337

everyone else was staring at the ground or points beyond the yard, she gazed at her husband. Despite his disappointment and anger, he'd taken it upon himself to defend her to her own parent.

"How dare you speak me to that way!" Louise exclaimed. Turning her gaze on Caroline, she demanded, "Did you put him up to this? Wait until I speak to your father! He'll have him terminated on the spot."

Albert, who'd concluded his business with the driver, finally reached them. "Come, Louise. You're overwrought from the long journey." Taking her arm, he nodded sagely to the group. "Please excuse us. Feel free to linger as long as you wish."

Louise tried to pry herself from his grip. "Did you hear the way he spoke to me? Imagine, a mere stable manager!"

Caroline winced. She'd spouted similar ugly sentiments not so long ago.

"A stable manager who is your son-in-law." Albert seemed to take pleasure in reminding her. "It's a difficult thing to fire family."

Irritated all over again, Louise wrenched free and, head held high, strode for the house.

"I apologize for that," Caroline said into the strained silence. "My mother and I haven't ever seen eye to eye, but we usually keep our disagreements in private."

"It's not your fault." Allison linked arms with her. "Like your father said, she was no doubt exhausted. Coming home to a yard full of people when what she desired was rest and quiet would've been upsetting for anyone."

Caroline sought Duncan's gaze and instead encountered his broad back as he strode away. He'd said his piece and wasn't willing to speak to her one-on-one. Desperate to speak to him once more before he left, she was tempted to run after him and throw herself at his feet. Anything to make him listen.

Jane's expression was hopeful. "That was very sweet of Duncan."

Jessica snorted. "Did you see your mother's reaction? She looked like a fish on dry land, gasping for air."

"That's not helping," Jane admonished.

"He's a man of many admirable traits," Caroline said, wishing with all her heart that she'd realized it sooner. Maybe then she would've tried harder to become a woman he could admire. Maybe then she could've won his heart.

But she wasn't what he wanted or needed. The sooner she accepted that, the better.

■ ■ ■ ■

Duncan stood on the busy streets of Boston, travel bag in hand, trying to absorb the familiar sights, scents and sounds at once. Nearby, a sausage vendor hawked his wares. Young girls balanced newspaper-wrapped bundles of flowers on their shoulders in the hopes of making a little income. Horse-drawn carriages shared the cobblestone streets with throngs of people hurrying about their business and the occasional stray dog.

He breathed in the briny air as nostalgia seized him. He'd changed so much during his absence that he felt as if he was a completely different man. As he made his way along the crowded streets, he tried to imagine Caroline's reaction. Would she like the city's hustle-and-bustle atmosphere? There were museums and art galleries, parks and libraries he could've taken her to if he'd allowed her to accompany him. Plays and musicals, too. Had she ever tasted lobster or crab? Oysters were a personal favorite. And clams. He'd convinced her to test frog legs. He was confident she'd be willing to try more new things.

Regret was a tangible thing. His wife

hadn't left his thoughts for one second since he left Gatlinburg two days ago. He'd had a lot of time to think things through, time to pray and seek God's guidance. Duncan had come to the conclusion that he'd allowed his hurt feelings to dictate his actions. Instead of hurling accusations, he should've given her a chance to explain. He should've said goodbye. That was his biggest regret . . . leaving in the predawn hours, his heart a stone in his chest as he'd walked past the big Victorian where she slept in her old bedroom, as if their marriage was already over.

Shaking off the troubling thoughts, he continued on his way. When he reached the gates at the entrance to his parents' estate, he felt the urge to break into a run. He'd missed them and his brothers more than he'd realized. Picking up the pace, he hurried along the path lined by trees on one side and vast green lawn on the other. The grand brick house looming above him looked the same. Before he could reach the stairs leading to the front entrance, someone shouted his name. Duncan turned and recognized his youngest brother running toward him.

He skidded to a stop mere feet away, his chest heaving and green eyes as huge as saucers. "Duncan? Is it really you?"

"Hello, Bram." Grinning, he held his arms out and received a hearty hug. "How are you? How's Maw and Da? And Alistair, is he home?"

Bram laughed and pulled him up the steps. "Everyone's fine. Ian is still his stodgy self. No' sure why Lorraine puts up with him. The kids are healthy and as mischievous as ever." Tugging open the door, he ushered Duncan in. "Alistair has met a lady who he believes may be worth keeping. He *willnae* shut up about her."

Duncan chuckled. "And what about you? How are your studies?"

"Challenging," Bram conceded on a more serious note. "I have little time for fun anymore."

"Welcome to adulthood, little brother."

His parents welcomed him with such joyous enthusiasm that he felt guilty for staying away as long as he had. The one thought at the forefront of his mind was that Caroline should be here. His family would adore her. They'd sat down to tea in what his mother referred to as the gold parlor when Alistair waltzed in. After more hugs and questions, they settled in their seats around the low table piled with refreshments. Duncan lifted his cup to his mouth and sipped the honey-sweet liquid.

Alistair surged to his feet, startling them all.

"What's that?" he demanded.

"What's what?" Duncan looked at his parents, who were as perplexed as he was.

"The gold band on your finger!"

His mother gasped. "Duncan, did you . . . are you . . . why *didnae* you tell us?"

Bram let out a whoop and rubbed his hands together. "Oh, this is goin' to be good."

Setting his cup on the table, he stood and looked at them each in turn. "I was married in early July. I sent a letter explaining the circumstances surrounding my marriage."

His father's thick auburn brows crashed together. "We *didnae* get your letter, son."

"Who is she? Why *didnae* she travel with you?" His mother demanded, lifting a handkerchief to her mouth with trembling fingers. "Did she not wish to meet us?"

"No, Mother." Heaving a sigh, he thrust his fingers through his hair. "Caroline would've liked to meet you. I chose to come alone."

Alistair arched a brow. "This *disnae* sound good. What's goin' on, Duncan?"

He explained how he wound up in East Tennessee working for the Turners, as well as the reasons for their forced marriage.

"I wish you'd never left Boston," his mother lamented. "You could've made a wonderful match from among our friends."

"Maureen would've made a fine wife," his father tacked on.

"No' for me, Da."

Duncan wandered over to an oversize window with a view of the gardens. A massive, curly-edged cloud had drifted in front of the sun, casting the fountains and flower beds in shadow. The largest fountain was a reminder of the time he and his best friend had dumped soap shavings in the water. His mother had been livid, the head gardener even more so. He'd lived without thought to consequences or others' feelings back then. He thanked God he'd gotten out when he had.

"I'm sorry that happened, son." His father's voice was heavy with sympathy.

"I'm not."

Not now that he'd gotten to know Caroline probably better than anyone else in the world knew her. He realized with a start what a privilege that was, considering how fiercely she guarded her heart.

Alistair was the first to break the stunned silence. "Have you grown to care for her then?"

"I have."

"Do you love her?" This from Bram, who suddenly seemed like a grown-up man.

"I *didnae* mean for it to happen," Duncan replied, almost to himself.

Rubbing both hands down his unshaven face, he pictured her as he'd last seen her, beautiful and untouchable and adrift. Not part of her parents' family and not truly part of his, either. Missing her became an ache in his chest that wouldn't be comforted. Duncan felt as if he'd lived a dozen lifetimes and had not an ounce of wisdom to show for it. His usual instincts had failed him in countless ways throughout their relationship. He felt inadequate and hopeless and desperate for a solution.

He wasn't supposed to fall in love with his own wife. But he had, and now he was miserable. *Father God, what am I supposed to do? How can I fix this?*

"Does she feel the same?"

"Doubtful. Caroline *disnae* trust me."

"That *disnae* mean she can't love you," his father said. Then, stroking his chin, he turned to his wife. "Does it?"

"Hold on," Alistair interjected, "how come she *disnae* trust you? What did you do, Duncan?"

"My guess is he was his usual pigheaded,

345

prideful self." Bram smirked.

"You're right. I was. Am."

In his initial anger over the marriage, he'd nursed bitterness that had blinded him to Caroline's needs. Throughout their time together, he'd mostly been focused on *his* ideas and *his* priorities. He hadn't considered what his wife thought about things, how her upbringing had molded her, made it difficult to rely on anyone except herself.

Instead of proving himself worthy of her trust, he'd pushed her away at the first sign of trouble. The question remained — would she accept his apology and give him a chance to be the husband she needed?

CHAPTER TWENTY-THREE

"Caroline? Are you in here?"

For a split second, Caroline thought the male voice belonged to Duncan. Then the lack of accent registered, and the bubble of hope burst. Patting Lulabelle, she rose from the stool and left the stall.

"Good evening, Ben. What can I do for you?"

The deputy entered the shaded interior carrying a small wooden box and sporting a sheepish expression. "I'm here on an important errand that completely slipped my mind."

"What sort of errand?"

"This." He indicated the box. "It's your birthday present." He grimaced. "*Belated* birthday present."

She peered inside. The contents were hidden by checkered fabric. "How did you know?"

Sinking his hands in his pockets, he

winked. "A gentleman never reveals his sources."

Bewildered, she found a seat on the nearest hay square and started to lift the fabric. "This is really thoughtful of you, Ben, but you shouldn't have."

"Oh, it's not from me. It's from Duncan."

Her head whipped up. "What? He's been gone three days."

"I know. That's why I feel so terrible." Leaning against the stall, he crossed his arms. "Duncan gave it to me after the party and asked if I'd deliver it to you the next day. I got busy and forgot."

"Oh." Delight warred with confusion. Why hadn't he given it to her himself?

Probably the same reason he didn't say goodbye. Because he can't bring himself to forgive me.

Unable to quell her curiosity, she uncovered the contents, an assortment of paints and brushes and even decorating items. She picked up a sack of acorns and laughed.

"What's that for?"

"Um, I dabble in art."

"With acorns?" He bent closer. "And feathers?"

"You wouldn't understand."

Her fingers brushed a folded white paper. Pulse leaping, she unfolded the letter.

348

Dearest Caroline,

I ken this gift would be considered useful, one that requires effort to enjoy. But I've seen you at work in your studio, and in my opinion, a certain amount of play is involved, too. I hope you agree. Happy birthday.

Duncan

Dearest. He'd called her dearest. Surely that meant something. Touched beyond words, she found her eyes filling with tears even as a smile lifted the corners of her mouth.

"You're crying now? Explain to me why a thoughtful gesture would make a woman cry."

Tucking the note into her pocket, she rose to her feet. "I miss him."

"I still don't understand. A gift should make you happy."

"Maybe if you stopped playing games and paid closer attention to the women you interact with, you'd understand."

"There's nothing wrong with flirting, Caroline. Everyone knows I'm not the serious type," he shrugged.

"Do they?"

"Why do you think I cultivate my reputation? I don't want anyone getting the wrong idea." He wiggled his left hand. "There ain't never gonna be a ring on this finger."

Since it was futile to continue the conversation, Caroline gestured to the box. "Thank you for bringing my gift."

They strolled outside into the dusk. "I asked for you at the main house. Sylvia said you were staying here. How come?"

She wasn't about to tell him the true reason, that staying in the cabin helped her feel a tentative connection to Duncan. "It's my home."

"Duncan thought you'd be safer with your parents."

"He said that?"

"He told me about Theo. He asked me to keep an eye on you until he returns."

"I'm not sure he's going to," she murmured.

His brow furrowed. "What?"

"Never mind. Look, I'm fine. I haven't seen Theo in weeks. The fact that my parents have returned will dissuade any more late-night visits from him or horse thieves."

"I gave him my word, which means you'll have to get used to seeing my ugly mug around here."

Caroline had to admit that his presence on the property would alleviate her anxiousness. She still wasn't completely comfortable spending nights alone.

"All right."

He tipped his hat and headed for his horse tied to the post. "Good night, Caroline."

"Good night."

After he'd left, she pulled out Duncan's note and reread it. *Dear Lord, please let Ben be right. Please let my husband come home. Oh, about that letter I wrote? Could You maybe help it get lost in the bottom of his bag? I thought I could do the noble thing and let him go. I know I don't deserve him, Lord, but he's mine. He's the only man I'll ever love.*

It felt strange being in his old room. Despite his fatigue, sleep was proving elusive. Folded onto the slim window seat, he studied the star patterns in the night sky. They weren't as bright here as they were in the mountains. Too many city lamps still flickering. He wondered if Caroline was having trouble sleeping, too, and if she was looking at the same stars from her old bedroom window.

As wonderful as this reunion with his family had been, he yearned for his wife's sweet embrace. He needed to see her smile again, her eyes shining with joy. They had much to discuss. Not only did he owe her an apology, but the truth about his feelings. He wasn't sure how she'd react, and that worried him a little. Still, he held out hope that she'd accept his love and learn to love him in return one day.

The grandfather clock at the end of the hallway clanged midnight. Stirring from his spot, he lit a lamp and went to retrieve his Bible from his travel bag. As he lifted the heavy book out, an envelope fluttered to the rug. He sank onto the cushioned chair and ripped it open. He recognized Caroline's writing style. His heartbeat slowed.

Dearest Duncan,

I hope by now you are safely ensconced with your family and enjoying your time together. This isn't easy to say, so I'll be blunt. I'm releasing you from your obligation to me. You didn't seek out this marriage. It's because of my selfish actions that you found yourself tied not only to a town not of your choosing, but to a wife you never would've picked for yourself. Please forgive me, Duncan. I pray that, someday in the future, you will be able to think of your time in Tennessee with a modicum of fondness. We had some good times together, wouldn't you agree? But I digress. I expect to receive proper documentation from you about the dissolving of our union. Don't allow guilt to prevent you from pursuing your dreams. Be happy, Duncan, and that will make me happy.

Caroline

Duncan sat there, unmoving, mired in disbelief.

She was *releasing* him, was she?

Without consulting him? What about what he wanted? Did his feelings not count?

"What am I supposed to do, Lord?"

Sorrow consumed him. How was he supposed to live without her? He *loved* her. He loved the life they'd built together in that humble cabin. And he knew, beyond a shadow of a doubt, that it could be so much more than they'd experienced thus far. Without the secrets and protective barriers between them, they could share something beautiful and wondrous.

If being rid of him was what she truly wanted, she'd have to tell him to his face.

He was in the midst of tossing belongings in his bag when he stopped. He'd spent their entire acquaintance thinking about what he wanted. Here was his chance to honor his wife's wishes. He had a choice to make — was he going to continue in his pigheaded, prideful ways? Or was he going to actually listen to Caroline and grant her freedom?

Caroline was done being the victim.

Leaving September's installment on the rock, she turned and picked her way along the steep trail. Anyone watching would assume she was returning home like every other time she'd met the blackmailer's demands. She wasn't. Instead, she walked out of sight of the stream and then ducked into the trees to retrace her movements. Caroline was going to discover her tormentor's identity and end this, once and for all.

Weeks had passed since she'd seen or heard from Duncan. Three lonely, horrible weeks. His scent was fading from his pillow, and the initial comfort she'd gained from sleeping in his bed was waning with it. Everywhere she looked, memories reminded her of her loss. It appeared he'd found her letter, after all. With each passing day, she dreaded the arrival of papers indicating her marriage had been dissolved. Thoughts of him with Maureen or some other gorgeous debutante tormented her.

This will get easier, she told herself. It had to.

Locating a sturdy tree to hide behind, Caroline settled on her haunches and prepared to wait. Little sounds became magnified. Her toes quickly became cramped in her shoes. If she hadn't been so distracted, she would've remembered to put on her boots. Her thighs and knees were aching by the time movement registered in her peripheral vision. Balancing one hand against the trunk, she leaned forward, her heart in her throat.

At first she rejected what she was seeing. She'd suspected Theo and Vivian were involved with each other — in a secretive romance, not ongoing criminal acts. As the pair neared the rock, Theo spoke forcefully and gestured with his hands. Vivian looked uncertain, as if she wasn't comfortable with their actions. He checked the contents of Caroline's pouch and, mouth pinching, pocketed it.

Although shocked by what she was witnessing, Caroline also felt relief. Her nightmare was nearing an end. She wasn't going to confront them here. All she had for protection was a kitchen knife in her pocket. Sheriff Timmons could handle their arrests.

"Enjoy your last moments of freedom," she murmured. "The game's over."

Pushing to her feet, she turned and cried out. "Sylvia! You frightened me." Belatedly registering the gun Sylvia had trained on her, she lifted her hands in a placating gesture. "What are you doing with that?"

"This may be a game to you, but to those of us unfortunate enough to work for the Turner empire, it's retribution."

Caroline stared. Sylvia didn't look like the meek maid she'd known for more than a year. Gone was the mobcap and gray uniform. Her brown hair in a long, thick braid, she wore a stylish white dress printed with tiny pink flowers and shiny brown boots. Her eyes blazed with hatred.

Fear snaked its way through her system, hindering rational thought. "My father has treated you well, has he not?"

She racked her brain for some instance of unfair treatment and came up empty.

"Indeed, he has little regard for anyone besides himself. If I hadn't been convinced of it before I came to work inside his home, I am now." She waved the pistol. "Come, let me show you."

Considering her options of escape, Caroline climbed the sloping hillside on unsteady legs. There didn't seem to be any. Sylvia's mental state, her ability to transform from appeasing employee to this irate woman with a weapon, made Caroline leery of attempting to flee. There were her accomplices to consider, as well.

The couple's conversation ceased the moment they caught sight of her. Alarm leapt to life in Theo's gray gaze.

"Sylvia, what are you thinking? This wasn't the plan."

Sylvia motioned for her to stop at the narrow stream's edge. Theo and Vivian stood on the opposite bank, frozen amid the forest foliage like two characters whose story had abruptly changed direction.

Caroline looked at Sylvia "You've been working with them all this time?"

"Not with them, honey." She let loose a high-pitched cackle. "They follow *my* orders."

"What has my father done to you?"

"He's the reason my mother is homebound," she spat. "He ruined her health and that of hundreds of others."

Caroline's heartbeat drummed in her ears, a steady rhythm of denial. "There was nothing on those documents to indicate employees' health had been impacted. If I'd known, I would've gone to the authorities myself. Were they falsified? Was the information about the soap ingredients false?"

"Oh, it's all too true. Albert Turner is not only a shrewd, greed-driven businessman. He's a magician. He's conjured up this grand lie . . ." Pressing her free hand to her chest, she mimicked, "Turner soaps contain rare plant extracts from the Mediterranean and Western Europe." She sneered. "But this isn't about stupid soap. Granted, his sins in that area aided my cause and goaded you into lining our pockets. Albert's true crime is in willingly and knowingly putting people's lives at risk in those handful of artificial-flower shops you employed to decorate your tea party."

"I don't understand any of this. How would making fake flowers endanger anyone? And how did you obtain your information about the soap recipes? They are fiercely guarded."

"Theo's connection with your family proved an advantage. I needed leverage and he delivered."

Caroline ripped her gaze from the gun barrel directed at her chest to a man she'd been acquainted with for years but had never truly known. "What did you do?"

Wearing an unhappy frown, he lifted his hands in surrender. "Your father has committed multiple offenses. He's hurt countless innocent people."

He turned to the young woman beside him. "Show her, Vivian. Remove your gloves."

Frowning deeply, Vivian did as she was

told. After removing the elbow-length gloves, she held out her hands. Caroline couldn't withhold a gasp. They were tinted green and covered with scars where once were sores. Her nails were yellowed and the top layer of skin around the tips of her fingers had peeled away.

"What happened?" she ventured, dreading the answer.

"Remember I was gone last summer?"

"You went to visit family."

Theo grimaced. "She came to visit my father and me. We're cousins."

"Theo got me a position in one of your father's shops making artificial flowers. We had no idea how deadly the arsenic dye was." Her anxious gaze flicked to Sylvia. "Sylvia's mother had worked there the longest, and she had started to display serious health problems by the time I arrived."

"But when she went to the manager, he threatened to fire her if she didn't keep her trap shut," Sylvia said hotly. "One day, the high-and-mighty Albert Turner happened to visit the premises. My mother intended to talk to him about her concerns. When she got close, however, she overheard him say that the people of Charleston would have their colorfast green flowers no matter what the price. He said to terminate anyone who dared complain."

Mortified, Caroline pressed a hand to her stomach. "I had no idea."

"Of course you didn't, Miss Caroline." Sylvia mimicked her previous submissive tone. "You were too busy enjoying the luxurious life of an heiress to care."

Sylvia's huge, catlike eyes were cold with condemnation. In those eyes, Caroline saw zero potential for forgiveness. She very well might die today. Would they hide her body? Would Duncan assume she left town?

Theo stepped closer to the water's edge. "Caroline isn't to be blamed for her father's actions. We've gotten more money than we initially agreed upon, enough to start fresh in a new town. The three of us can leave right now."

"It's not enough. Weren't you the one who told me her new husband's riches exceed the Turners'? There's plenty more to be had."

His jaw tensed. "I suspect it'll never be enough for you, Sylvia. You've allowed your thirst for revenge and your greed to exceed common sense."

"You're not the one who's had to see to your parent's every single need, day in and day out, all the while holding a full-time position. The Turners destroyed my mother's life, and they destroyed mine."

Sylvia's arm trembled. She was growing tired holding the heavy pistol aloft. Caroline inched in the opposite direction and, because she wasn't looking where she was going, her feet became submerged in the cool water up to her ankles. Her hem became sodden.

"And what of Caroline?" He flung out his arms. "Duncan isn't going to give you money if you harm her."

The thought of Duncan made her want to weep. If she didn't come out of this alive, he'd never know how much he meant to her.

"I'm not going to harm her." Her gaze lit once more on Caroline. "I'm going to hold her for ransom."

"Sylvia, you can't!" Vivian exclaimed.

Storm clouds gathered on Theo's face. "That's sure to land us in prison."

"I'll stash her in my shed. No one will suspect I had anything to do with poor Caroline McKenna's disappearance. While I'm faithfully performing my duties, you two can see she's fed at least once a day."

Horrified, Caroline moved farther away. The water around her feet stirred.

"I won't be part of this," Theo stated uncompromisingly. "And neither will Vivian."

Caroline took another step. The silt beneath her left foot shifted and she looked down in time to see the thick body of a snake. Twin points of pain exploded in her calf. Her scream rent the air.

Sylvia's eyes went from startled to aghast. "Copperhead!"

"Caroline!" Theo splashed through the water to get to her.

"Where is it?" Lungs heaving, Caroline scrambled away from the stream, her heavy skirts tripping her. She landed on her side in the grass. A burning sensation crawled up her leg.

Theo crouched beside her. "It swam away."

"I don't feel so good," she murmured, dizziness assailing her. Flat on her back now, she stared up at the chubby clouds floating past and the blue sky framed by interwoven tree branches. It was so beautiful she wanted to cry. "I'm going to die, aren't I?"

"Don't say that."

Vivian's white face came into view. "She needs to stay calm. Remember what happened to Johnny?"

"I know," Theo bit out. Bent over her, he smoothed her hair and peered into her eyes. "I'm going to have to make incisions at the wound site. I'll try to get as much of the

362

venom out as I can."

Nausea roiled. The pain was unbearable. Her heart throbbed in her chest.

Her fingers digging into his arm, she pleaded, "Get a message to Duncan. Tell him I'm sorry. For everything. And tell him that I l-love him."

Denial pulsed in the gray depths of Theo's eyes. "You'll tell him that yourself."

She saw the glint of a knife blade and squeezed her eyes tight.

A small, gloved hand enclosed hers. "Squeeze my hand, okay?" Vivian hovered on her other side.

All Caroline could manage was a tiny nod. Then Theo clamped down on her leg, and she screamed again. Blessed darkness crept over her, her final thoughts of Duncan's beloved face.

CHAPTER TWENTY-FOUR

Where was Caroline? Duncan left the barn and walked to Tammy's pen to greet her, all the while surveying the property. He'd gone to the main house first, fully expecting to find her there. Albert had informed him that she'd been staying in the cabin since his departure. He hadn't expected that. It gave him hope that she'd come to cherish their life as much as he had. Anxious to see her, he'd stopped in the stables in the hopes of finding her in her art room. He'd encountered Wendell instead, who'd been none too pleased with him.

Duncan had promised to endure his lecture later. First he had to find his wife.

She wasn't at the pond. Had she decided to visit one of her friends?

He crouched at the goat's pen. "Hey there, Tammy. Looks like Caroline's been taking good care of you."

"McKenna!"

Duncan automatically reached for his gun. Theo Marsh had no business here, especially in the wooded area behind the cabin —

The sight of Caroline's unconscious form stopped him cold. Theo carried her in his arms, and the man's energy seemed to be faltering. Duncan vaulted toward them.

"What happened?" he yelled. "What's wrong with her?"

"She needs a doctor." Theo was panting and sweating profusely. "She was bitten by a copperhead."

Fear seized him. "Give her to me."

Theo obeyed. Caroline was a deadweight, her head lolling back and her arms limp. *God, please don't take her.* Praying as he never had before, he bore her toward the cabin.

"How long ago did this happen?" he called over his shoulder.

There was no answer. Turning, he saw Theo on his knees in the grass, expelling the contents of his stomach. Vivian tripped out of the tree line, her eyes as huge as saucers.

"Theo!" Rushing up to him, she laid a hand on his back. "You shouldn't have sucked the venom out. I told you it was dangerous."

He waved her away. "I'm okay." His gaze flickered to Caroline. "Had to be done."

A mass of emotions pummeling Duncan, he pushed out, "You will tell me exactly what you were doing with my wife and how this happened. But first, one of you needs to fetch the doctor."

"I'll go." Vivian started then stopped. "Sylvia's still up there. She's armed."

"Sylvia the maid?"

Theo struggled to stand. "I'll get the sheriff."

"Just hurry," he commanded. "Take my horse."

Inside, he gently laid her on his bed. Her complete lack of color scared him.

Duncan framed her cheeks. "I *didnae* come home to watch you die. Fight, Caroline. You have to fight this. Do it for me. For us."

She didn't respond. Her breathing was rapid and shallow, her hair damp with sweat.

With a muttered oath, he peeled back her muddy skirts and got his first glimpse of the wound. He sucked in a sharp breath. The skin around the punctures was discolored, and the limb itself appeared slightly swollen. Theo had removed her shoes and wrapped a wide strip of material several inches above the bite. Duncan tested it to be sure it wasn't too constricting. He hadn't witnessed a venomous bite before, but he guessed this was to slow the venom's spread through her body.

She groaned. Lashes fluttering, she curled onto her side. "Sick," she whispered. "Going to be sick."

Duncan dashed to the kitchen for a pail. He returned to her side and, squatting beside the bed, gingerly caressed her hair. "It's all right, lass. I'm here."

"Duncan?" Her navy gaze hazy with discomfort searched his face. "Am I dreaming?"

"I'm really here, lass."

Her lids glided closed. "I'm sorry I lied. Sylvia. The money . . ." Grimacing, she sucked in a ragged breath.

"None of that matters. What matters is that you pull through this. I *cannae* lose you."

The wait for the doctor seemed interminable. Caroline slipped in and out of consciousness. Duncan remained by her side, praying she'd be strong enough to fight this. At long last, he saw Doc Owens riding into the yard through the open door.

"Doc's here, Caroline. He's going to examine you."

She lifted her hand. "Don't leave me."

He enfolded her fingers in his and lightly squeezed. "You *dinnae* have to worry about that. I'm never leaving you again."

Doc Owens shuffled inside, his black bag in hand.

"I hear you've suffered a grievous injury, young lady." He strode over, his probing gaze revealing nothing. "I thought you knew better than to tangle with a copperhead."

There was no response. In his grasp, Duncan felt her hand go limp.

His heart stuttered. "She's going to be okay, right?"

"Fetch me clean water and soap. This wound needs cleaning."

Aware he hadn't answered his question, Duncan gathered cloths and a bowl of water. When the doctor ordered him outside, he balked. "I promised I *widnae* leave her."

"I'm not asking you to. But her parents need to be informed, do they not? You can deliver the news and come straight back." His gaze was steady, his manner matter-of-fact. "It's unlikely she'll wake in the few minutes you're gone."

Torn, Duncan studied her wan features for long moments before brushing a kiss on her brow. "I'll be right back."

Not looking at the doctor, he strode

outside into what looked like a normal day. Birds sang their merry tunes, the honeysuckle-scented breeze teased his skin, butterflies flitted along the fence line. It was odd, being surrounded by sun-drenched beauty. He'd entered a nightmare cloaked in normalcy. Because his world was in chaos, the rest of the world was supposed to follow suit.

Duncan had journeyed home intending to ask his wife's forgiveness. He'd planned the perfect speech. He was going to confess the depths of his feelings and ask for a true marriage. Now he may be denied that chance. Because she'd been in the wrong place at the wrong time. If he hadn't postponed his return, she might not be battling for her life.

Fear coiled tight inside him. Pausing on the top step, he fought to maintain composure. *Have You given her to me only to take her away, Lord? Are You trying to teach me a lesson?* He hung his head. *I'm sorry, Father. I'm desperate here. Please spare her.*

Forcing his feet into motion, he walked the familiar route to the Turners' home. A distracted Albert admitted him.

"No one knows where that mousy maid disappeared to." He started to return to his study. "What can I do for you, Duncan?"

"I *dinnae* know how to tell you this." At the tremor in his voice, Albert turned with furrowed brow. "Caroline has met with an accident. She, ah, sustained a bite from a venomous snake."

The man paled. "How bad is it?"

"I *dinnae* know. Bad. Theo was there when it happened. He made incisions at the wound site to drain the venom and apparently tried to draw the rest out with his mouth."

"Barring death, she could lose a limb."

Seized with grief, Duncan blocked those thoughts. "Is your wife here?"

"No, she's at the mercantile. I'll go to her and explain the situation."

Nodding, he made for the exit. "I'll see you at the cabin."

"Actually, I think it best if we stay away. You'll keep us apprised of her condition?"

"You're not going to see her?"

At Duncan's incredulous tone, Albert's gaze slid away. "Louise is a delicate person. Besides, our presence won't change the outcome."

"She's your *daughter.*"

"We'll say a prayer for her. And of course, you can count on Cook for meals. As soon as she's up to visitors, we'll stop by."

Temples pounding, he clamped his jaws

closed and stalked out. Colder, more callous people he'd never met. No wonder his wife had trouble reaching out to others. She'd been rejected by her own parents in subtle ways. To compound matters, Duncan had rejected her, too, in the beginning. Regret hounded him. He needed to make things right, yearned for a chance to treat her as the precious, valuable woman that she was.

The thundering of hooves alerted him to visitors. The sheriff rode into the yard, followed by Theo and Vivian riding double on a second horse.

When he'd dismounted, Shane clasped Duncan's shoulder. "How is she?"

"No' good."

"I'm so sorry, Duncan."

Unable to stomach the other man's grave expression, he shook him off. "*Dinnae* act like she's already gone."

"That's not what I intended —"

Duncan pushed past him and advanced on the pair. "What were you doing with my wife?"

Shane wedged in front of him and, ordering Theo to remain in the saddle, prevented Duncan from closing the gap. "Let him have his say. You need to hear the whole story."

"Spit it out," he growled.

Theo swallowed hard. "Vivian and I met Sylvia last summer in Charleston. Vivian came to visit us — our mothers are sisters — and I got her a position in one of Albert's flower-making shops."

"We didn't know until after I started working there that the employees were suffering from a variety of ailments." Vivian removed her gloves, exposing her ravaged hands. "We learned later that the green dye contains arsenic. I quit that very day. Others, like Sylvia's mother, depended on the income. She waited until her health had deteriorated to the point of being bedridden to quit."

"What's this got to do with Caroline?"

"Sylvia and Vivian had struck up an acquaintance," Theo said. "She came to us with a plan. She and her mother would move here and find a way to get close to Albert. Then she was going to blackmail him. Her mother's health couldn't be regained, so she was going to go after his money."

"The idea of revenge sounded good to me," Vivian confessed. "My hands are permanently damaged. Looking back, I would've made a different decision."

"She decided to target Caroline, didn't she?" Duncan said, his gut roiling. He'd accused her of spending the money on clothes when in fact, she'd been protecting her father. "Why?"

"Albert intimidated her. Caroline was an easier mark." Shame cloaked Theo's sickly visage. "I'd heard rumblings of trouble at Albert's soap factories. Sylvia asked me to do some digging. I discovered that the supposedly pricey ingredients in his exclusive soaps were actually common, everyday ones. That was all the proof we needed to spur Caroline to act."

Spots danced before his eyes. He could literally feel his blood pressure rising. Straining against the sheriff's hands, he said through clenched teeth, "How long? How long did you torment her?"

"Since January."

In a quiet voice, Vivian related the day's events, as well as Sylvia's terrifying plan of kidnapping Caroline.

Spinning on his heel, Duncan buried his face in his hands. His wife had been shouldering a horrendous burden for months, doing everything possible to preserve her father's reputation. Albert didn't deserve such a sacrifice.

"Ben and some of the locals have formed a search party for Sylvia," Shane told him. "I'm going to keep these two in custody until I can figure out what to do. Go be with your wife, Duncan."

Time ceased to make sense for Caroline. Hours or days could've passed since that ordeal at the stream, she couldn't determine. She drifted in and out of consciousness. During those times when she was aware of her surroundings, there were two constants — pain and Duncan. She still had trouble accepting that he was here and not merely a figment of her imagination.

Raised voices brought her to wakefulness. Lanterns set around the room dispelled the shadows.

"Why isn't she getting better?" Duncan moved into her line of vision. He looked haggard. "You said the willow bark would break her fever."

"You have to give it time to work."

"It's been two days!" He tunneled his hands through his hair. "Try something else."

"I'm doing everything I know to do."

"Then I'll send for another doctor. I'll do whatever it takes . . ." His gaze fell on her and widened. "Caroline!"

In an instant, he was at her side, his large palm cupping her cheek. "You're awake," he breathed, his gaze devouring her. There were shadows under his eyes. Brow furrowing, he shifted on the mattress. "She's still hot."

Doc Owens loomed behind Duncan. "How do you feel, Caroline?"

Her mouth felt sawdust dry. "My leg hurts. And my head. Can I have water?"

While the doctor went to fetch it, she reached up and stroked Duncan's jaw. The bristles tickled her skin. "You look exhausted."

Capturing her hand, he kissed her knuckles. His lips were cool. "I kept my promise. I *havnae* left your side."

That made her smile. He helped support her upper body while she sipped the water. Nestled against the pillows once more, she closed her eyes for what felt like a minute. When she came to, however, it was morning.

She blinked up at the rafters, relieved to discover her vision was no longer fuzzy. The nightgown skimming her body felt crisp and clean, as did the sheet beneath her. A soft snore disturbed the quiet hush enveloping the cabin. Duncan was slumped over the bed, his arms a cushion for his head.

She tested the softness of his hair. "Duncan?"

He stirred. "Hmm?"

Caroline rested her fingers on the column

of his neck. He was warm and solid. Here, with her. Not in Boston.

"Why did you come back?"

He opened his eyes and focused on her. Sleep's hold on him loosened. Lifting his head, he slowly sat up and stretched, a cautious smile tipping his lips. "You're awake again," he said huskily. "For how long this time?"

"I feel different."

Moving to sit beside her, he tested her forehead. "Fever's gone. Praise the Lord." The worry clouding his eyes lessened but didn't completely dissipate. "Is your leg paining you?"

"It's not as bad as it was. My head isn't aching anymore." She glanced around. "Where's Doc Owens?"

"He left last night to see to another patient." He started to get up. "Do you want me to get him?"

"No, that's not necessary."

Today marked the first time she felt alert since finding herself flat on her back on the stream bank, staring up at the summer sky and convinced she wasn't going to see Duncan again. *Thank You, Lord Jesus, for bringing me through the worst of it. And for bringing my husband home.*

He helped her sit up, propping more pillows behind her back and rearranging the coverlet. He treated her as if she were made of the finest porcelain. She couldn't tear her gaze away. His shirt was wrinkled and half untucked from his waistband. He probably hadn't slept or shaved or changed clothes since she'd wound up in this bed. She didn't know what had brought him back to Tennessee. She didn't have to know, but she did have to tell him how precious he was to her. Her brush with death had taught her the importance of being honest.

"I have to tell you something."

"I know about Sylvia and what she's been doing to you." Frowning, he resumed his spot beside her. "She's no longer a threat. She's in jail awaiting transport to Knoxville. Ben guessed she'd come home to check on her mother. He was right. As for Theo and Vivian, they are being held until Shane decides what punishment to mete out."

The events at the stream came rushing back. "They helped me. If not for Theo . . ."

His eyes darkened. "I know. Shane said he'd take that into consideration. Theo admitted to stealing the horse as a device to get you alone. Seems he does have feelings for you, as twisted as they are."

"I didn't realize how mixed up his thinking had become."

"I'm just grateful he brought you to me. He could've left you up there."

"Are you willing to forgive me? I should've told you what was going on."

His expression grew fierce. "There's nothing to forgive. You did what you had to do to protect your father. I'm sorry you *didnae* feel that you could share your burdens with me. My behavior didn't inspire your confidence." He took her hand, his thumb rubbing a slow pattern across her skin. "I was convinced my way was the only way. I'm sorry for that."

"We've both made mistakes. It's understandable. One minute we were strangers at odds, the next we were pledging to love, honor and obey each other." She gathered her courage once more. "Why did you come back?"

"I regretted leaving you every second I was away. Then I got your letter. I tried to honor your wishes, but I was weak. I needed you too much."

"I didn't *want* to give you up, Duncan. I wrote that letter because my greatest desire was for you to be happy. I thought you'd be happy in Boston." Her heart began to pound. Revealing her deepest feelings didn't come naturally. "To be honest, I prayed the letter would get misplaced. I love you. I want you here with me, every day for the rest of our lives, teaching me new things, giving me goats —"

"Hold on." Scooting closer, he cupped her cheek, his eyes suddenly sparkling. "Did you say you *love* me, Caroline Turner Mc-Kenna?"

Smiling shyly, she encircled his wrist and held on tight. "I did."

Leaning close, he pressed his lips ever-so-gently against hers. "Am I glad to hear you say that, because I love you. You own me, sweet wife, mind, heart and soul."

"Oh, Duncan." Despite her body's weakness and lingering soreness, Caroline experienced such sweet acceptance and joy that she couldn't imagine ever being happier. Her husband loved her. He'd seen the best and worst parts of her, and still he accepted her. Wanted her.

"I want to start anew," he said with urgency. "Are you willing to give us another chance? Allow me to prove I can be the kind of husband you can confide in?"

"I'd be miserable without you, you know."

"Is that a yes?"

Caroline held out her arms. "Yes, my darling. There could never be any other answer."

Duncan's answering smile struck a balance between relief and delight. He wrapped his strong arms around her and held on as if afraid she might disappear. She snuggled closer, too full of gratitude for words.

EPILOGUE

Two weeks later

The feeling of panic sweeping over Duncan when he couldn't locate Caroline was all too familiar. He strode out of the barn, hollering for her.

"I'm over here."

Her voice calmed him. The knot in his chest slowly unraveled as he approached her spot beneath a silver maple beyond the vegetable garden. Seated with her legs tucked under her on a rainbow-hued quilt spread out in the grass, she was concentrating on one of her masks, her lip pillowed between her teeth. Tin cans sat at precarious angles around her, likely holding her various crafting tools. Since she'd been ordered by Doc and Duncan to avoid strenuous activity, she'd taken to spending time outside with a book or sewing project.

His gaze soaked her up, automatically searching for any signs her recovery might be suffering a setback. Despite her and Doc's reassurances, he was still haunted by the memories of her on the brink of death. He shoved the troublesome images away and prayed they would fade quickly. In her summery white dress printed with dainty pink flowers, she was the picture of good health. A wide celery-green sash highlighted her trim waist. A ribbon of the same color trimmed the edges of her short sleeves, giving him a glimpse of her strong, sleek arms. Her complexion was sun kissed, her lips a soft coral hue, and her eyes were bright. Lately she'd been leaving her long hair loose, a shining blond curtain that reached the middle of her back. He loved the simple style.

He crouched in front of her, careful not to soil the quilt with his boots. *"But to see her was to love her, love but her, and love forever."*

"Quoting Robert Burns again?" A content smile graced her mouth.

"What can I say? The man had a way with words." He winked at her. "What are you working on?"

"My butterfly mask. It's finished." She held it up for inspection.

"This one's my favorite." Reaching out to test one of the aquamarine stones, he said,

"Are you going to sell it?"

After the curiosity shop had sold her masks and requested more, she'd decided to sell most of her inventory and distribute the money among the women who'd worked in the now-shuttered artificial-flower shops.

"I think I'm going to keep this one."

"Good." Resting his knees on the ground, he produced a paper-wrapped box from his pocket. "I'm hoping you'll want to keep this, too."

"What is it?"

She turned it over in her hands. "It's obviously not a living thing, and it's too small to be a cleaning tool."

"It arrived today in the mail. I forgot to pack it while I was in Boston, so I contacted my parents. They were happy to oblige me." His parents and brothers were as eager to meet Caroline as she was them. When she was fully recovered, they planned to embark on a long holiday. He couldn't wait to show her the best parts of Boston.

Aiming a questioning smile his way, she quipped, "It's not my birthday."

"Consider it a wedding gift."

Gingerly unwrapping the packaging, she opened the lid and peered at the contents. Her eyes widened and her lips parted on a sigh. "Duncan, it's lovely."

She lifted the wedding band his grandfather had crafted for his beloved and presented to her on their wedding day decades before. His grandmother had worn it until her death and, according to her wishes, it had passed to Duncan. The gold band was twisted into the shape of a Celtic knot and graced with three miniature diamonds. While the knot meant different things to different people, in his family it represented the endless bonds of matrimony viewed in the eyes of a holy God.

"My grandfather had this ring especially designed for my grandmother. I was always her favorite." He winked at her. "She promised it to me while I was still a young lad. She wanted me to give it to the woman of my choosing, the woman who tamed my adventurous heart. That woman is you, Caroline."

He carefully removed her plain band and replaced it with his grandmother's. "It fits."

Her eyes soft with emotion, she leaned over to hug him and, in the process, knocked over several of the tin cans.

"Hold on a moment." He started moving the cans to the ground beside him.

"What are you doing?"

"It's nap time." Grinning, he tugged off his boots and tossed them, one by one, over his shoulder.

Her cheeks pinked, and her smile took on that shy, we-share-a-secret quality. "Ah, so it is."

Duncan joined her on the quilt and, pulling her into the circle of his arms, shifted onto his back. "This is my favorite part of the day," he mused, studying the patterns of clouds drifting past.

They'd sort of fallen into this habit in those initial days after her fever broke and she was still confined to the sickbed.

"Mine, too." Tucked against his side, her fingers playing with the buttons on his shirt, she sighed. "I wish we could do this every day, but I'm pretty well healed. I can resume my usual chores, which means there won't be time for naps. Besides, I'm sure my father wonders where you go every day."

"If your father noticed, he hasn't said anything. Wendell, on the other hand, recognized the pattern. He approves." Duncan chuckled. He'd developed a deep fondness for the older man. The fact that Wendell adored Caroline had a lot to do with it.

"In about a week's time, I'll be the boss around here, which means I can take a nap with my beautiful wife if I'm so inclined."

As expected, Caroline raised up on one arm to stare at him. "Care to explain that?"

Smoothing her hair behind her ear, he said, "Your mother and father have decided to move to Virginia. He sold his soap factories. He deeded us the house and the property."

Her lips parted. "I knew they were thinking of traveling, but I had no idea they planned to move away. Why Virginia?"

"They have friends there, he said. With everything that's happened, they aren't ready to return to Charleston."

Nodding, she assumed the expression of puzzlement and hurt that accompanied thoughts of her parents. Albert and Louise hadn't come to see her until several days after the accident. She'd requested that Duncan remain by her side, and the exchange had been fraught with tension. Albert, who'd been apprised of the blackmailing situation, had offered a stiff apology. Louise had been oddly silent. They'd left after a brief time and hadn't returned. Duncan had wrestled with feelings of anger on his wife's behalf and had had to offer frequent prayers for God's help. There was nothing he could do to repair her relationship with them, but he could offer her a listening ear and a shoulder to cry on whenever she needed.

Their move would be good for her, in his

opinion.

"What are you thinking?" he said.

Her mouth curved into a dreamy sort of smile. "That I'm blessed to know you. I didn't know what love was until you came into my life."

Her palm against his chest for support, she leant down and kissed him. He cradled her head, reveling in the waterfall of her silk hair across his skin. The moment ended too soon.

"We have a decision to make," he said.

"You're talking about moving into the main house." She surveyed the tiny cabin. "I can't believe I'm saying this, but I'd be a little sad to leave the cabin. It feels like home to me."

"To me, too."

They'd made changes during her recovery. The quilt barrier and extra bed had been relegated to the storage area in the hayloft so that they could share his. At long last, theirs was a true union, heart, body and soul. Being able to drift to sleep each night with Caroline in his arms made him feel like the most fortunate man in the world. He treasured the love they shared and the new life they were knitting together as a couple. Duncan prayed that, in time, the Lord would bless them with a child.

"The cabin suits us now, but when babies start to come along, we'll need more space."

She blushed prettily. "You'll make a wonderful father."

"And you, fair lass, will shower your children with love and affection."

"I will, indeed." Her navy gaze burned with conviction. "I would never allow a child of mine to feel unloved."

"I realize that house doesn't hold many good memories, so we can stay here and build on as necessary. Or we could redecorate the house to suit your tastes. We could even change the rooms around."

"That's an idea. We could use my old bedroom." Wearing a thoughtful expression, she tapped his chest. "And my parents' room could be my new art studio."

He chuckled at that. "Louise would be scandalized."

"That's part of the appeal." She laughed along with him, then sobered. "We don't have to rush the decision, Duncan. We can remain where we are and still use the house for entertaining our friends or ladies' meetings."

"I'm content no matter where we live, as long as I'm with you."

Her answering smile and the affection shining in her eyes filled him with such inexplicable emotion he couldn't speak. Sliding his hand beneath the curtain of her hair, he cupped her neck and, tugging her down once more, funneled everything he couldn't express into a kiss that melted both their hearts.

ABOUT THE AUTHOR

Karen Kirst was born and raised in East Tennessee near the Great Smoky Mountains. She's a lifelong lover of books, but it wasn't until after college that she had the grand idea to write one herself. Now she divides her time between being a wife, homeschooling mom and romance writer. Her favorite pastimes are reading, visiting tearooms and watching romantic comedies.